A DANGEROUS
MAN

A DANGEROUS MAN

WILLIAM W. JOHNSTONE
with J. A. Johnstone

PINNACLE BOOKS
Kensington Publishing Corp.
www.kensingtonbooks.com

PINNACLE BOOKS are published by

Kensington Publishing Corp.
119 West 40th Street
New York, NY 10018

PUBLISHER'S NOTE
Following the death of William W. Johnstone, the Johnstone family is working with a carefully selected writer to organize and complete Mr. Johnstone's outlines and many unfinished manuscripts to create additional novels in all of his series like The Last Gunfighter, Mountain Man, and Eagles, among others. This novel was inspired by Mr. Johnstone's superb storytelling.

All Kensington titles, imprints, and distributed lines are available at special quantity discounts for bulk purchases for sales promotions, premiums, fund-raising, educational, or institutional use. Special book excerpts or customized printings can also be created to fit specific needs. For details, write or phone the office of the Kensington special sales manager: Kensington Publishing Corp., 119 West 40th Street, New York, NY 10018, attn: Special Sales Department; phone 1-800-221-2647.

PINNACLE BOOKS and the Pinnacle logo are Reg. U.S. Pat. & TM Off. The WWJ steer head logo is a trademark of Kensington Publishing Corp.

ISBN-13: 978-0-7860-3350-8
ISBN-10: 0-7860-3350-9

First printing: September 2014

10 9 8 7 6 5 4 3 2 1

Printed in the United States of America

First electronic edition: September 2014

ISBN-13: 978-0-7860-3351-5
ISBN-10: 0-7860-3351-7

CHAPTER ONE
Scar of the Noose

Two men rode through the freezing night, revolvers in their holsters and evil on their minds. Behind them lay a dead man, murdered for the few dollars in his pocket, his gun, horse, and new boots.

Wild Bill Longley had not known who the man was, nor did he care.

He needed boots, the man had them, so he shot him. Gut shot him, just to watch him die slowly and in agony, as was Longley's way in such matters.

As snow flurried in the icy wind and settled among the pines like streaks of wan moonlight, Longley drew rein and kicked away the dead man's ten-dollar horse as it pulled alongside him. "Damn it, Booker, you sure there's a town at the end of this trail? I'm freezing my nuts off here."

Booker Tate nodded. An uncurried, dangerous brute, his red beard spread to the middle button of his mackinaw and long hair fell over his shoulders in greasy tangles. "Comanche Crossing is there all right, Bill, and it's ours for the taking. Man, I've been there afore, and it's prime."

"What about the town sheriff?" Longley asked. "Is he a gun?"

"Hell, no. The sheriff is elected, Bill. Fat feller by the name of Frank Harm. We can take him, real easy."

"Maybe so, but I don't want no slipups on this venture, Booker. I mean, I don't want to come up against no big name draw-fighting lawman aiming to mess things up."

"Hell, Bill, there ain't a named draw fighter within two hundred miles of the Crossing," Tate said, grinning. "The only one I can think of is Con Collins and he never leaves the San Juan River country. Like I said, the town is there for them as wants it. Come the spring melt, we can ride out rich men."

"A hick town in the middle of nowhere ain't going to make us rich. And that's a natural fact."

"Yeah, maybe so, but we'll have enough to keep us in whiskey and women fer a year," Tate said.

"Well, that's always something, ain't it?"

"Damn right it is."

Longley lifted a whiskey flask from the pocket of his sheepskin and took a swig, then a second. He passed the flask to Tate.

Unlike his muscular simian companion, Bill Longley was a tall, dark, and handsome man. He sported a trimmed imperial that set female hearts aflutter and usually affected the dress and languid, Southern manner of the riverboat gambler, though he possessed none of those gentlemanly traits.

The eyes he turned to Tate were a spectacular blue, but cold as floe ice, tinged with a lurking insanity.

"I say Bill, that time you was hung when you ran with Tom Johnson an' them, how did it feel?" Tate said. "I was always meaning to ask."

"Why do you ask me such a question, at this place and time? And you a man who has been my acquaintance only for two weeks?" The gunman's voice was flat, toneless, like lead coins dropping onto the trunk of a dead tree.

Tate heard that dead voice, accepted its warning, and stepped carefully. He smiled, or tried to. "Well, I figure when it's time to finally turn up my toes I'll be shot or hung. I know what getting shot feels like, but I ain't never been hung afore."

Longley undid the top button of his sheepskin, pulled the collar away, and craned his neck. "Take a good look. This is what it's like." A dull red scar about an inch deep, banded with distorted white tissue, circled his neck.

The terrible scar still bore its scarlet anger, but the vertical bands were white as bone and looked like small, writhing snakes.

It took a great deal to shock Booker Tate, but the livid legacy of a hemp rope did. "My God, Bill, an' you was only half hung," he said, wonder in his small, black eyes.

Longley adjusted his collar. "The posse as done it didn't stay around. They should've lingered awhile and made sure the hanging took."

"What happened to Johnson?"

"His neck broke like a dry twig. I heard it snap."

"You was lucky, Bill, an' no mistake."

Longley shrugged, his hard face empty. "If the vigilantes hadn't bungled it, I would have swapped one hell for another just a tad before my time. Luck don't even come into it."

"You're a rum one, Bill," Tate said. "An' no mistake."

"No, I'm a man who should be dead on a hell-firing trail to nowhere."

Tate smiled. "Comanche Crossing ain't nowhere. It's somewhere. Any place you can sleep in a bed is somewhere."

"Every town is nowhere to me." Longley smirked. "And Comanche Crossing will be nowhere after I get through with it."

CHAPTER TWO
The Man Hunter

Tam Sullivan sat across the table from a man he'd just met. The raging snow and wind had forced him to look for shelter and the rancher had graciously obliged.

"It's a dugout saloon and hog farm, owned by a man name of Rufus Brooks, and he's a real bad 'un," the rancher told him. "Hell, boy, you can't miss it. Well, you can, but follow my directions and they'll take you right to the front door."

The man raised a lascivious eyebrow and smiled.

"Huntin' fer a woman, are ye? Young buck like you."

"Nope," Sullivan said. "I'm hunting a man. Feller by the name of Crow Wallace. You heard tell of him?"

"Who ain't heard tell of him? He's another bad 'un like Brooks, maybe worse. Stranger passin' through tole me Crow killed a man in San Antone real recent, then badly cut up another in a saloon down El Paso way."

Sullivan nodded. "The stranger said it right. But

two weeks ago Crow made the mistake of robbing a Butterfield stage. He shotgunned the guard and got away with ten thousand dollars and a passenger's gold watch."

The rancher pushed the bottle of whiskey across his kitchen table, closer to Sullivan. "Ye don't say?"

Sullivan was not, by inclination, a talking man, but the rancher was a widower and lonely. That, the whiskey, and a reluctance to again brace the wild weather outside loosened his tongue a little. "Seems like the passenger set store by the watch and added five hundred dollars to Crow's bounty."

"How much is he worth?" the rancher asked, a gleam of avarice in his eyes.

"Right now, two thousand five hundred dollars and ten per cent of all monies recovered."

"And you mean to collect?"

"Seems like."

"Well, I'd like to help you, but—"

"I don't need any help," Sullivan said. "I'm a man who works alone."

"You said you tracked Crow this far?"

"Yeah." Sullivan waved a hand in the direction of the window. "Then this winter weather cracked down hard and I lost him."

"Well, if'n he ain't already skipped out of the New Mexico Territory, Brooks' dugout is the only place he could be."

"No towns farther north?"

"One. A burg called Comanche Crossing maybe twenty miles south of Grulla Ridge, but nobody goes there. It's a straitlaced town if you know what I mean. Well, except for Montana Maine, that is. She's the big attraction, but they say she's mighty choosy about who she keeps company with." The rancher leaned back in his chair, like a man ready to state an undeniable case.

"No, if a man's looking fer shelter an' a willing women and whiskey to go along with it, he takes his life in his hands and heads fer Rufus Brooks' hog ranch."

Sullivan nodded again. "Crow Wallace isn't a man who's easy to kill. If he's at the Brooks place, he'll be the toughest, baddest hombre there." He smiled. "That is, until I arrive."

Through snow flurries that bladed horizontally in a keening wind, Sullivan made out the glow of oil lamps in the distant darkness. He reckoned that was the place, unless the rancher had no liking for bounty hunters and had steered him wrong.

Well, he'd soon find out.

He urged his tired horse in the direction of the lights, then picked up an eyebrow of trail that led to an undercut limestone shelf about as high as a tall pine.

Under the torn sky, the area seemed a bleak, lonely, and dark place for a saloon and cathouse, but as Sullivan drew rein and looked around him, he decided that its isolation was probably one of its attractions. To an outlaw on the scout, a man who avoided the settlements and johnny law, it would be a haven of rest and plenty indeed.

Sullivan let his mount pick its way through a stand of Ponderosa pine then crossed a brush flat where a few struggling Gambel oaks rustled in the raw north wind. He came upon a well-marked trail, a wagon road that ran parallel to the base of the ridge then followed a gradual ramp to a broad shelf of rock.

Across a hundred yards of flat, a second ridge ascended like a gigantic step, its top thick with pine.

Most of Rufus Brooks' place, a saloon and adjoining structure, had been cut out of the rise, but they were fronted by a mud brick façade that gave them a Spanish flair.

To the left of the saloon's timber door, where Sullivan dismounted, was a painted blue coyote tall as a man. Its howling head was turned to the moon represented by a chipped white platter fastened to the wall.

The effect was quite artistic and he wondered if it was Brooks' work or that of a bored saloon girl.

If he were a betting man, his money would be on the girl.

The door swung open just as he slid his Henry from the saddle boot. He left the muzzle drop when he saw that it was a boy, a small, underfed Mexican with a mop of black hair and huge eyes.

"Take care of your horse, mister?" the boy asked.

"Seems like you ain't tall enough to rub him down," Sullivan said.

"I stand on a box. Brush him good."

It was only then that the bounty hunter noticed a barn set in a clump of oaks, most of its front obscured by a massive limestone rock that had tumbled from the ridge during some ancient earthshake. "You got hay and oats in there?"

His question was answered by a thin man who stood framed in the doorway. "Hay with a scoop of oats, seventy-five cents."

Sullivan frowned. "A shade high, ain't it?"

As though he hadn't heard, the man continued. "Beer, ten cents. Whiskey, a dollar. The stew in the pot is a dollar a bowl if you provide your own eatin' iron."

Then, like a man who'd recited it many times before, "One hour, two dollars. All-nighter with bed, six dollars, and the young lady will expect champagne at ten dollars a bottle."

"What do you call this place?" Sullivan asked.

"Call it what you want to call it," the thin man said.

"Judging by your prices, I'd call it the Savoy."

"Take it or leave it,"

Sullivan tossed the reins of his sorrel to the Mexican boy. "Brush him down good and feed him hay and oats, and don't skimp on the oats."

"Nice looking hoss," the thin man said as the boy led the sorrel away. "How much you pay for a big American stud like that."

"Too much." Sullivan unbuttoned his sourdough, a tan-colored canvas coat with a heavy blanket lining that reached to his lean hips. His .44 Army Colt was holstered high in the horseman fashion.

He had killed four men with the graceful revolver, all of them fugitives with dead or alive bounties on their heads. His conscience didn't keep him awake nights.

"I'm looking for a man goes by the name of Crow Wallace. Is he inside?"

The thin man shook his head. "I never ask a man his name. If he don't give it out, then it ain't none of my business. But mine's Rufus Brooks. Well known in these parts for my sweet, generous nature." He had the quick eyes of a bird of prey and his tall scrawniness did not suggest physical weakness, but rather a lean, latent force that could move fast when called on to do so. Like a rapier blade.

"I don't doubt it," Sullivan said. "Now if you'll give me the road."

The inside of the saloon was pretty much what he expected. From the Mexican border to the Missouri Breaks, he'd been in a hundred just like it—dark, dingy dens where the oil lamps cast shadows and men with closed mouths and careful eyes stood still in the gloom. Every dugout shared in common the same stink, a raw mix of whiskey, spilled beer, sweat, vomit, and cheap perfume.

The bar was a couple of timber boards laid across barrels, a few bottles displayed on an old bookshelf behind, and above the bottles an embroidered sign.

Have You Written to MOTHER?

"What will it be, stranger?" Brooks asked.

Sullivan had already taken stock. Two shaggy men in bearskin coats sprawled on an overstuffed sofa that was spilling its guts. A young Mexican girl in a state of considerable undress sat between them. The dugout behind the bar, a half-dome cut out of living limestone rock, was wide enough to accommodate two tables and some chairs. Three men holding greasy cards sat at a table sharing a bottle of whiskey.

One of the men, a breed with lank, black hair that fell over his back and ended at the top of his gun belt, looked up from his cards and saw Sullivan. "The game is poker, mister. Table stakes."

Sullivan took time to order a rye, then said, "I reckon not."

"Then go to hell," the breed said.

Sullivan smiled and said to Brooks, "Friendly folks."

The man shrugged. "He gave you an invite. That's neighborly."

"Man shouldn't refuse an invite," one of the bearskin coats said. "I mean, it ain't genteel."

"True words as ever was spoke, Clyde," his companion said. "I wonder what he'd say if old Queen Vic offered him a chair at her poker game."

The Mexican girl giggled. "That is silly." Her naked breasts were brown and small.

Sullivan ignored the comments. There was no profit in doing otherwise. He took off his gloves and reached into the inside pocket of his coat. He produced two things, a slender, silver cigar case and a piece of paper folded into a rectangle.

He chose a cheroot, lit it, then unfolded the paper and smoothed it out on the bar. "Another rye." He turned toward the table. "Crow, your likeness don't do you justice. Makes you look almost human." He held up the wanted dodger to the breed and the men sitting with him.

"Can you read, Crow?" Sullivan asked. "Them big words where my finger is say Wanted Dead or Alive."

Crow Wallace rose slowly to his feet, the chair screeching away from him along the stone floor. His right hand clawed over the handle of his Colt. "That ain't a dodger, mister. It's your death warrant." He had a strange way of talking, a lisp so pronounced that *mister* came out "mithter."

Sullivan could see his thick tongue move.

Wallace was a skinny little runt with buckteeth that gave him the look of a malignant teenager—which he was.

According to the dodger, Wallace was nineteen years old that winter, one of the new breed of draw fighters Texas had spawned by the hundreds after the War Between the States.

But young though he was, Wallace was a killer, fast and dangerous as a striking rattler.

"Here's how I see it, Crow," Sullivan said. "Unbuckle and drop the iron and bring them saddlebags over to me. Then we both walk out of here alive. See, that word right there says *Alive.*"

Wallace smiled, a twisted, vicious grimace. "Then read this, bounty hunter." He drew.

He was fast. Real fast. Smooth as silk.

Wallace fired, fired again. One shot tugged at Sullivan's sleeve, the second split the air less than an inch from his ear.

Tam Sullivan jerked his gun and then adopted the duelist position, revolver extended in front of him with a straight arm, the inside of his left foot against the heel of his right. He thumbed back the Colt's hammer and fired.

Wallace took that shot smack in the middle of his forehead.

Already a dead man, Crow triggered his Colt dry and .36 caliber balls ricocheted off the floor then *spaaanged!* from wall to wall, precipitating a hasty stampede from the card table.

Sullivan shifted aim and centered on the chest of one of Wallace's companions. "You in? State your intentions."

"Hell, no, I'm not in," the man said. "I was only playing poker."

The older man hurrying behind him yelled, "I'm out of it. Don't shoot."

A movement flickered at the corner of Sullivan's eye.

Rufus Brooks eared back the hammers of a scattergun and flung the butt to his shoulder.

Sullivan fired by instinct.

The big .44 ball struck the side plate of the Greener. Badly mangled, it ranged upward into Brooks' throat just under his chin. By some strange quirk of velocity and energy, the ball continued its upward momentum and exited in an exclamation point of blood, brain, and bone from the top of the man's head.

Brooks stumbled back and the shotgun fell from his hands. He crashed against the bookshelf that toppled over and the *Have You Written to* MOTHER? sign fell across his chest.

Sullivan glanced at the dead man. "She must be mighty proud o' you."

Both bearskin coats were on their feet and the young Mexican girl had vanished.

"You taking a hand in this?" Sullivan asked.

As the sound of hooves receded outside, the man called Clyde, a tinpan by the cut of his jib, shook his bearded head. "No we ain't, mister. Just don't expect no po-lite invites from me an' Jules here."

"He means to a fiddle soiree and such," Jules said with a French-tinged accent.

"I take that real hard," Sullivan said. "You boys disappoint me."

"Nothing personal," Clyde said. "But you shouldn't be around folks."

The door to the adjoining quarters opened and a slim woman who looked a tired and worn age stepped inside. She glanced at Sullivan's leveled Colt, dismissed it, then moved to the wreckage of the bar. For a moment she stared in silence at Rufus Brooks' lifeless body, then spat in his face.

Sullivan smirked. "Not one to hold a grudge, are you, honey?"

CHAPTER THREE
Death of a Yankee

Bill Longley stood at his room window of the Bon-Ton Hotel and stared out sullenly at the sluggish river of mud the good folks of Comanche Crossing, New Mexico Territory, were pleased to call Main Street. Snow flurries cartwheeled in the wind and a wooden sign hanging outside a general store banged back and forth with the sound of a muffled drum.

By times, he was a past-thinking man, especially when it came to reminiscing about women he'd enjoyed and kills he particularly relished.

A grandfather clock in the hallway chimed midnight. The mud outside reminded him of another road in another time and place. . . .

The Camino Real, the old Spanish royal highway between San Antonio and Nacogdoches, ran within a mile of the Longley farm. On a cold, early December day in 1867

*sixteen-year-old Bill was warned by his father to stay close
because mounted Yankees had been seen patrolling the road.*

*Campbell Longley, who'd been a close friend of General
Sam Houston and had helped bury the American dead
at Goliad, had passed on two traits to young Bill. One
was a virtue—his skill with firearms. The other, a vice—
a pathological hatred of Yankees and blacks.*

*As snow flurried and the Camino Real turned to mud,
Bill took his father's Navy revolver. Never one to avoid the
chance of a confrontation with Yankee soldiers, he sneaked
out of the house and headed for the highway.*

*"There are Yankees on the road! Stay away!" a woman
wrapped in a blanket yelled at him from the shelter of a wild
oak, frantically waving her hands.*

"Where are they?" Bill hollered.

*The woman pointed back down the highway. "That way.
Stay clear. They'll kill you and eat you."*

*He walked up a gentle rise that led to the road. Snow
clung to the brush and salted the trunks of the bare trees. As
he stepped closer, he saw that the woman was old. Her gray
eyes had faded to the color of smoke and the hair that showed
under her bonnet was white. She was thin and looked
hungry.*

*She carried a wicker basket, as did all the old men and
women who scavenged along the Camino Real. She'd already
found an old horseshoe and what looked to be a dented can
of meat.*

*"Go back, son," the woman said. "That Yankee up there
will arrest you and then you'll get skun an' your hide stretched
on a frame."*

"Who, grandma? Who'll arrest me?"

*"Black man on a hoss, wearing a blue coat. He's got
stripes on his sleeves and a rifle."*

"Did he say anything to you?"

The woman shivered, from cold or memory he couldn't tell.

"He told me to get the hell off the road. Said there's too much thievery going on along the highway."

Bill's dark, sudden anger flared. "A black man spoke to you like that?"

"Son, since the war ended, a black man can speak to a white woman any way he damn pleases. Or didn't you know that?"

"Not in San Jacinto County, he can't. Where the hell is he?"

"That way. Down the road apiece."

Bill nodded and laid his hand on the woman's skinny shoulder. "You go home now. I'll take care of the black. He'll never sass a white woman again." He opened his coat and revealed the Navy in his waistband. "I got me some uppity negro medicine right here."

He watched until the old lady vanished from sight behind a hill, then followed her directions, avoiding the worst of the mud puddles as he walked, head bowed against the chill wind and slashing sleet.

He saw the soldier sitting his horse under the thin cover of an oak. A Spencer carbine lay across the pommel of his McClellan saddle as he intently peeled a green apple with a folding knife.

The corporal spotted Bill and took account of his ragged coat, pale, underfed face, summing him up as local white trash. Taking a bite of the apple, the soldier made a face and tossed it away. He wiped his mouth with the back of his hand and kneed his horse into motion, approaching Bill at a leisurely walk. The Spencer was upright, the butt resting on his thigh.

When he was a few feet away, the corporal drew rein and

*again studied the lanky teenager, not liking what he saw.
"You, Reb. Git off the damned highway. We've had enough
of thieves and footpads preying on decent folks."*

"And if I don't?" Bill said, his anger simmering.

*The soldier leveled his rifle. "Then I'll damn well blow you
off the road."*

*Bill whimpered a little. "Please, mister, don't. I didn't
mean no harm."*

*"You look like dirty, thieving Reb spawn to me," the soldier
said. "Now get off the highway and run home to your mama
and ask her to dry your tears."*

*The solder then made a mistake. He turned his back
on Bill.*

*It was a gesture of contempt that cost Corporal Thetas
Washington, age twenty-six, his life.*

*Bill drew from the waistband, aimed at a spot between the
shoulder blades and pulled the trigger. The .36 caliber ball
shattered the black man's spine as he cried out in pain and
rage at the time and manner of his death.*

*The sixteen-year-old didn't fire a second time. Powder and
ball cost money his father didn't have. He waited until the
soldier toppled from his horse then stepped beside him.*

A clean kill!

The man was as dead as he was ever going to be.

*Working quickly for fear of being discovered, Bill searched
the man's pockets. He took twenty-three Yankee dollars, a
nickel watch and chain, and a whiskey flask. Made from
pewter, the Bonnie Blue Flag was engraved on its side. Under
that was another engraving.* Lieut. Joseph Herbert, 17th
Georgia Infantry.

*Longley uncorked the flask, fastidiously wiped it off, then
took a swig. He gathered the reins of the dead man's horse,
picked up the Spencer, and walked back to the farm.*

He had his first kill, a black carpetbagger at that, and he was so elated that even the icy wind and spinning sleet could not chill him.

Bill Longley was pulled from his pleasant reverie by a shadow of movement on the street. A careful man, he turned down the oil lamp and stepped to the window again, one of his beautiful .44 Dance revolvers in his fist.

The night was so torn and dark it took his eyes a few moments to adjust to the gloom. When they did, he saw a tall man on a sorrel horse stop outside the town sheriff's darkened office.

After a few moments, the rider swung out of the saddle and stepped to what Longley at first thought was a packhorse. Only when the tall man dumped the horse's burden into the street did he see that it was a body.

While the tall man worked the kinks out of his back and looked around him, Longley quickly moved away from the window. Suddenly he felt an odd sense of unease . . . as though a goose had just flown over his grave.

CHAPTER FOUR
A Dead Man for Breakfast

Tam Sullivan stepped onto the boardwalk and studied the sign that hung on the door. Suspended by a cord over a tarnished brass hook, it said simply SLEEPING GO AWAY. He smiled. At least it was a change from the small town lawman's usual GONE FISHIN'.

Spurs chiming like silver bells above the wail of the wind, he walked into the street again, grabbed the late Crow Wallace by the back of his coat and dragged him, boot heels bumping, up the boardwalk to the door. Sullivan, a big man and strong, removed the sheriff's sign and hung Wallace's skinny body from the brass hook.

Dangling as he was, the dead man looked like a trussed chicken, his glazed eyes staring into a street he could no longer see.

Sullivan hung the sheriff's sign around Wallace's neck then stepped to the edge of the boardwalk. He peered through the tumbling snow. Across the street

stood a false-fronted building with a sign outside.
BON-TON HOTEL.

The big bounty hunter nodded, fished inside his
canvas coat for tally book and pencil, and wrote *Tam
Sullivan—Bon-Ton*. He reckoned the town lawman
would figure that out, folded the sheet. and stuck it in
Wallace's open mouth. "Don't choke on that, Crow."

Sullivan crossed the street to the hotel.

When asked for a room at the late hour, the sleepy
desk clerk replied, "Yes, I have a room, and no, you
are wrong. It *is* an uncivilized hour to wake a man."

"Livery?" Sullivan had a notion the clerk didn't like
him much.

"Down the street that way." The clerk pointed to his
left. "Last building in town."

"Is the livery man awake? Seems that Comanche
Crossing is an early to bed town."

"We roll up the boardwalks at eleven, when the
saloon closes. And no, Clem Weaver ain't asleep.
Damned old fool never sleeps and he keeps a Sharps
.50 close, so don't get your head blowed off."

"Who's the town law?" Sullivan asked .

"Questioning man, ain't you, mister?"

"Learn stuff that way."

The clerk dredged up a sigh, as though recalling
the lawman's name was a chore. "Feller by the name
of Harm."

"Frank Harm?"

"You heard of him?"

"Maybe so. There used to be a bounty hunter by
that name, operated out of Denver. Got wounded up
Montana way by Henry Plummer in the spring of '62
and gave up the profession."

"Yeah, well, Sheriff Harm walks with a limp, so it could be the same man. How come you're so interested in our lawman? You on the scout, mister?"

"Nope. But Frank Harm is the feller who's going to pay the bounty on Crow Wallace, the outlaw I brought in tonight."

The clerk looked past Sullivan at the door. "Where is he?"

"He's hanging around somewhere."

"I hope he ain't dangerous. I mean, an outlaw on the loose like that."

Sullivan shook his head. "Crow isn't dangerous. He's changed his ways quite a bit recently."

"Seen you coming in, leading that American hoss," Clem Weaver took hold of the bridle on Sullivan's horse. "Know who the buckskin over there belongs to?"

Sullivan's eyes followed the jerk of the liveryman's thumb to a stall. "Can't say as I do."

"Wild Bill Longley, as ever was," Weaver said. "Wanted oats fer his hoss."

"I heard he'd been hung a few years back."

"Half hung. Somebody cut him down in time."

"How do you know he's Longley?"

"I recognized him. But he didn't remember me, an' that's a good thing. Coffee?"

"I don't mind if I do," Sullivan said.

The hour was late, but it seemed that Clem Weaver was a talking man. "I remember Bill Longley as a strutting bully. He made a reputation as a draw fighter by picking on men who were unarmed, scared, drunk, or unskilled. Sometimes all four.

"I first saw him up in the Montana Territory at Fort Brown where he had a job with the army as a civilian teamster and pack master. That would be . . . let me see . . . the winter of '71. A bad winter that, snow and bitter cold. Hell, kinda like this one."

Prepared to be sociable, Sullivan said, "You were in the army back then?"

Weaver shook his head. "Nah. I was a surveyor for the Northern Pacific Railroad. They planned to lay rails across the Yellowstone country, but of course the Sioux had something to say about that. I damn near lost my hair a couple times."

Weaver said Longley and an army quartermaster by the name of Nathan Gregory were selling off army stock, but they lowballed the number of animals they sold and pocketed the profits.

"Making money hand over fist, was ol' Bill back in them days. Smoking big fat cigars and drinking nothing but the best whiskey. But the good times ended when he and Gregory had a falling out. It seems that Longley sold a team of Missouri mules for five hundred dollars but told his partner he only got three."

The liveryman blew on his coffee to cool it some. "It seems that Gregory, being a crook his ownself, knew there was chicanery afoot and he called Bill out for a cheat and a damned liar. Ain't hard to figure what happened next."

"Longley shot him," Sullivan said. "That's my opinion."

"You opine right, young feller. Ol' Bill cut him near in half with a scattergun, grinnin' like a possum the whole time. On account of how Gregory was good with a gun, Bill shot him in the back. Gregory lingered for a whole day in agony, cussin' Longley for a yellow-bellied coward and lowdown."

"Scattergun can sure put a hurt on a man, even if a coward pulls the trigger," Sullivan added.

"Well, Nathan Gregory made a big mistake," Weaver said. "He tried to put the crawl on a man who was a whole sight meaner than himself."

"Well, ain't that always the way of it?" Sullivan drained his coffee cup and rose to his feet. "I'd appreciate if you could sell the gray I brought in. And see what you can get for the saddle and traps."

Weaver was a foxy little man with red hair and mustache and quick hazel eyes that never rested on any one thing for too long. "I'll give you a hundred for the hoss and twenty for the stock saddle. Cash in hand."

Sullivan disagreed. "The gray is worth that much by itself."

"Maybe, but folks don't like grays much. Say they smell bad."

"Maybe it's the folks that smell bad."

Sullivan saw Weaver's face close down and said, "All right, a hundred and twenty for the gray and twenty for the saddle."

"Done and done. You hold right there, young feller." The little man made a show of picking up his Sharps before he stepped into a small office built against the stable wall.

Sullivan smiled. It seemed Weaver was not a trusting man.

He heard a tin box open, some muttering, and then the liveryman rejoined him.

"One hundred and forty dollars," he said, handing Sullivan the money. "You know why I'm eatin' beans today instead of steak? Because go anywhere west of the Mississippi and you won't find a hoss dealer more on the square than honest Clem Weaver. Yup, it's what's making me a poor man, my honest dealings with folks."

"Mind if I count it?" Sullivan asked.

"Count away, young feller. It's all there to the last cent."

The sum was correct and Sullivan shoved the bills into a coat pocket. He offered his hand to seal the deal.

Weaver shook his hand. "Pleasure doing business with you."

"How come you quit the surveyor profession? On account of the Sioux?"

Weaver waggled a forefinger in front of his eyes. "Nah, the peepers ain't so sharp anymore."

"Sharp enough to see this sucker coming." Sullivan left the livery and strolled toward the hotel.

He was quite pleased with the deal he'd made for Wallace's horse and saddle. He'd turned a quick profit and that was what the bounty hunting business was all about.

Like all outlaws, Crow Wallace was a big spender. Sullivan had managed to recover only the gold watch and six thousand dollars of the stage holdup loot. His percentage and the reward for the watch totaled eleven hundred dollars in addition to the two and a half thousand reward owed by Butterfield.

All in all, he considered it not bad for an evening's work.

As he neared the hotel, Sullivan thought he caught a flicker of movement at one of the upstairs windows. It was there for just a moment and then was gone.

He wrote it off as a sleepless gent stretching his legs or using the chamber pot, and thought no more about it.

Sullivan entered the hotel and went straight to his room on the ground floor, just off the lobby. It contained a brass bed, a couple of chairs, a dresser with a blue earthenware basin and jug, and a small writing table with an inkwell and steel pen.

On the wall above the bed hung a portrait, draped in black crepe, of General Robert E. Lee. The great man stared grimly into the room as though he thoroughly disapproved of its present occupant.

"Now don't fall on top of me, General," Sullivan said as his head hit the pillow.

If the general made any reply, Sullivan didn't hear it.

He was already asleep.

CHAPTER FIVE
Doing Business with the Devil

Tam Sullivan woke to someone pounding on his door.

"Open up in the name of the law."

"It's open," Sullivan ground out. "The key only works sometimes."

The door slammed open and a big-bellied man with a walrus mustache and eyebrows to match stomped inside. A few flakes of snow clung to the shoulders of his mackinaw. "All right, what's the big idea? And give me no sass or backtalk either."

"Town sheriff Frank Harm, I presume?" Sullivan said, sitting up in bed. Robert E. Lee scowled at him from his perch on the wall.

"Damn right it is," the lawman said. "You the one who left a dead man on my front stoop?"

Sullivan picked up the dodger he'd laid on the side table by the bed. "Is this him?"

"Yeah. It's him all right."

"Then he's mine." Sullivan said.

Harm scowled in thought, his head cocked to one side like a great, prehistoric bird of prey, as he tried to place a face. "Here, I remember you. Big Tam Sullivan. You done fer Salty Stidger down in Fort Worth that time."

Sullivan nodded. "He was notified, but Salty never was a listening man."

"He was good with a gun," Harm said.

"Well, he thought he was, but he wasn't. Fast on the draw and could shoot all right, but he had a problem hitting what he shot at. Kinda like Crow in that respect."

Harm frowned. "I have no liking for bounty hunters, Sullivan."

"Hell, Frank, you was one yourself."

"Yeah, I was, but I suddenly got religion."

"A bullet can incline a man in that direction, I guess," Sullivan said.

"The dodger says twenty-five hundred dollars," Harm said. "I don't have that kind of money."

"You got a Butterfield stage depot?" Sullivan asked.

"No. Hell, mister, we got but one hoss in this town and we share it around."

"Two. I sold Crow's horse to Clem Weaver."

"Then he robbed you."

"He surely did. But beggars can't be choosers. Isn't that how the old saying goes?"

"I wouldn't know about no sayings, but it seems to me you have a choice, Sullivan. Either wire Butterfield direct or ride to the nearest town that has a stage depot."

Sullivan shrugged. "You have a wire?"

"Yeah, at the train station."

"I didn't know there were rails around here."

"There aren't. We built a station, but the railroad spur never came. That's where the wire is. In the stationmaster's office."

"You still have a stationmaster?"

"Yeah. His name is Isaac Loomis. The Acheson, Topeka, and Santa Fe never got round to firing him, so there he sits, year after year, getting a check in the mail every month."

Sullivan smiled. "Must get pretty lonely for him, huh? A man waiting for a train that never arrives?"

"No, it doesn't. Isaac thinks the trains arrive every day. Get me? He'll sell you a ticket to Timbuktu if you want, only you won't go nowhere."

Harm read the doubt in Sullivan's face.

"The wire works just fine between here and Santa Fe, unless the Apaches have cut it again."

"Then I'll send a wire."

The sheriff watched a cockroach crawl up the far wall then lost interest. "I'll identify Crow Wallace should Butterfield ask. He wasn't much."

Sullivan nodded. "All draw and no shoot."

"Give me three dollars, Sullivan," Harm said.

"For why?"

"To bury your dead, that's for why."

Sullivan picked up his wallet from the bedside table and gave the lawman a five. "Bury him decent, Frank."

Harm took the money and turned to leave, but Sullivan's voice stopped him.

"You hear that Bill Longley is in town?"

The lawman said, "Yeah, I heard. Him and a lowlife by the name of Booker Tate. Two rotten apples in any barrel."

"I'd keep a watch on your bank, if I was you. Them boys could be inclined to a robbery."

"I already spoke to Perry Cox, the banker, but he don't care. He's a church deacon, but he says he'll do business with the devil himself if there's profit in it. Kind of like you, Sullivan."

"You got a dodger on Longley or Tate?"

"Nope. And if I did, I wouldn't tell you."

"Prefer outlaws to bounty hunters, huh?"

"One's as bad as the other, but that's not the reason. I don't want you to get your damned fool head blown off in my town. Sullivan, you ain't in Bill's class. You never was and you never will be."

"And what class is that?" Sullivan needled.

Harm smiled, a picket fence of teeth under his great mustache. "Draw down on him and you'll find out pretty damned quick."

CHAPTER SIX
Bad Day on Boot Hill

"Who do you suppose he is?" Booker Tate said. "I mean the dead guy."

"Do you care?"

"I guess not, Bill. But it seems they'll bury him decent, nice coffin an' all. The big feller with the gimpy leg is Frank Harm, the town sheriff I told you about."

"You didn't tell me anything about him except he's fat," Longley said.

"Yeah, but I said you can take him. That's all you need to know."

A heavy, sleety downpour clicked and clacked like castanets on the tin roof of the hotel porch. Longley and Tate sat in rockers, watching Harm and a couple of men manhandle the coffin onto the bed of a spring wagon. The Morgan in the traces snorted and pawed at the ground, kicking up gobs of mud.

Raising his voice a little above the racket of the

sleet storm, Longley said, "I recognize that law dog's face from somewhere."

"Wasn't you in an army stockade fer nine months at hard labor, Bill? Maybe Harm was a guard back in them days."

"Maybe. But I seen him somewhere, that's for sure."

Their wet slickers gleaming, the three men left the coffin on the wagon and stepped back into the sheriff's office. The morning was icy cold and Longley figured the lawmen planned to whiskey up before heading for the graveyard.

Longley lit his first cigar of the day and its plume of blue smoke drifted from under the porch roof and quickly got battered into nothingness by the sleet. Where the hell had he seen Harm before?

The question troubled him.

Longley did not care for any kind of uncertainty. It could get a man killed.

After the killing of Gregory, he'd tried to escape on a stolen army mule, but a couple Pawnee scouts tracked him down and dragged him back to Fort Brown. He'd protested his innocence but was tried and sentenced to thirty years at hard labor for murder.

"An Iowa State Prison gun bull, maybe," Longley said.

Tate turned his head and looked at him. "Huh?"

"They sent an iron cage and a four man escort to take me to the pen," Longley said. "Them fellers all had scatterguns and bad attitudes. Nowadays cons call them gun bulls, especially the blood-sweatin' Negro gangs in the cane fields."

Tate smiled. "Hell, Bill, the law must've took ye for a mighty dangerous feller."

"I reckon they did, but I fooled them. One of the army guards was a Texan and he helped me break out of the stockade. Left them Iowans in my dust. I think maybe Harm was one of them."

"We'll ask around. Find out for sure."

Longley shook his head, letting smoke drift from the O of his mouth. "I can't take a chance on him, not with thirty years hard time on the line." He thought about it, weighing his options. "I'll kill him today," he said finally.

"Hell, Bill, it's a chore to kill a man in this weather. Takes the sport out of it, like."

"You can stay here. I'll go this one alone." Longley got to his feet, stubbed out his cigar in the ashtray beside him, and stepped into the hotel lobby.

A harassed-looking woman stood by the front desk attempting to pry a stick of pink and white candy from the pudgy fingers of her squealing offspring. Longley smiled at her as he passed.

He emerged onto the porch ten minutes later, a Henry .44-40 hidden under an army oilskin cape. The brim of his hat was pulled down over his eyes and he wore black leather gloves. He congratulated himself. He'd timed it perfectly.

Harm, up on the seat of the spring wagon, urged the Morgan into a walk. His two companions sat behind him, flanking the jolting coffin.

The relentless north wind cut to the marrowbone. As the morning had grown colder, the sleet had piled up into small, icy parapets where the boardwalks met the mud. The street looked like a crocodile infested river somewhere in darkest Africa.

"Hell of a day for a killing, Bill," Tate said. "You'll get soaked to the skin."

Longley grunted and stepped off the walk into mire.

The bad weather kept people off the street but for one intrepid matron. With her small, meek husband in tow, she bustled into the general store, a shopping basket over her arm. Loudly, she demanded service.

Bill Longley followed the spring wagon but kept his distance. Trudging through ankle-deep mud, he watched Harm swing onto a narrow ribbon of wagon road that headed north out of town.

The Morgan strained into its collar as the trail began a fairly steep climb between rows of wild oaks and a few pines. Beyond the trees, on both sides of the road, lay flat expanses of brush, rock, and stands of prickly pear. Near a row of cottonwoods stood the remains of a stone cabin—three walls and a broken-backed roof—in mute testimony to an old Comanche raid and the deaths of a ma, pa, and kids that no one could remember anymore.

The day was bleak, the landscape bleaker. It was a desolate, achingly lonely place that tried a man's soul.

Soulless, Longley was unaffected by his surroundings. His only consideration was to find an ideal spot to hole up for a rifle shot.

The wagon climbed the hill and topped off at the crest. The graveyard took the entire space, an open, windswept area about ten acres in extent. Harm let the wheezing Morgan rest.

As though in competition with the sleet that clicked

through the tree branches, a mist the color of smoked
cotton laced among the wild oaks.

Longley left the road and stepped into the cover of
trees, the Henry hanging from his left hand. He
moved through the haze like a vengeful gray ghost.

The reason for the large burial ground was not because Comanche Crossing produced an inordinate
number of dead. It didn't. Five years before, the town
fathers had cleared timber from the cone-shaped
crest of the hill and then cut off the top like a boiled
egg, creating a last resting place with room to grow.

It might have looked like any other Boot Hill in
scores of frontier towns but for one thing—a few of
the dead were buried in above ground tombs.

The first mayor of Comanche Crossing, Armand
Babineaux, was a Cajun and he'd introduced the idea
of a City of the Dead, as was the practice in his
beloved New Orleans. He was the first to be interred
within a marble vault built in a Greek style, but few
others had the fortune, or the will, to become his
neighbors.

As the wagon rolled through wind-tumbled sleet to
the pauper section where graves went unmarked, Bill
Longley saw his chance. He crouched behind a stone
angel that stood head-bowed over a low, sun-bleached
tomb that was already scarred by a creeping black
moss, and laid the Henry in front of him.

Then he waited. Smiling, his eyes glittered.

As Harm helped the other men haul the coffin off
the wagon, one of the cheap pot metal handles broke
off. The box tilted and thudded to the ground.

Longley was close enough to hear the sheriff curse

then yell, "Hell, don't lift it again. We'll dig the hole and push the damned thing into it."

"How deep?"

That also carried to Longley.

"Just deep enough to cover the damned thing and keep the coyotes away," Harm said. "I don't care. He's not one of my dead."

Harm stood to one side, his sleet-slashed slicker glistening, and watched his men dig. Their shovels threw up muddy clods of earth.

As the grave grew deeper, Longley smelled dank dirt and the loamy tang of rotting vegetation. Gunmetal clouds hung low in the sky and the mist prowled through the cemetery like a stalking beast.

Melted sleet ran down the stone angel's face like tears.

Only when the work at the grave slowed, and the men laid down shovels and arched their aching backs, did Bill Longley pick up his rifle.

He aimed at Harm's chest then moved up the sights to a point between the top of the lawman's right ear and the rim of his hat. Longley smiled, anticipating the mule kick against his shoulder, the acrid smell of black powder, and his noise-deadened ears that would follow the shot.

He'd been there before. None of those things troubled him.

He took a deep breath and thought *steady now.* He let out a little breath . . . squeezed. *Don't jerk the trigger . . .*

Fired.

Frank Harm's skull exploded and his hat blew clean off his head.

The two other men were not lawmen but laborers hired for the grave-digging job, and they were unarmed. Standing stiff as boards, their scared, horrified expressions pleased Longley.

He didn't wait to see the sheriff fall. He got to his feet and walked toward the men, working the Henry as he walked, levering shot after shot into the diggers.

Both men tumbled into the grave and Longley whooped in triumph.

When he reached the muddy hole, one of the men still showed life, his bloody, open mouth gasping like a trout on grass.

"Time to take your medicine, old fellow," Longley said. "No hard feelings, I hope."

He shot the man between the eyes.

Gun smoke and mist curling around him, Longley grinned as a good joke popped into his mind. He dragged the coffin and let it slide onto the bodies of the diggers then grabbed Harm by his boots and lugged the lawman on top of the heap he'd created.

Longley stood back and admired his handiwork. He grinned, delighted.

The piled-up grave, its bottom already an inch deep in watery blood, was a good prank he'd played on the town of Comanche Crossing.

CHAPTER SEVEN
The Mayor's Daughter

The weather was no damned joke, Tam Sullivan told himself as he stared morosely from the shelter of the hotel porch at sleet blowing inside the wind. To his left a big man with the features of a belligerent ape sat in a rocker and used a fingernail rimmed with dirt to fish cigar ash out of his coffee.

Sullivan turned. "Lousy weather, huh?"

"So you say," the man said.

"You don't agree?"

"Rain, hail, or shine, it makes no difference to me."

"If I was a guessing man, I'd say your name is Booker Tate," Sullivan said. "And I'd say you're running with Bill Longley."

Tate watched a lumber wagon trundle past, mud lacing off its wheels. The driver sat hunched over, huddled inside an old Confederate army greatcoat that still bore the faint scar of three stripes on the sleeve.

"I never give out my name," Tate said. "Are you some kind of law?"

"No, not any kind of law."

"But you're a stranger in town. You the man that brought in Crow Wallace?"

"Maybe."

"He was a good man, was Crow."

"Yes. Those of us who knew and loved him will miss him terribly." Sullivan was being sarcastic.

Tate rose to his feet. He was big all over, huge in the shoulders, chest, and belly, and he had the dull, merciless eyes of a carrion eater. An engraved Colt with carved ivory grips he could never have come by honestly was shoved into his waistband.

Handy for the draw, Sullivan noted.

His own revolver, holstered under his coat, was out of reach for the draw and shoot. The extra seconds spent unlimbering the gun could be the death of him. It was a rube's mistake and he cussed himself for his carelessness.

"I don't like you, mister. It all of a sudden come on me, like." Tate had the piggy, hostile eyes of a rutting boar.

"I'm afraid that if you don't take a bath soon, the feeling will be mutual," Sullivan was on the prod, despite the voice inside him that whispered *You'll be too slow. Step back from this, Tam.*

But Tate saw something in Sullivan's eyes that troubled him. With the air of a man resigned to postponing an important task for another day, he shrugged and let it go. "You stay out of my way, bounty hunter."

"Until you take a bath, depend on it."

Death glinted in Tate's eyes as he turned away and stepped into the hotel.

Sullivan watched the man go then smiled at his uncanny knack for making enemies in low places.

The growl in his stomach told him the time was nigh for breakfast, but the sea of mud between him and the restaurant on the opposite boardwalk kept him on the porch.

He considered his options. Apart from going hungry, he had none.

Back in the Dark Ages, a philosophizing monk might have gazed at the iron sky and tumbling sleet and said to his fellow friars, "That's it, boys, down on your knees. Seems like God's destroying the world again."

In Tam Sullivan's opinion, the monk could have been right.

There was no sign of a letup in the bad weather. The sky was one gigantic bruise, swollen masses of black, mustard, and purple smeared together like oil paint on a mad artist's palette. The gusting north wind continued to fuss and fluster the sleet, blowing it in every direction but straight down.

It was a morning for a brandy bottle, a couple of inventive ladies who were a credit to their profession, and a scarlet fire crackling in the grate.

Sullivan had none of those things. Only the bleak prospects of the aborning day.

He sighed, removed his spurs, and prepared for his muddy odyssey.

* * *

It seemed the good folks of Comanche Crossing had decided not to hazard the weather, preferring to stay warm and dry at home and forgo steak and eggs for buttered toast.

Besides himself, there were only a few customers in the restaurant, a businessman of some kind in broad-cloth and brocade, a couple of drifters who looked like hardcases, and a young blond girl who sat at the counter talking with a woman twice her age and three times her size.

"You tell your pa that the state of the street is a dis-grace," the woman was saying as Sullivan stepped inside and chose a table in a corner where he could sit with his back to a wall.

"Pa's talking about bringing in crushed shell rock, Ida Mae," the girl said. "Spread it around, like. Put up our taxes a few dollars, though."

"Shell rock ain't the answer, Lisa. And neither is new taxes."

Sullivan thought the girl's frown was real pretty.

"Then what do you suggest, Ida Mae?"

"Don't ask me. Your daddy's the mayor and he's being paid to figure these things. If he won't do any-thing, speak to your ma. Polly will get to the bottom of the problem."

"Shell rock will work," Lisa said, her little chin stub-born. "All we have to do is build up the level of the street a couple feet."

"That's a lot of shells. I don't think there's that many shells in the ocean." Ida Mae pushed herself off the counter, grabbed the coffeepot from the stove, and walked to Sullivan's table.

She was a thick-bodied woman with heavy black eyebrows and a wide thin mouth that seemed compressed, as though she was forever holding back an insult that sulked on the tip of her tongue.

She filled Sullivan's cup. "Hi, sweetie. What can I get you?.

"Burn me a steak then add four—nah, make it six—fried eggs."

"Takes a lot to feed up a man as big as you, huh?"

"Well, at a guess, I'm missing my last six meals," Sullivan said.

"Then you've come to the right place to fill that hole. The girl's name is Lisa York, by the way. She's the mayor's daughter."

"That obvious, huh?"

"Other men look at her the way you do. Nothing new in that."

"Anybody walking out with her?" Sullivan wanted to know.

"All the single men in town and the occasional army officer passing through."

"A heap of competition, I'd say."

"What do you expect? Have you ever in your life seen a gal prettier?"

"Maybe just once. A spotted pup down El Paso way. But it's a close run thing."

Ida Mae smiled. "Mister, if you think that, you've got rocks in your head. Talking about that, what do you know about crushed shell rock?"

"Nothing," Sullivan said.

"Me, neither," Ida Mae said, walking away.

The coffee was good, but the steak, eggs, and sourdough bread spread thick with butter were better.

After he'd eaten, Sullivan leaned back in his chair, a contented man.

The girl was gone, her bustle swaying and ankle boot heels pounding on the wood floor after she and Ida Mae got into another heated discussion about the muddy street, the duties of a mayor, and the advantages, or lack thereof, of shell rock as a paving medium.

Sullivan felt a pang of disappointment that Lisa hadn't even glanced in his direction. He'd shaved close and trimmed his mustache just that morning.

He was about to call for his bill when a tall man who'd stopped on the boardwalk to kick mud off his boots opened the door and stepped inside.

Sullivan pegged him at a glance. By his high-headed arrogance and bully's swagger, the tall man was a gun.

The man carried a Henry rifle. He removed his dripping Army cape and hung it on a peg. His coat was open, revealing a pair of revolvers butt-forward in a fancy two-gun rig.

Sullivan reckoned he could only be Bill Longley.

The two hardcases that had been sitting by the window glanced at the man, did a double take, and decided it was no time or place to linger over coffee. They paid their score and left in a hurry.

Longley stared at Sullivan as though he expected him to do the same. The bounty hunter merely smiled and said a good morning.

Longley grunted then crooked a finger at the waitress.

Ida Mae filled his coffee cup and Longley said, "What you got to eat besides steak and eggs?"

"The cook can make you a nice bacon or salt pork sandwich."

"Two slices of toast. One dry, the other spread thin with molasses. And don't burn the toast."

"Will that be all?" Ida Mae said, her face stiff.

"Yeah, pour me more coffee. This is cold."

Ida Mae protested. "I just took the pot off the stove."

"I don't give a damn when you took it off the stove. It's cold. Now do as I tell you."

Ida Mae stepped back into the kitchen, making more noise than was strictly necessary.

Driven by need and covered in heavy coats against the sleet, more basket matrons shopped along the boardwalks. The skirts of their morning dresses flapped in the wind, revealing lacy petticoat hems that swirled around their ankles like snowflakes.

Outside Tom Archer's dry goods store, a dog stared balefully at the black and white cat in the window. The cat's name was Precious and the dog had chased her a hundred and seven times, catching her once. After what had turned out to be a painful and humiliating experience, he'd licked his wounds and vowed off bird-dogging cats forever.

Tam Sullivan returned his attention to Longley. The man's uneaten toast was turning to leather on his plate.

Irritated at the way he'd treated the waitress, Sullivan said, "So you're Wild Bill Longley. Heard about you."

CHAPTER EIGHT
Longley on the Prod

The eyes Bill Longley turned on Tam Sullivan were cold as the muzzles of a Greener shotgun. "What did you hear?"

"Damn it all, Bill, I've been sitting here racking my brain trying to recollect," Sullivan said. "Nothing too interesting, I guess."

"Well, don't rack too hard. You'll give yourself a headache." Longley picked up his plate, stared at it for a while, then tossed the toast on the floor.

"I'm sure there must have been something good, you being such a nice feller an' all," Sullivan said.

Ida Mae stepped up to Longley's table. "I'll have to charge you for that."

Longley glared at her. "The hell you will. In this town everything Bill Longley wants is on the house."

"Not in this restaurant, it isn't," Ida Mae said. "Simeon!"

A tall, well-made man with a blue-black skin and

dark, wounded eyes, seen so often in his kind, stood behind the counter. He wore a white apron, much stained, and a blue bandana with a paisley pattern around his neck.

"This man won't pay his bill," Ida Mae said.

"Seen you when I first came in," Longley said. "I won't eat food a black man's hands have touched." He rose to his feet, the two Dance revolvers on his hips exclamation marks of danger.

Five years before he'd arrived in Comanche Crossing the man called Simeon had fought an unsanctioned, bare-knuckle bout with the great American champion John Camel Heenan. All the New York smart money was on Heenan, at that time a tough, six-foot-two, 200-pounds brawler who was hard to put down.

Two inches shorter and twenty pounds lighter, Simeon took Heenan to twenty-four rounds in a fight that lasted two hours and twenty minutes. Finally, with five ribs broken and his battered face a bloody mess, Simeon's seconds threw in the towel.

Heenan's manager gave him a cigar and a silver watch.

As he faced Bill Longley, the watch was in Simeon's pocket and his face bore the scars of every punch of John Heenan's that cut him to the bone. The black man didn't lack for sand, but a draw fighter like Longley was a visitor from hell that was beyond his experience.

Longley grinned and ground the two pieces of toast into the floor with the heel of his boot. "Pick it up, boy."

Sullivan saw Simeon's fists clench and it looked like

the man was willing to walk into a wall of lead to land a punch.

"Hell, Bill, now I recollect what I heard about you," Sullivan said. "It was in the summer of sixty-seven down in Lexington, Texas, way." He slapped the table. "I know I'd remember eventually."

"What the hell are you talking about?" Longley said, his eyes ugly.

"Mind that time you, Johnson McKowen, and Slick Williams lost all your money at the racetrack? I remember hearing about it because I later had the pleasure of killing Slick when he was on the scout with five thousand dollars on his head for rape and murder." Sullivan shook his head and made a *tut-tut-tut* sound. "Poor ol' Slick, where did he go wrong? Maybe it was you led him astray, Bill."

Longley's eyes went to Simeon, then back to Sullivan. "Back there in Lexington, you're talking about darkie shooting."

"Why yes, you do remember," Sullivan said. "You shot up a street dance as I recall. Left five or six dead and twice that number wounded, woman and children among them."

"Yeah, well say your piece, but darkie shooting ain't murder. It's a long overdue reckoning, the damned scalawags."

"Bill, Bill, I'm surprised at you," Sullivan said. "What an awful thing to say. How cold."

"Well, you tell me what right them savages had to hold a street dance when the South was bleeding and the tears on the faces of our widows and orphans wasn't even dry yet?"

Sullivan smiled. "You're a patriot, Bill. True blue."

He raised an eyebrow. "You sure you don't have paper on you? How about Booker Tate?"

"Go to hell."

"Then I'll take that as a no. But I don't believe you." The bounty hunter rose to his feet, coat open, hand close to his Colt. "Pick it up, Bill."

For a moment Longley looked like a man who's just had a sewing needle rammed into his ass. "Are you talking to me?" His startled eyes were big as coins.

"I certainly am, Bill. The cook is too busy to clean your mess, what with lunchtime coming up an' all. I'm sure you understand, huh?"

Longley jabbed a furious forefinger at Sullivan. "You go right to hell. And stay out of my way." He stomped to the door, trailing mud, grabbed his cape and walked into the street.

After the door slammed, rattling its glass panes, Ida Mae smiled at Sullivan. "Thank you, stranger. You put the crawl on him."

"I didn't put the crawl on him. He just postponed the day is all," Sullivan said. "He didn't pick up the toast and he didn't pay his score. I'd say he won that round."

Simeon grinned, revealing teeth as large and white as piano keys. "Mister, I was about to tackle him, take the hits, and keep on coming. If you hadn't intervened, I reckon I'd be dead right now."

"From now on leave Bill Longley the hell alone," Sullivan said. "You see him come into the restaurant, leave by the back door."

"I'm not scared of him," Simeon said.

"You should be. You heard of the Marquis of Queensberry Rules?" Sullivan said.

"Sure," the black man said.

"Yeah, well just remember there ain't no Marquis of Queensberry rules in a gunfight."

The big chocolate-colored dog that had earlier stared into the window of the dry goods store, bitterly lamenting his fate at the hands of its belligerent cat, nosed around the restaurant door.

Sullivan opened the door to the dog and pointed to the toast on the floor. "Pick that up."

The dog's brown eyes stared into Sullivan's face with a *You-got-to-be-kidding-me* expression. He cocked a leg, pissed against the door, and trotted away.

Tam Sullivan shook his head and studied the puddled floor at his feet. "This just isn't my day."

CHAPTER NINE
Bushwhacked!

Where the boardwalk stopped, the walk to the train station with its telegraph office began, a state of affairs that didn't set well with Tam Sullivan.

The station sat high above a sea of mud and put Sullivan in mind of the abandoned hulk of Noah's Ark grounded on a reef. A pair of wet, matted coyotes nosed around the mired gully where the rails should have been.

Looking for their long-gone fellow passengers, he decided.

Due to a quirk of the wind, the sleet spun in frenzied circles and a cold mist drifted down from the surrounding hills like campfire smoke.

Like a mariner plotting a course, he stood at the edge of the boardwalk and chartered his best route, using his extended right hand to point the way.

Of course there was no best route, just less bad ones.

He pulled his hat lower over his eyes, turned up the

sheepskin collar of his canvas coat, and stepped off the walk. His feet squelched deep into mud and he lifted his knees high, like a Spaniard treading grapes.

Stepping carefully, Sullivan angled to his right, heading for higher ground where Ponderosa pine and clean grass prospered among scattered slabs of limestone. His plan was to follow the rise, then loop west, giving him only about a hundred yards of mud to navigate before he reached the station.

Around him lay a hostile, unforgiving wilderness of deep canyons and high mesas, the unwanted children of the Sangre De Cristo Mountains, twenty miles to the west. He was a long way from the polished brass, red velvet, and down-soft beds of the New York and Boston cathouses and gambling dens where he spent his money before heading back west again.

That tracking down dangerous and violent criminals was hardly worth a few weeks pleasure in the big eastern cities never occurred to him. For a short while, it was pleasant to move among well-mannered men and beautiful, sophisticated women in a world far removed from the mud, blood, and violence of the frontier. But even in the city, he always carried a derringer under his evening dress. A gun was an alluring mistress from whom a man couldn't bear to be parted for too long.

Sullivan reached the grassy high ground and followed the tree line north for fifty yards. Sleet ticked from the branches of the pines and the wind's cruel, serrated edge found every opening in his coat and sawed deep. He became one with the day, a drab, seemingly aimless figure slogging through a swirling, merciless tempest of slashing sleet and wolfish cold.

Numbed and stiff as he was, it took him several seconds to react to the bullet that kicked up a startled V of grass and mud at his feet.

The flat crack of a rifle sounded again.

The bullet zipped past his head and rattled into the pines as he dived for the ground and rolled, but fetched up hard against a rock.

He was still a sitting duck.

Sullivan crawled behind the rock. He got to his feet, cleared away his coat, and grabbed his Colt as he looked around for a target. Nothing moved or made a sound but for the wind and sleet. The tattered mist covered up any drift of gun smoke, but the shots had come from his left, a stretch of flat, open ground with patches of brush, cactus, and a few piñon.

He saw no sign of life, but he knew who'd tried to bushwhack him. "Bill Longley, show yourself!" he yelled.

The wind tore his words from his mouth and scattered them. The echoing silence that followed mocked him.

Sullivan holstered his revolver, but his eyes still scanned into murky distance. He tried to figure it. Maybe Longley thought his second bullet had dropped him and he'd scampered. Either that or having missed with two shots he didn't dare risk a third.

Sullivan had pegged Longley as a braggart and a bully, not a man with any true depth of morality or courage. But the bounty hunter knew the most dangerous creature on earth was a coward with a gun, and he'd already learned that it was a deadly mistake to underrate the man.

As he waited behind the rock, he remembered that

a gambling acquaintance, a trail boss named Hank
Rector had learned that truth the hard way. . . .

*Back in the spring of 1869, Rector hired Longley as a
drover, but when the herd reached the Indian Territory, the
gunman eagerly sought out and killed a Choctaw boy who'd
stolen a biscuit from the camp cook.*

*The boy was only about thirteen years old, but Longley
mounted and rode him down. By the accounts of those who
were there, he shoved the biscuit into the Indian boy's mouth,
choking him, then put a ball into the kid's head.*

*Longley threw a loop on the boy's body and dragged it into
camp behind his horse while he shot his revolver into the air
and bragged that he was the best damned Redskin killer in
the Nations.*

*Hank Rector, a hard-nosed but basically decent man,
dragged the gunman off his horse, called him out for a murdering scoundrel, and dropped him with a crashing right to
the chin. Furious, Rector challenged him to get up and take
his medicine like a man. "Fists, knives, or guns. The choice
is yours."*

*"You go to hell," Longley said, staying where he was in the
dirt as he wiped blood off the corner of his mouth.*

*Rector, well known as a reliable trail boss and Christian
gentleman, then told the hired man to draw what wages were
owed him. "Hit the trail back to Texas as you are finished
here." He turned and walked away.*

*Longley yelled, "You fool. I'm damned if I will." He drew
his murderous revolver and with a vile curse, fired three balls
into Rector's back.*

*The unfortunate trail boss immediately fell to the ground,
weltering in his blood, and said to his friend John Black who*

kneeled by his side, "He's killed me, John. My backbone is shot through and through and I cannot long survive."

Longley then mounted and rode around the camp, hurling curses at the dying man before he stole the contents of a moneybox kept in the chuck wagon for emergency expenses. He rode away, vowing to "kill any man stupid enough to follow me."

Rector lingered in great pain until the following morning.

As Sullivan left the high ground and once more descended into mud, he swore to himself that he'd never repeat the mistake Hank Rector had made.

He'd never turn his back on Wild Bill Longley.

CHAPTER TEN
The Phantom Railroad

A small, wiry man wearing the blue uniform and gold-braided cap of the Atchison, Topeka and Santa Fe Railroad stood on the station platform and watched Tam Sullivan until he was close enough to get on speaking terms. "The nine-o-twenty left an hour ago, young feller, but there's a midnight cannonball goes right through to Santa Fe if that's to your liking."

Sullivan walked onto the platform and much to the stationmaster's chagrin stomped mud off his boots.

Isaac Loomis was in his early sixties with shrewd brown eyes and a pair of little round glasses perched on his sparrow's beak of a nose. His skin was pale, not the ghastly gray of sickness but rather the white pallor of a man who spends much of his time indoors. A silver watch chain hung across his small, rotund belly and all his brass buttons were sewn in place and shined.

"I'm here to send a wire," Sullivan said.

"Business or pleasure?"

"Business."

"Not much call for business wires . . . or pleasure wires, either," Loomis said, his little birdlike face tight. "Seems that the folks of Comanche Crossing don't have anything to say." He hesitated a moment. "Can I sell you a ticket for the midnight cannonball?"

Sullivan frowned. "You don't have any rails, or haven't you noticed?"

"So you say, big feller, but the rails are there if you look hard enough. What I do got is coffee on the bile. It's for passengers, like, but since you're giving me wire business, I'll make an exception this time."

"I'm obliged," Sullivan said, touching his hat brim.

Loomis smiled. "You're a real polite young feller. Did you fire them two shots I heard?"

Sullivan didn't want to get into it. "Thought I saw a wolf."

The stationmaster shook his head. "Haven't been wolves around this neck of the woods in years."

Sullivan nodded. "I know. I was mistaken."

"Probably a coyote. Plenty of them. But they ain't a patch on timber wolves."

"I'd sure appreciate that coffee before I send the wire," Sullivan said.

"Yup, it's a rip-roaring day, ain't it? Come inside and set."

Sullivan nodded and they went inside.

Loomis poured coffee. "Give 'er a taste, young feller. See if she's to your liking." He lit his pipe.

Sullivan was fascinated by his ceramic cup. It was big enough that it was decorated with a fine locomotive and the words, *Terre Haute & Richmond, Madison & Indianapolis, and Bellefontaine Railroads.*

"Beauty, ain't it?" Loomis said. "Good railroads, them."

"Their trains stop here, huh?" Sullivan smiled through a cloud of cigar smoke.

"Think I'm crazy, don't you, young feller?"

"As a loon," Sullivan said.

"Well, that's what you think, but it ain't necessarily true."

Sullivan raised an eyebrow but said nothing.

"I still get paid by the Acheson, Topeka and Santa Fe, right?"

"So I heard."

"Well then, work it out fer yourself."

Sullivan considered the situation. "As long as they keep sending you a check, you'll go on pretending this is a real railroad station. Am I right?"

"Right as ever was. You're a smart young feller."

"You're crazy alright, Loomis. Crazy like a fox."

The stationmaster grinned and tapped the side of his nose with a forefinger. "Isaac Loomis by name, Isaac Loomis by nature, my old ma used to say."

Sullivan let that fly over his head. "I guess I should send my wire."

Loomis pulled a yellow pad across the table and then looked at Sullivan, pencil poised, a question on his face.

"Make it to County Sheriff, Santa Fe, New Mexico Territory.'

"Got it," Loomis said after a while.

"Um . . ."

"You want the *um?*"

Sullivan stabbed the man with a look. "Have killed

Crow Wallace and claim reward. Stop. Have recovered silver watch and six thousand dollars from Butterfield stage robbery. Stop. Please advise. Stop. Urgent. Stop."

"Well spoke, young feller."

"Send it right away, huh?"

"Once I know what name you want to use."

"Tam Sullivan."

"Tam? What kind of name is that?"

"My kind," Sullivan said.

Loomis rose to his feet, the slip of paper in his hand, but he never made it to the wire key.

The door burst open and a young towheaded boy hurled himself inside along with a blast of cold air and sleet. "Send a wire!" he yelled.

"Who to?" Loomis said. "And slow down, younker."

"The law," the boy said, asthmatically gulping for breath. "Mayor York says send a wire to the law."

"What law?" Loomis asked.

Sullivan took over. "What's your name, son?"

"Matt Hardy."

"Tell us what's happened," Sullivan said.

"Sheriff Harm has been shot along with Pete McPherson and Clete Miller."

"Are they dead?" Loomis asked.

"Yeah, all three of them, up at the cemetery," the boy said. "Shot through and through an' tossed in that outlaw's grave."

Sullivan frowned. "Crow Wallace's grave?"

Matt shrugged. "I guess that's his name." He looked hard at Sullivan. "You're the one that brung in the outlaw, ain't you?"

"Yeah, that would be me," Sullivan nodded.

"Can I see your gun?" the youngster said.

"No." Sullivan looked at the stationmaster. "Loomis, I guess now you've got two wires to send to Santa Fe."

"Like the county sheriff is going to care about what happens in Comanche Crossing." Loomis shook his head. "Like he's going to come all the way up here."

"Oh, I don't know." Sullivan grinned. "He can always take the train."

CHAPTER ELEVEN
Some Bad Enemies

"Well, lookee, Bill," Booker Tate said. "The golden boy is headed our way."

Longley's eyes went to the tall man crossing the street. "Let him come."

"I could kill him real easy, Bill. Drop him right in the mud."

"Later. This hick town can't handle four killings on one day." Longley watched Tam Sullivan step onto the hotel porch and kick mud off his boots. He noticed the bounty hunter's coat was open, his Colt clear.

Longley nodded at Sullivan. "Howdy. I ain't seen you since breakfast."

"Funny you should say that, Bill. I figure you saw me real recent."

"Over a gun sight, like?" Longley smirked.

"That's about the size of it," Sullivan said.

"You're talking about them two rifle shots I heard. Oh, about thirty minutes ago."

"Yeah, them two."

Longley shook his head like the news surprised him. "Man, if I'd taken a pot at you, I'd have needed one shot, only one."

"Bill's right," Tate said. "Ain't nobody better with a long gun than he is."

"You listen to them shots, Sullivan? That's your name, right? Tam Sullivan? I got it off the hotel register."

"Who read it for you?" Sullivan asked.

Longley smiled. "You're a funny man, Sullivan, a real hoot. You an' me are gonna give this hick town some snap."

Sullivan quickly disagreed. "You and me aren't gonna do anything. Try to ambush me again, I'll come shooting, not jawing."

"Damn it, I thought you were smart," Longley said. "Didn't you listen to the shots?"

"No. I was too busy running for my life."

Longley shook his head again. "I carry a forty-four Henry. Them shots fired at you were from a big gun, a Sharps fifty or a fifty-five sixty Spencer. A Henry don't make a big bang like that."

"You know your rifles, huh?" Sullivan stomped more mud off his boots.

"Well, I was in the army, at least for a spell."

"What caliber was used on Sheriff Harm?" Sullivan asked.

"I'm not catching your drift."

"He was murdered this morning along with two other men."

"Was that what all the stir was about?" Longley shifted on the rocker.

"This morning I saw you follow the wagon carrying

Crow Wallace's body. Seems like you'd something hidden under your coat, a Henry rifle, maybe."

Longley and Tate exchanged glances, then Tate said, "Bill likes to take a stroll of a morning. He calls it his constitutional."

Sullivan waved a hand in the direction of the windy, sleety turmoil of the street. "In this? With a rifle?"

"Bears," Longley answered. "I always carry a rifle when I go for a walk as protection against big, growly bears. Ain't that so, Booker?"

"You murdered the sheriff and two other men and took pots at me." Sullivan looked Longley in the eye. "I want to hear the reason from you, not Booker."

The bounty hunter raised a hand when Longley opened his mouth to speak. "What I can't figure out is the why of it."

"There ain't no why of it," Longley said. "And I'll shoot any man who accuses me of killing Harm and them other fellers."

"I just did," Sullivan said.

"Yeah, but Bill never shoots the village idiot," Tate said. "He likes to keep him around fer laughs, like."

Sullivan turned to Tate. "Booker, you're really starting to be a burr on my butt. Don't irritate me any longer, because when I get irritated bad things happen."

"Booker means no harm," Longley said. "Just joshing with you."

"Joshing with me can get a man killed," Sullivan said.

"Look at us, Sullivan," Longley said, spreading his arms wide. "What do you see? I'll tell you what you see—just two honest, peaceful citizens who plan to winter in this town and then, come spring, ride on."

"After you rob the bank, I imagine."

"All righty then, maybe that's part of my plan. So now we come down to it . . . are you with us or agin us?"

"Neither, I'm standing pat." Sullivan leaned against a pole holding up the roof.

"Then you can expect no trouble from us. Ain't that right, Bill?" Tate put in.

Sullivan said, "Don't let him speak again, Longley. I'm too close to drawing down and scattering his brains, if he's got any."

"Booker, shut your trap. Can't you see you're getting on the gentleman's nerves?"

One fact about a sure-thing killer, if you tell him to shut the hell up he will. It's when you turn your back on him that he'll kill you.

So Tate sat in silence, took what Sullivan was dishing out and said nothing, biding his time.

"I'm taking over this town between now and the spring thaw, Sullivan," Longley said. "You catching my drift?"

"It ain't difficult to figure out."

"Then you stay out of my way and I'll stay out of yours. Can I say fairer than that?"

"Sure. But step on my toes and I'll take a side."

"Hell, Sullivan, there ain't no sides. You don't give a damn for this dung heap."

"You're right about that. But if another bullet is fired in my direction, I'll come looking for you, Bill."

"Fairer words was never spoke," Longley said. "Ain't that right, Booker? Oh, I plum forgot, you've been struck dumb."

Tate glared at Sullivan, the hate in his eyes a burning thing.

"Well, live and let live, I always say." Longley stuck out a hand. "Let's shake on it, Tam."

Sullivan stared at Longley's outstretched hand for a full second, then walked past him into the hotel.

Tate made a strange *eee, eee, eee* sound in his throat. "Bill, I want to kill that man real bad."

Longley looked at him. "Be patient, Booker. Your time will come."

CHAPTER TWELVE
The Fat Lady Sings

Lashed by wind, snow, and sleet, the open overloaded wagon trundled south from Cimarron, the settlement that marked the cutoff from the old Santa Fe Trail. To the west, the wagon and two harnessed mules were dwarfed by the massive, jagged bulk of the Tooth of Time Ridge and beyond that, hidden by lowering clouds, the tall peaks of the Cimarron Mountains.

"This is gonna be another wild goose chase, Helga," the man at the reins yelled to the fur-wrapped woman sitting in back. He'd raised his voice above the roar of the wind.

"Sure is," agreed the man beside the driver. "Crow Wallace ain't around here. He's probably in Old Mexico by now."

Helga Eckstrom wailed, shook her head and set her yellow pigtails flying. "I must find my darling Crow. He needs his Helga now more than ever before."

"Hell, he could even be hung by this time, Helga," the driver said.

She shrieked, a significant sound from the throat of a three hundred and fifty pound woman. "Don't you dare say that, Dan Culp. I know my Crow is alive and waiting for me."

Culp and the man next to him exchanged glances.

"What do you think, Jack?" Culp said. "Is it a go or are we turning back?"

"Don't whisper!" Helga screamed. "I can't hear you when you whisper."

"We ain't whispering, Helga," Culp said. "We're planning a route."

"It's over there! The man in Cimarron said it's over there!" The woman jabbed a fat forefinger at the Tooth of Time Ridge.

"We can't go over them peaks, and the passes are blocked, damn it all, Helga," Culp said. "We got to keep on this heading then swing west at Rayado Peak."

"The man said it's over there! Over there!" Helga wailed. "Over there!"

Culp drew rein and turned in the seat, a white maelstrom of the snow cartwheeling around him. "Helga, the damned ridge rises near two and a half thousand feet straight up," he yelled. "God Himself couldn't get a wagon and two worn-out mules over that."

"Besides, there ain't no towns in this wilderness south of the Turkey Mountains," the man called Jack said.

"Over there! Over there!" Helga shrilled. "It's over there!" Her round face was bitten by cold, her cheeks like two red apples in a pink ceramic bowl. One of her pigtails had become undone and strands of her hair coiled and uncoiled in the wind like yellow snakes.

Helga Eckstrom was twenty-six years old that winter, a schoolmarm by profession. Crow Wallace's short visit to Cimarron a couple of months before had left her with a small problem in her belly that was rapidly growing larger.

Crow had told her he was on the scout. He believed the law was closing in on him and that he'd be gone when the baby was born.

Cimarron was fast becoming a boomtown, the center of a gold rush that attracted thousands of miners and some of them had already struck it rich. Fancy women and gamblers had arrived first, followed by grifters, goldbrick artists, claim jumpers, gunmen, whiskey peddlers, hangers-on, and dance hall loungers, all of them conducting business in a wide open town free from church bells.

According to Crow, where sin comes easy but never cheap, the law was bound to follow. When he became convinced that hard-eyed men were beginning to look at him strangely, he decided to leave town.

The note he'd left on Helga's bedside table stated his intentions.

Going sowth. See you in sum other town.

Helga, of an excitable Nordic nature, immediately panicked and the Viking in her took over. She retrieved her life savings from under the mattress and hired a couple of shifty characters to take her south in a mule wagon.

Dan Culp and Jack Flood, in imminent danger of being hung by vigilantes for being damned nuisances, had readily agreed to Helga's terms.

But adrift in a land of vast distances, brooding mountains, and black, ominous shadows, the two men were about to renege on their part of the bargain.

Culp climbed down from the wagon seat and walked back to Helga. Her enormous body was wrapped in a buffalo skin coat and she was angry enough to spit.

Snow circling around him, the man's breath smoked as he said, "We're turning around. Me an' Jack will take our chances back in Cimarron. I'd rather get hung than freeze to death."

Helga's rage grew as the berserker in her made her throw caution to the winds. "I paid you fifty dollars to take me to Comanche Crossing, and that's where we're going." She pointed at the ridge and shrieked, "Over there! Over there!"

Flood, his gray eyes set close together, bookending the bridge of his broken nose, produced a massive revolver. "One more word out of you, lady, and we'll dump you right here. You can walk to Comanche Crossing."

In her haste to leave, the only thing of value Helga had brought with her was her porcelain chamber pot, made in Sweden by her late father, a potter by trade. She threw the vessel at Flood, but the man did not react as it bounced off his chest.

The Ute arrow bristling from his throat had already killed him.

Appalled, Dan Culp was frozen to the spot for a moment, then he picked up Flood's revolver, his eyes probing through the snowfall. He saw them then, five Ute warriors wearing rabbit skin capes, their long hair falling over their shoulders. They were painted for war.

A rifle bullet thudded close to Culp's feet and an arrow flashed over his head.

Knowing he was moments from death, fear and desperation drove the man. He dragged Helga from the wagon, dumped her onto the ground and then jumped into the seat, Helga cursing him in a language he did not understand. Nor did he care.

Culp gathered up the reins, screamed as an arrow bladed deep into his right shoulder, and hoorahed the mules into a turn.

The Utes were almost on top of him.

He slapped the team into a run, grabbed the revolver from his waistband and snapped off a shot. Then another.

Both missed.

A long way off their home range, the Utes were wary. Pressed hard by vengeful Apaches, they'd already lost four of their number and had been forced to release the horses they'd stolen. Never a numerous tribe, the loss of four young braves was already a disaster. Culp's shots had come close, and they could not afford to lose more.

They fired at the man as he slowly disappeared into the gloom, the parted snow closing behind him like a lace curtain.

There was only Helga left.

A short, sturdy figure, she struggled to her feet and

stared at the Indians coming closer to her, walking their horses.

"Get away from me," she yelled. "Go away."

Had they been a hunting party, the Utes might have taken Helga with them. But in fear of the Apaches, a woman of her great size would only slow them down and eat too much.

The Utes drew rein, but for one warrior astride a gaudy Appaloosa who rode forward, a bow in his hand.

The man's face was painted black, a sign of mourning, and his amber eyes were hard and merciless.

It took five arrows to bring Helga down.

Later, the Utes would say that she was a strange creature, half human, half buffalo, and her medicine was strong.

In search of her beloved Crow Wallace, Helga Eckstrom died a long way from her native Sweden. Her skeletal remains were not discovered until 1928. She was identified when her name was discovered on the bottom of a ceramic chamber pot.

CHAPTER THIRTEEN
Vigilante Talk

The day after the deaths of Sheriff Frank Harm, Clete Miller, and Pete McPherson, Mayor John York called an emergency town meeting and inquest, doddering old Judge Matthias Brooke presiding.

Brooke, in his late eighties and prone to incontinence, was quick to declare that the three men were most foully murdered by a person or persons unknown. He then banged his gavel and declared, "This inquest is now concluded."

It wasn't, of course, and as the judge fled for the outhouse, the finger pointing began.

Tom Archer, the owner of the dry goods store, was the first to speak. "There are three strangers in town, all of them violent men."

To a ripple of "Hear-hear" and "Well said," Archer felt emboldened. Holding up his thumb, he said, "One. Bill Longley, a desperado well known to the law." A forefinger now joined the thumb. "Booker Tate, a frontier tough and ruffian." He raised his middle finger. "Tam Sullivan, a bounty-hunter and the killer of the outlaw Crow Wallace."

After the muttered comments died away, Archer said, "Any one of those men, or all three in league, could have murdered Frank Harm and the others."

"I say we arrest the rogues and string 'em up after we find them guilty," stated a florid-faced man with blue pouches under his eyes.

This brought cries of agreement and even a couple "Huzzahs!"

Mayor York rose to his feet. "Do we all agree that the three men mentioned are desperate characters and no doubt skilled gunmen?"

"They're draw fighters all right, a class of violent Texans spawned by the late war and I despise each and every one of them, seed, breed, and generation," Archer said. "Remember Bodie Burgess?"

Silent nods confirmed that everybody in Comanche Crossing remembered the thin, sallow man whose skin was pitted by childhood smallpox. He'd ridden into town two years before bringing with him a reputation as a named draw fighter and killer.

Archer, not trusting to people's memories, recounted that Burgess had been in town two days when he got into an argument in the saloon over a card game.

Irritated, the gunman knifed one man and shot another and only the quick thinking of Sheriff Harm saved the day when he blew Burgess's backbone apart with two barrels of buck.

"Now we have three such gunmen in our fair town, and one or all of them must answer to a court of law for poor Frank Harm's death." Archer sat down in his chair with the air of a man who has fairly made a compelling case and nodded sagely as people whispered congratulations into his ear.

To everyone's surprise, Lisa York got to her feet, a pretty girl with a fine straight back and bright, intelligent eyes. "I'd like to ask Mr. Archer a question."

"Ask away, little girlie," the storeowner said, grinning.

Lisa knew she was being patronized and tilted her chin. "It's about the three gunmen you mentioned."

Archer nodded. "Good, you paid attention. So what's your question?"

"Who's going to arrest them, Mr. Archer? You?"

The storekeeper hesitated a moment. Then he said, "We'll go in force, armed with rifles and shotguns."

"How many more widows and orphans can this town afford?" Lisa asked.

"I'm not catching your drift, young lady." Archer was irritated and it showed.

"You'll be going toe-to-toe against three professional gunmen. I ask the question again. How many widows and orphans can this town afford?"

Archer made no reply, nor did anyone else.

The faces of the women in the crowd were stiff, as though it was a problem they'd never anticipated.

Lisa glanced around the crowd and spotted the liveryman. "Clem, you've been in some wild towns in your time. Ever see a skilled Texas draw fighter shoot?"

Weaver smiled, somewhat embarrassed that the limelight had shifted to him. "A few, I reckon, in my time. They're a rare breed, mainly because so many of them die young."

"If the men of this town try to arrest three skilled draw fighters, how many widows after the smoke clears?" Lisa asked him.

The old man didn't hesitate for even the space of a heartbeat. "A dozen. Give or take one or two."

Above the babble that followed this pronouncement, Weaver raised his voice. "Bill Longley is probably the fastest there is. I don't know nothing about that Tate feller, but I reckon the bounty hunter is hell on wheels with a six-gun when he's riled. He done fer Crow Wallace, and nobody ever took Crow fer a bargain."

Lisa kept at it. "What about it, Mr. Archer? Is it to your liking that a dozen women will be made widows in one afternoon?"

For a while the room was quiet but for the wind shuddering against the windowpanes and the quiet sobs of a pregnant young woman who was helped outside after declaring that she'd, "Suddenly come all over faint."

The silence stretched and grew taut. It seemed that everybody present had lost the will to talk.

Finally Mayor York said, "Lisa, that will do."

The girl glared at her father, defiance in her eyes. When she noticed strain cutting lines into his face and the defeated slump of his shoulders, she finally sat down.

"I will consider what has been said here tonight and decide on a course of action," York said. "We'll meet again tomorrow morning at ten."

It was lame and all present knew it was lame, but no one volunteered an alternative course of action.

Three skilled gunmen in one town at the same time were a force to be reckoned with and suddenly it seemed that Comanche Crossing had lost the will to take on such a power. As Lisa York had pointed out, the butcher's bill was too high.

Coming on the heels of the deaths of Harm, McPherson, and Miller the loss of a dozen more of its best and bravest would sound the death knell of the town.

After York declared the meeting over, the fifty or so people in the room huddled into small groups and discussed what had been said.

"What the hell is that?" a man standing near the window yelled.

Then people crowded close to him to see what he was seeing.

A black silhouette of something large was out there, standing still and silent in the lashing wind and sleet.

CHAPTER FOURTEEN
Dead Man at the Reins

Bill Longley watched as folks from the town meeting spilled out onto the street, attracted by a wagon drawn by an exhausted pair of mules. A sleepless, restless man, he shouldered off a post and stepped to the edge of the hotel porch.

Tam Sullivan stepped through the door and stood beside him.

"A window-watcher like me, huh?" Longley commented.

"Man in my profession lives longer that way," Sullivan said. "I make it my business to know what's going on."

Longley glanced at the black sky. "Hell of a night."

"Is the only weather in this country wind and sleet?" Sullivan asked.

"I don't know. My first time here." Longley shivered. "It will turn to snow soon." He looked back to the street. "They're getting a man down from the box."

"I got a bad feeling about this. I reckon I'll go take

a looksee." Sullivan made a little bow and extended his arm. "After you, Bill."

Longley thought that amusing. "I'd hardly shoot you in the back in front of all those people."

"I don't think there's any way of telling what you'd do, Bill," Sullivan said.

Longley adjusted the hang of his guns. "Damn, I just got my boots cleaned."

"We all have a cross to bear. Lead the way, I'll be right behind you."

"Yeah? Well don't get any ideas, bounty hunter."

Sullivan grinned. "Me, Bill? Why, I wouldn't dream of putting a bullet into the back of your skull."

The body lay facedown on the boardwalk and no one seemed willing to pull the arrow out of its back.

"Here, I recognize that ranny." Clem Weaver lifted the dead man's shoulder with the toe of his boot. "Yup, it's him all right. His name is Dan Culp, runs with a feller by the name of Jack Flood. He was here in town for a spell afore we run him out."

Mayor York nodded. "I remember him. Chicken thief as I recall."

"And a damned nuisance," Weaver said. "He should've been hung fer a pest years ago."

"Apaches?" Tom Archer threw the question out to everybody.

Weaver shook his head and yanked the arrow out of Culp's back, bringing blood, flesh, and bone with it. After a while he said, "It's Ute. And it's a war arrow, judging by the strap iron head. If'n the savages had been hunting, they'd have used flint."

"What the hell are Utes doing this far south?" York said. "They never come this far into Apache country."

"Long time ago, they took a notion to mount winter raids against the Apaches. The Ute are friends with the Jicarilla and they know the young bucks like to hole up with their womenfolk and young'uns in the cold weather, then raid into Old Mexico come spring. That's how come the Utes figure December is a good month for hoss stealing." Weaver nodded at the Culp's body. "And that's how come he's dead. Must've bumped into the Utes while they was out conducting business."

"I say we mount a punitive expedition," Archer said quickly, his anger showing. "Make those damned savages pay for killing a white man."

The storeowner was met with blank stares and a stony silence.

Weaver said, "Tom, Ute warriors are fellers you don't want to tangle with. They're mean as hell and don't know when to quit."

"Seems like you're on your own again, Mr. Archer," Lisa York said.

Sullivan who'd been listening to the talk, wondered what she meant by that, then dismissed it from his mind.

Even at that late hour and in the middle of a sleet storm, she was so dazzlingly pretty that the big bounty hunter's breath caught in his throat. Amid the gray night, surrounded by gray buildings, torn by a gray storm from a gray sky, Lisa York burned like a candle flame that lit up the gray recesses of his soul.

He admitted to himself that he'd . . . no, not loved her . . . but certainly admired her from the first moment he'd seen her. But she'd never even glanced at him or acknowledged that he was alive.

He vowed to change that just as soon as he could.

"We'll bury this man in the morning." Mayor York looked around him. "Jim, can we put him in your icehouse for the night?"

"Hell, no," James O'Rourke, the saloon owner said. "I don't want him bleeding all over my ice."

"Stick him in the livery," Weaver said. "He'll keep pretty fresh in there, and I'll take care of his mules and wagon."

"I bet you will, Clem," declared a voice from the crowd.

The remark relieved the tension and for the first time that night people laughed.

Bill Longley turned away, a smirk on his face.

Sullivan followed him and caught the gunman just before he stepped back into the hotel. "Hey, Longley."

The man turned, scowling. "What the hell do you want now?"

Sullivan stepped closer. "Let's say you didn't take a pot at me on my way to the train station."

"Let's say I didn't," Longley agreed.

"All right then, a person or persons unknown tried to cut my suspenders. Right?"

Longley looked bored. "If you say so."

"Suppose the Utes have gotten the Apaches all riled up, and suppose it was an Apache who took a pot at me."

"So what?"

"Might be a good time for you to leave town."

"You trying to get rid of me, Sullivan?"

"Yeah. You're a bad influence."

"You mind that Sutton-Taylor business down Texas way?" Longley said. "Jim and Hays Taylor and John Wesley Hardin and them?"

"The feud still going on," Sullivan said. "As far as I know."

"Yeah, it is. Worse than ever before. Anyhoo, a couple years ago, back in Yorktown, Texas, the army mistook me for one of the Taylor boys and came after me with a rope."

"A travesty of justice, Bill," Sullivan said, his face empty.

"Well, the month before I'd shot an uppity black in a town called Evergreen, and I figured the soldier boys was aiming to hang me for that killing."

"Careless of them, Bill. Misleading a man like that."

As though he hadn't heard, Longley continued his story. "The sergeant in command of the damned Yankee hanging squad had a better horse than mine and soon came level with me." He drew himself up stiff and straight like a drill instructor. "'Surrender,'" shouts he, "'in the name of the law.'"

Longley relaxed his back and shoulders. "'You go straight to hell,' says I, drawing my revolver, this one here in my right holster. I shoved the muzzle into the sergeant's side and blew his Yankee guts out."

"You're a stern man, Bill," Sullivan said, "when all is said and done."

"Wait, there's a moral to this story," Longley said. "Maybe a couple morals. One is that I don't pull the trigger until I know I can kill my man. That's why it wasn't me who took a pot at you. If it was me, you'd be dead."

Sullivan opened his mouth to speak, but Longley

held up a silencing hand. "The second is that I don't scare easy, so your Apache talk is falling on deaf ears. I'm gonna take this town, Sullivan, and all that's in it, so stay out of the way. Do you *comprende*?"

"I've got no friends in Comanche Crossing. What do I care?"

"Yeah, that's true, but all the same I saw you making calf eyes at that little York gal tonight."

"Keep her out of it."

Longley smiled. "I would if I could, but I can't. See, pretty Miss Lisa is getting hitched."

"To whom?" Sullivan said.

"*To whom?* I like that. Very good grammar as befits a fine gentleman like yourself. Lisa York is getting hitched to my dear friend and colleague Booker Tate. The happy couple plan Christmas Eve nuptials and I will be Booker's best man and maybe even read from the Book."

Longley coughed. "How's this. '*May your fountain be blessed and may you rejoice in the wife of your youth. A loving doe, a graceful deer—may her breasts satisfy you always, may you be captivated by her love.*" He grinned. "That's from Proverbs 5:18-19. My pa learned me that from the Bible when I was a younker."

Sullivan was too stunned to speak. Beautiful Lisa York planned to be the bride of a savage animal like Booker Tate? It was beyond his understanding.

Longley's hands made pictures in the air. "Candles, pine wreaths, frost on the window panes, the blushing bride in white silk, her mama sniffing into her handkerchief and Mayor York all puffed up proud as a pup with a new collar . . . I can see it all."

Finally Sullivan found his tongue. "Yup, Booker is

a son-in-law to be proud of all right. When did Miss York say yes?"

"Oh, she hasn't yet, but she will."

"You mean Tate hasn't asked her?"

"He hasn't even met her, but he saw her at a distance and right away started mooning over the little gal he calls his Miss Pretty. That's when I began to make wedding plans."

A sense of relief flooded through Tam Sullivan. "Lisa York won't marry a violent, smelly brute like Booker Tate."

"Oh yes, she will," Longley said. "Trust me, she will."

"You mean you'll force her?"

"A harsh word, Sullivan. I prefer to say that we'll persuade the young lady to give her heart to Booker. After a couple years and a few beatings, she'll learn to love him." The gunman's eyes narrowed. "I've told you how it's going to be, so now it's time to back off. Just stay out of my affairs." Longley turned on his heel and stomped toward the hotel door.

He hesitated, turned, and grinned. "Sleep tight. Don't let the Apaches bite."

Sullivan heard the man's laughter echo until it he slammed shut his room door.

The sleet had turned to snow and the big bounty hunter watched pure white flakes fall onto the black mud of the street and disappear. His face troubled, he asked himself some hard questions. What if Lisa York came to him for help and asked him to make her problems his own? How should he respond?

He had no answers, nor did he seek any.

After all, he was only passing through.

CHAPTER FIFTEEN
Apaches in the Snow

By morning the snow had stopped, but storm clouds piled up above the Sangre de Cristo peaks like massive black boulders, threatening another avalanche of bad weather. The air was frigid, so cold it was sharp to breathe and the people who passed Tam Sullivan on the boardwalk were wrapped to the eyes in great woolen mufflers.

"I tell you I seen them with my own two eyes," he heard a man say as he took his seat in the restaurant. "A dozen maybe, and painted for war they was."

"So how come you're still alive, Eddie?" said the speaker's companion, an affable-looking man in a gray woolen topcoat and plug hat of the same shade.

"Because I hid, didn't I? And I didn't look at them direct. Look at an Apache direct, and he can feel your eyes burning him, like."

"And smell you if the wind is blowing right," the affable man said.

Ida Mae, looking as tired as always, came up to Sullivan's table. She gave him a half-smile as she poured coffee. "All this talk of Apaches is scaring me half to death."

"Where did the gentleman see them?" Sullivan asked.

Ida Mae turned her head. "Hey, Eddie, where did you see them savages?"

"Over to Angel Fire Peak, Ida Mae. Just yesterday morning. Seen them clear as day."

"What the hell were you doing over there in this weather?" Ida Mae said.

"You know the crazy lady?" Eddie said.

"Yeah."

"She asked me to guide her over there and stand by with my rifle while she gathered"—he hesitated—"potsherds."

Ida May jerked back as though amazement had just slapped her. "What the hell is a potshard?"

"Broken pieces of clay pots an' jugs and the like, Ida Mae. An' the crazy lady wanted old Injun skulls."

"What does she want them for?"

"I don't know. She says she collects them. Anyhoo, that's when I seen the Apaches and wished I hadn't."

The affable man said, "Eddie, you're as nuts as the crazy lady."

Ida Mae shook her head, then turned to Sullivan. "Maybe he saw Apaches and maybe he didn't. That crazy lady is no companion for a sane man. Make him as tetched as she is. Still hungry?"

"Enough for bacon and eggs," Sullivan said.

"Comin' right up." Ida Mae hesitated a moment, bent toward Sullivan and her voice dropped to a whisper. "Your name was mentioned at the town meeting last night as maybe being involved in the murder of Sheriff Harm and them two others."

Sullivan smiled. "You believe that?"

Ida Mae straightened up and shook her head. "No, I don't. You look like a born killer to me, but not a cold-blooded murderer."

Sullivan laughed outright. "Well, that was a double-edged compliment."

Ida Mae smiled. "I meant born killer in a nice way."

After Tam Sullivan ate, he asked Ida Mae about the crazy lady, some kind of amateur collector of antiquities, he'd guessed . . .

Or maybe a raving lunatic.

"She calls herself Lady Clotilde Wainright," Ida Mae said. "And I guess that's what she is. She's from England but came to live here about two years ago. She keeps to herself and accepts no visitors."

"Old? Young?"

"She's young, no older than thirty, and quite lovely in my opinion. Of course, I've only see her once and that was when she first arrived. She has a hired man who does her shopping, an Oriental gentleman."

"She lives in the hotel?" Sullivan asked.

"No, in the yellow house at the edge of town. You can't miss it. It's got a painted dragon weather vane that the Oriental gentleman keeps bright. Several times a year, he climbs up onto the roof with a can of red paint and a brush."

"Seems like an interesting lady," Sullivan said.

"She's a widow and she's crazy, collecting broken pots and old skulls. Before you get any ideas, she does not encourage gentleman callers. Perry Cox the banker tried and she left him standing at the door like a great booby. And in the summer heat, too."

"I'd like to ask her if she saw the Apaches. I sure don't cotton to them getting in my way out of town."

"Eddie Lewis was out there in a snowstorm and maybe he saw something or maybe he didn't," Ida Mae said. "The eyes of a scared man standing on guard with a rifle can play tricks on him."

"Lady What's-her-name would know."

"Wainright. Yes, she'd know, but she won't tell you." Ida Mae refilled Sullivan's cup. "You're safe here in Co-manche Crossing. Why not stay here until the Apache thing blows over?"

Sullivan shook his head. "No, I don't want to do that. Just as soon as I collect the bounty on Crow Wal-lace, I aim to head south. If Lewis is right about what he saw, there's a chance I could lose my hair real quick."

Ida Mae shrugged. "Well then, try to talk to Lady Wainright. But you could lose your hair real quick at her place, too."

CHAPTER SIXTEEN
A Mysterious Lady

Tam Sullivan returned to the hotel. He saw no sign of Bill Longley.

He damped down his unruly shock of hair, combed it in place, and trimmed his sweeping dragoon mustache. The mirror told him he looked all right, but he wished he'd one of those . . . what did they call it? Oh yeah, a *carte-de-visite* with his likeness on one side and a sentiment on the other.

A card like that would be sure to impress a highborn lady.

But he didn't have one of those so he settled his hat on his head and went as he was.

The morning remained cold and the clouds so low Sullivan figured a man could reach up and grab a fistful of iron-colored mist and watch it fade away like a fairy gift in his hand.

He crossed the street, wading through five inches of mud, then walked south until he reached the end of the boardwalk. He turned and touched his hat to a respectable-looking woman who'd just stepped out of a store. "Good morning, ma'am."

The woman cast him a horrified look, lifted her skirts, and hurried away.

"Yup, Tam, you're a real charmer with the ladies," Sullivan said to himself.

A yellow, gingerbread house of considerable size, six small-paned windows showing to the front, stood on a low, timbered hill to his left. The ground floor was of worked stone, but the upper level was clad in shingles. A roof of the gambrel type, of moderate steepness, ended in a broad gable. The house had several chimneys, an extensive porch, and multilevel eaves.

Sullivan stepped through a front yard haphazardly laid out with miniature Chinese and Indian temples, Greek columns of white marble holding up nothing but sky, statues of ferocious oriental gods, and a classical statue of a shapely nymph covering her feminine parts with a strategically placed veil.

But what held Sullivan's attention was the weather vane in the shape of a red, snarling, Chinese dragon, its tusked and fanged snout telling anyone who cared to know that the wind was blowing from the north.

The oak door was weathered, but the brasses shone as though they were polished every day. Also in brass, and just as shiny, was a plaque that read: GUN KAI.

Sullivan had no idea what that meant.

He lifted the door knocker, yet another dragon, and rapped sharply four times. Echoes knelled inside the house and he heard a woman say something in a rapid foreign tongue.

He fixed his smile in place and waited . . . and waited. . . .

After what seemed like several minutes, the door opened slowly and hesitantly.

Sullivan's smile that had slipped was back in place. He expected to see a fine English lady, but in her place stood a small, Chinese man, slender as a girl, wearing tiny little slippers, a red silk jacket embroidered with silver dragons, and black pants.

Sullivan recovered from his surprise quickly. "I'm here to see Lady . . ." Damn! He'd forgotten her name again.

The little man, who stood as tall as the middle button of Sullivan's coat, scowled and pointed to the brass sign. "You no read?" His voice had a belligerent edge.

"I don't know what the hell it means," Sullivan said.

"Last word *off.* You work it out, big shot." The Chinese man moved to close the door, but Sullivan grabbed him by the front of his shirt.

"I still want to see the lady of the house."

The first lesson the bounty hunter had learned was to never underestimate an opponent. But he broke that rule and it cost him.

The little man did something quick and the next thing Sullivan knew he was on his back in the yard, stunned, his ribs and jaw throbbing.

"Gun kai!" the Chinese said, not even breathing hard, and slammed the door.

Sullivan hurt all over. For the moment, he stayed where he was, staring up at the glowering sky that threatened to snow on him at any minute. He figured he'd had warmer welcomes.

After a minute or so, he heard the door slowly creak open again.

Still groggy, he got to his feet, made fists of his gloved hands and yelled, "You want to try that again you little—" The words died on his lips when a young woman appeared at the door.

"Are you badly hurt?" she asked. "I do hope not."

Sullivan unclenched his fists. "I guess I'm still all in one piece."

"Cheng can be so rough. And he has a quick temper."

"I noticed." Sullivan rubbed his jaw.

The woman was tall, of stately bearing and handsome rather than beautiful, but the dark auburn hair that cascaded over her shoulders in tumbling waves was lovely beyond measure, as were her steady, emerald green eyes. She hesitated on the doorstep a moment, then said, "You look most unwell. I suppose you'd better come inside and have a cup of tea. My name is—"

"Lady Clotilde Wainright," Sullivan said, smiling, the woman's name flashing back to him.

"And yours?"

"Tam Sullivan, from down Texas way."

A faint, fleeting smile touched Clotilde's lips. "Yes. How nice for you. Do come inside."

As he stepped into the drawing room, the first thing he realized was that he was too big for the furniture. It seemed that the spindly, antique chairs were made at a time when people were smaller and women in crinolines weighed about a hundred pounds.

In the fashion of the period, the room was overcrowded and stuffy with too many tables and settees, paintings on the walls, and delicate vases and ornaments on every surface.

Afraid to move, he stood in the middle of a Persian rug and turned his hat brim in his hands, a tall, wide-shouldered man feeling as out of place as a preacher in a courtesan's boudoir.

The room smelled of incense, like a Catholic church on a Sunday.

Lady Wainright, who had the British aristocracy's instinct to spot unease in others, smiled. "Perhaps we should repair to the kitchen, Mr. Sullivan. There's a nice warm fire in the stove."

She seated him at a more substantial pine table then glided into the chair opposite. "Cheng will bring the tea directly, but first he'll look at your forehead. You have quite a bump and some grazing, I fear."

"It's fine. It doesn't hurt any." Sullivan smiled. "Well, not much."

"But, I insist, Mr. Sullivan. Cheng was a fine physician and anatomist in his native China and he's very skilled at treating bumps and bruises."

Sullivan grinned and gingerly touched his head. "And very skilled at putting them there."

"Yes, indeed. Cheng has made a study of many ancient martial arts and he can be quite the rowdy at times." She turned as the little man entered the kitchen. "You may proceed, Dr. Cheng."

Sullivan tensed as the man advanced on him, but Cheng wore a wide smile and carried a bowl of water, a towel, and a small alabaster jar.

The Chinese kowtowed, then straightened up. "Welcome to the home of Lady Wainright, honorable sir. It is indeed a prodigious pleasure to see you here. Now, if you will permit?" As gentle as a woman, he dabbed at the graze on Sullivan's head with a damp towel.

"I think you may have taken a bad fall," Cheng said. "It is most distressing." He spread some ointment on the wound that smelled of pine but didn't sting then stepped back like an artist admiring his work. "There. You'll soon feel right as rain."

"You may serve the tea now, Cheng," Lady Wainright said. She gave Sullivan her slight smile. "Cheng is a treasure. He and my late husband were both physicians and they met when we did missionary work in China."

"I'm sorry your husband is no longer with us," Sullivan said, trying to be polite.

"Sir Arthur was killed during the Second Opium War, trying to save China from being annexed by the Western powers. I'm afraid he failed."

"And the Chinese killed him, huh?"

"No, Mr. Sullivan, the British killed him. On Christmas Eve three years ago, they stood Arthur against a wall in Nanking and shot him as a traitor. Ah, here's the tea at last."

Cheng poured tea into thin, china cups. "Cream? Sugar?" he asked Sullivan, bowing.

"No. This is just fine." The big bounty hunter looked at Lady Wainright over the rim of his steaming cup. "You must have been very young when your husband was killed."

"Not so young. I was twenty-eight. Arthur was forty years older than me, but he was a fine, intelligent, and energetic man and a first-rate anatomist. As it happened, I was spared execution, but Lord Elgin, the British commander, warned me that if I ever returned to England, I most certainly faced the hangman's noose."

A log dropped in the stove and erupted a shower of sparks that glowed bright red in the morning gloom. A solemn, round-faced clock ticktocked on the kitchen wall and the wind had picked up, rattling the windowpanes.

"So that's why you came to the United States?" Sullivan held up his cigar case. "May I beg your indulgence, ma'am?"

"By all means. Sir Arthur enjoyed a cigar and I became quite enamored of the fragrance." Lady Wainright's mouth hardened. "We'd lived in this country before, in Louisiana, where Sir Arthur was famed among his peers for his profound knowledge of human anatomy. I returned to recover from my husband's martyrdom and to do what I can to save yet another ancient culture facing destruction at the hands of the Anglo-Saxons."

"The Indians, you mean? I guess they're doing all right—which brings me to the reason I came here. I want—"

"They're not doing all right, Mr. Sullivan. They will be slaughtered and humiliated, just like the Chinese. Have you finished your tea?"

Sullivan nodded.

"Good. Then come with me. I have something to show you." Lady Wainright rose and in her dark gray day dress she glided across the floor like a ghost.

Sullivan mentally compared her to Lisa York. If Lisa

was a pretty china doll, Lade Clotilde was a white marble statue like the one outside in the falling snow.

Lisa was alive, vivacious, and her skin would be warm to the touch. But Lady Wainright was cold, aloof, a vital part of her closed off and locked up tight. The woman part of her.

Sullivan reckoned Clotilde could arouse strong emotions in a man . . . but love would never be among them.

"As Chinese art is defined by her bronzes and porcelain, the history of the native tribes of America is written in their pottery," Lady Wainright said. "And in their bones. Do you understand?"

"Yeah, I guess so," Sullivan said, completely baffled.

"I am cataloguing all the pottery shards I can find and thus will preserve something of the Indian heritage before it's all destroyed." The woman stared directly into his eyes. "Have you ever killed an Indian, Mr. Sullivan?"

"Well, I recently shot a breed, feller by the name of Crow Wallace. But he was a murdering skunk and lowdown."

Lady Wainright's eyelids flickered as though Wallace's name had struck a nerve. "He was a lowdown because white men made him that way. Don't you agree?"

"Well I heard tell that his white part was a mountain man, and they generally got along pretty well with Indians," Sullivan said.

"Cheng told me there are Indian-killers in this very town. I thought you were too, Mr. Sullivan, after Cheng said you brought in a dead man who looked like an Indian."

"Hell, no . . . oh, excuse me, ma'am . . . heck no,

Crow Wallace was half-Irish, half-Cheyenne and all damn bad . . . excuse me again, ma'am. He was called Crow because one time his pa took to liking birds and named him after one."

"I plan to return to China next year and continue my ministry. Until then, woe betide any man or woman I hear has been abusing our Indian brethren."

Sullivan nodded, smiling. "I'll keep that in mind, ma'am. Now, you were going to show me something?"

"The door, Mr. Sullivan." Lady Wainright led the way. Cheng, once again tense and menacing, was her shadow.

She turned the handle on the door and Sullivan said quickly, "Ma'am, did you see Apaches yesterday when you were out by Angel Fire Creek with Eddie Lewis?"

"Yes, yes I did."

"Ten of them?"

"Twice that number, Mr. Sullivan. I'm afraid they were hidden behind falling snow and it seems that Mr. Lewis doesn't see very well."

"That's a heap of Apaches. Enough to put the wind up a man."

"A question for a question. Is there a man in town who goes by the name Wild Bill Longley?"

"There sure is," Sullivan said. "He's not a real sociable fellow."

The woman nodded, but said nothing. She opened the door and held out her hand.

Sullivan didn't know if he was supposed to shake the hand or kiss it, like he'd seen highfalutin' menfolk do. He settled for a handshake that Lady Wainright readily accepted.

"*Au revoir*, Mr. Sullivan. And remember me to dear Mr. Longley."

A moment later, Sullivan found himself on the doorstep, the door slammed in his face.

CHAPTER SEVENTEEN
A Scream from Hell

Tam Sullivan walked down the rise toward the street. The buildings looked like a fleet of old wooden men o' war adrift in a sea of mud. The landscape, in somber shades of tan, gray, and olive green, stretched away on all sides of him and even the branches of the pines cresting the surrounding hills were thin and sparse and brown.

Winter was cracking down hard and the north wind, flecked with snow, bit deep.

In the course of practicing his profession, Sullivan had acquired the highly-strung instincts of a lobo wolf. Someone, or something, was watching him.

He turned and looked back toward the house, in time to see a hulking figure at a second floor window. The man—judging by his bulk that's what Sullivan figured it was—vanished almost instantly and the concealing curtain twitched into place again.

He'd only caught a fleeting glance of the man but

registered what he saw with shock—a bald head and an almost featureless face, as though the skin had melted to the skull, leaving only holes for the eyes and mouth. It was the kind of sight that could come back to a man in his sleep and make him wake in a sweat, fear spiking at him as he reached for his gun in the scarlet campfire glow.

Tam Sullivan would not soon forget the face, or the fact that the man was lurking in the house the whole time he spoke with Lady Wainright.

Who was the man and why was he there?

Sullivan had no answers for that question as he regained the boardwalk and saw a dozen men gathered outside the saloon, the lean, scowling, malevolent figure of Bill Longley among them.

Tom Archer nodded to Sullivan as he approached. "Do you want to get your horse and join us?"

"To do what?" Sullivan said.

"We're mounting a punitive expedition against the Utes, teach them that they can't kill white men with impunity."

"Ride with us, Sullivan," Longley said. "It will be a lark."

"Seems to me that anything that involves killing blacks and Indians is a lark to you, Bill," Sullivan said.

"Yeah, and rightly so. But don't forget Mexicans. I ain't too fond of greasers either."

Booker Tate laughed. "You tell him, Bill."

Sullivan ignored that and said to Archer, "How come you've made a deal with the devil?"

The storeowner's eyes flickered, moved to Longley, then back to Sullivan. He seemed uncomfortable. "We need guns. Indian fighters."

Sullivan glanced around the gathered men, young

faces, old faces, faces in between. A few of them, like Eddie Lewis, had been in the war, but Utes and Apaches didn't stand in line and fight under banners.

The group in front of the saloon would be up against a very different kind of enemy.

"You sweet-talked these men into joining you, Archer?" Sullivan asked.

"No sweet-talking was needed. These fine men are all volunteers. And they are determined to punish the savages."

A ragged cheer greeted those words. Emboldened, the storeowner said, "Well, Sullivan, will you join us?"

"The Apaches are out," Sullivan said. "You know that."

"Yes, we do, and we'll sweep them aside," Archer said. "It's the Ute murderers we want."

"Apaches don't sweep aside worth a damn," Sullivan pointed out.

"That's because they ain't met men like me and Booker Tate before," Longley butted in.

Sullivan's smile was neither warm nor friendly. "Bill, Apache warriors are not scared, unarmed Negroes and Mexicans. They shoot back."

"So you say, Sullivan," Tate said. "They'll take one look at me and Bill an' run like rabbits."

Archer had had enough talking. "Mount up, men. Let's quit the gabbing and go get us some scalps."

"You're making a big mistake, Archer," Sullivan said.

"Mister, if you ain't got the belly for it, step aside," the storekeeper said. "Mount up, boys."

Sullivan caught the flash of Longley's triumphant grin.

And then he knew.

Longley and Tate had no intention of fighting Indians.

At the first sign of trouble, they'd scamper and leave Archer and the rest to their fate. Longley intended to take over the town and empty its bank. For that he needed to kill off the gutsiest fighting men first.

All he had to do was step aside and let the Utes and Apaches do it for him . . . at no risk of harm to himself.

Sullivan watched Longley swing into the saddle. "Hey, Bill, I almost forgot. Lady Clotilde Wainright sends her regards."

The color drained from Longley's face. "She's here? In Comanche Crossing?"

"As ever was, Bill," Sullivan said, puzzled by the gunman's reaction. "Big house on the hill back yonder."

Longley surprised everyone. He savagely put spurs to his horse, and the big buckskin reared then galloped along the street, great gobs of glutinous mud pelting from its pounding hooves.

Archer's baffled posse followed at a walk, and Sullivan hurriedly retraced his steps along the boardwalk.

By the time he reached the end of the boards, Bill Longley had already drawn rein about twenty feet from the house. His words carried in the wind, all tangled up with blowing snow. "You don't scare me, Clotilde!" he yelled. "Don't call in favors! You hear me? We're not going back to what we used to be. I'm done with it."

The silent house stared at him with blank eyes.

"Come after me, damn you!" he shrieked. "Bring your dead man if you want and I'll kill him all over again!" Longley laughed an I-don't-give-a-damn burst of hysteria. "I know how to destroy you! I know, Clotilde!"

A moment's silence, then the only sound was the soft sigh of the sloughing wind.

A scream erupted, echoing from the house, a piercing, venomous cry . . . godless inhuman rage distilled to its essence.

Terrified, Longley's horse got up on its hind legs, white arcs showing in its eyes, turned and dashed down the rise. The gunman battled the horse and finally managed to draw rein when he reached the street.

"What the hell was that?" Tom Archer cried.

"Bobcat," Longley answered quickly. "Let's go kill some Redskins." His face was still white as bone and he coughed continually as though his throat had gone dry.

Sullivan watched the posse leave, Longley in the lead, smiling as he talked with Tate as though nothing strange had happened.

Like any man who has spread his blankets in the woods, Sullivan had heard the screech of a bobcat. The sound that had come out of the house was louder, harsher, almost demonic.

He stared at the house, saw only shadowed windows and shook his head. "Longley, what kind of enemy have you made? And what kind of woman"—he almost said *creature*—"was Lady Clotilde Wainright?"

CHAPTER EIGHTEEN
"A Man Could Get Himself Killed"

By the time Tom Archer and his posse reached Angel Fire Peak their enthusiasm for Indian fighting had seriously waned. The three-hour ride across wild, broken country had tired the men and horses.

The day had grown colder and the snow fell thicker. The land lay bleak and lonely under a leaden sky, streaked here and there with snow and ice that gathered in every crack and fold of the frozen ground.

Five miles to the west, the gray bulk of the Cimarron Mountains, banded by pines that marked the timberline, stood cold and aloof.

Archer turned in the saddle and said to Bill Longley, "Where the hell are the hostiles?" He pointed at the peaks. "Up there in a canyon or a hanging valley?" The storeowner's mustache and beard were crusted with white and snowflakes rimmed his eyelashes.

"They're holed up somewhere, I reckon, but real

close." Longley said. "I thought I caught a whiff of smoke, maybe a mile back." That last was a lie, but Archer accepted it as truth.

As his riders crowded around him, he said, "Boys, we'll backtrack a mile, see if we can pick up the scent again."

Longley felt danger in the air, and even his horse sensed it, holding its head high, ears pricked. "Keep a sharp watch, Archer. Like I said, the Utes are mighty close so be on your guard."

Archer's face frowned into a question.

Longley answered it. "Me and Booker will head west and take a scout around the Cimarron foothills. If we spot the savages, I'll keep watch and send Booker back for you."

"I thought you said you smelled smoke south of us," a man said.

"Maybe I did," Longley said. "I'm not sure. The wind is blowing from the north, so the smoke could've come from the Cimarrons."

The posse was almost done. Frozen stiff, their heads bent against the icy wind, they seemed all used up.

Concealing his outlaw contempt for small town rubes, Longley pretended to be concerned for their welfare. "Archer, if you and your boys see no sign of hostiles, head back for Comanche Crossing. We don't want to be caught out here come nightfall."

Archer was surprised. "What about you and Tate?"

"We'll scout east like I told you. If we see no Indian sign, we'll rejoin you."

"And if you do see the Utes?" Archer said.

"I'll fire three shots, and that means come like hell."

Archer nodded. Suddenly he looked old. Worn out. "All right boys. We'll head back down the trail."

Longley watched the posse leave . . . ten tired men slumped in the saddles, wishing that they'd never left home. "Let them boys put some git between us and them, then we'll do what has to be done."

"Ain't we gonna scout the Cimarron foothills?" Tate asked.

"No, you idiot. Hell, I don't want to bump into Utes or Apaches. Man can get himself killed that way."

Tate's brutal, thick-lipped face revealed his confusion. "So what are we gonna do, Bill? Tell me."

"We passed a limestone ridge about half a mile back that overlooks the trail. It's got timber along the crest where a couple of men can take cover." His thin lips curled into a smile. "You catching my drift, Booker?"

Tate shook his head and said nothing.

A heavy snow flurry gusted over the two riders and for a moment they were hidden from view. The pines shook and sent down small avalanches from their branches. Tate shivered in his thin mackinaw.

The air was as hard as iron.

"We got a chance to thin 'em out, see," Longley said. "The rubes in the posse are the best Comanche Crossing has got. I say we can cut them in half real easy. And then—"

"We take over the town." Tate's ugly grin was quick as though he saw everything crystal clear. "I wed and bed the little York gal and then we empty the bank and go on our way rejoicing."

"You'll be a respectable married man after all that, Booker," Longley said.

Tate's mouth widened. "Well at least fer a spell until I've had enough of her. Then we can sell her down Old Mexico way for a pile of money."

"Sounds like a proposition. We'll head for the ridge and make like Injuns. When I fire the three warning shots, them rubes will come a-hootin' and a-hollerin' and we pick 'em off like ducks in a shooting gallery."

"Bill, damn it all, you're a genius," Booker said, his eyes shining.

"Don't I know it."

The limestone ridge was shaped like the prow of a steamship, its crest covered by a mix of aspen and ponderosa pine. At its highest point, the rise stood fifty feet above the flat. To the south, it ended in a sharp drop, but on the northern side a gradual, pine covered gradient sloped down to the trail.

Longley and Tate rode up the slope, dismounted, then stashed their horses in the trees. They bellied down with their rifles at the top of the ridge overlooking the trail. Longley grinned at Booker. "You ready?"

"Damn right I am," Tate said. "I bet you ten dollars I knock down five of them plowboys."

"It's a bet, Booker." Longley turned on his back, levered off three shots, and reloaded his rifle. "Now the fun begins."

The rate of fire of the .44 Henry was twenty-eight shots a minute. In the hands of expert riflemen like Longley and Tate, it was a devastating weapon. Each man's rifle was fully loaded with sixteen rounds in their tube magazines and one in the chamber.

Tom Archer didn't know it yet, but his punitive expedition faced slaughter.

After a couple of minutes ticked past, Tate turned his head to Longley and whispered, "Where the hell are they?"

"They'll be here," Longley said. "It's a hard trail. Just be patient."

Poor advice from an impatient man.

The snow fell, lying thick on the backs of the prone riflemen. More time passed . . . three minutes . . . four . . . five . . .

Tate voiced Longley's own thought. "They ain't comin'. Damn it, Bill. They'd be here by now."

"I don't believe it. Archer ignored my shots." Longley shook his head as though trying to clear the wonderment of it all.

"The damned traitorous swine sold us down the river. They left us here to die like dogs."

"Scum," Tate said. "That's what they are, Bill. Just yellow-bellied scum and lowdown."

A bullet, ranging upward, missed Longley's face by inches and punched a hole in his hat brim. He yelped. "What the hell!"

Apaches!" Tate's voice was clamoring like an alarm bell.

"Where?"

"Every-damn-where!"

His eyes wild, Longley sprang to his feet. "Hold them off, Booker. I'll go get help." The gunman sprinted to his horse and swung into the saddle.

"Wait! Wait for me, Bill!" Tate yelled.

But Longley ignored the man. He was already at

the top of the rise. He spurred his horse onto the slope.

Then he spotted the Apaches.

Six . . . no seven . . . fifty yards off, sitting their horses on the flat.

He swung south and winced as a bullet burned across his left shoulder. Then he felt his horse stagger. The big buckskin pecked, but Longley hauled on the reins and kept the animal's head up, using bloody spurs in brutal, raking sweeps.

Behind him, he heard Tate yell something that was swallowed by the wind and the pound of hooves on muddy ground.

Scared, Longley pushed his faltering horse. The buckskin kept running, but its pace slowed and blood and foam flew back from its mouth, the bit stained scarlet.

Shots racketed behind him, then a rider drew level with him and his eyes widened in fear. But it was Tate. He held his Henry like a revolver, shooting behind him without turning.

"Get them off me!" Longley shrieked.

"Bill, they ain't after us. They gave it up."

Longley spared a glance over his shoulder. He saw no Apaches, only the lacy curtain of the falling snow and the steely sheen of ice that covered every tree and rock. Slowing his wounded horse to walk, he said, "I thought Apaches were great warriors. Damned cowards. They were afraid to face us."

Tate said nothing, his face empty but for a trace of the wound Longley had inflicted on him.

"I killed three of the savages," Longley said.

Tate looked surprised. "You did?"

"Yeah, I dropped three before I hit the flat. Damn it, man, didn't you see?"

"Sure, Bill, sure. I seen them savages fall with my own two eyes."

"They got lead into me, though." Longley showed Tate the tear in the shoulder of his coat. There was a smear of blood on the fur. "That's why I didn't hold up for you, Booker. I mean, me being wounded like that. And the hostiles put a bullet into my hoss."

"Will he last until we reach town?"

"I'll make him last." Longley thought for a moment, then smiled. "Keep a sharp eye out for blanket Indians or Mexicans, Booker. Maybe we can go back to Comanche Crossing with scalps."

CHAPTER NINETEEN
"Born to the Reckoning"

Tam Sullivan stood at his hotel room window and watched Tom Archer's posse ride in, a group of exhausted, frozen men. They'd suffered no casualties and showed no signs of wounds, so they'd obviously been defeated by weather, not Utes.

But where were Longley and Tate?

Those two boys knew how to take care of their own skins and must have fallen behind for some reason.

Sullivan smiled. Probably stopped off to rob somebody.

He watched as the riders dismounted then followed Archer into the saloon in search of whiskey to defrost their bones.

Thinking about it later, Sullivan reckoned it might have been better for the storekeeper if he'd gone straight home to the bosom of his family.

Sullivan moved from the window and put on his hat and coat and wrapped a yellow muffler around his neck. It was a purchase he'd made that morning after the saleslady had assured him that yellow mufflers were all the rage since Queen Vic's cousin, a German prince, had been seen wearing one grouse shooting in Scotland.

"Just feel the quality," the woman had said. "The wool is of course from Scottish sheep."

"Smells like Scottish sheep, too," Sullivan had said, but he bought the muffler anyway.

"Nothing from Santa Fe for you yet, Mr. Sullivan," Isaac Loomis said.

"I should have heard by this time." Sullivan was disappointed.

"Maybe the lines are down," the stationmaster said. "This has been a severe winter so far. Coffee?"

"Yeah, please." Sullivan took a seat after Loomis poured the coffee, wondering when the lines might be repaired.

"Depends," Loomis said.

Sullivan tested his coffee. "On what?"

"On how the weather shapes up or if there's Indian trouble. I hear tell the Apaches are out."

"Seems like, from what I've heard."

"Maybe two, three days for an answer from Santa Fe," Loomis said. "It's my best guess."

"That's a lifetime in a burg like Comanche Crossing."

The stationmaster shrugged like a little bird ruffling its feathers. "Oh, I don't know. We got a real nice church and there's a choir."

"I don't go to church."

"Neither do I, but we got a real nice one if you felt inclined."

Sullivan lit a cigar and puffed until the end glowed. "What do you know about Lady Clotilde Wainright? Lives in the big house at the edge of town?"

"She's never caught a train here," Loomis said.

"That's not telling me much. Nobody's ever caught a train here."

"But if we did have trains, and I'm not saying we don't, Lady Wainright never caught one."

Sullivan didn't even try to work out the logic of that. "So you know nothing about her, huh?"

"Only that she's a strange one. Keeps to herself." The stationmaster leaned across the table and said in a conspiratorial tone, "But I tell you what, though. Sometimes she keeps strange hours. I've seen her lamps burn all night and she only turns them off at sunup."

"Maybe she can't sleep," Sullivan said.

"That could be," Loomis agreed, "but there are them who say she has visitors arriving after midnight and sometimes in closed carriages." He sat back in his chair. "What do you think of them shenanigans?"

"You ever hear tell of a ranny by the name of Bill Longley?" Sullivan asked.

"Wild Bill Longley, the Texas outlaw? Sure. Telegraph operators keep each other informed. We call it professional courtesy."

"Why would Lady Wainright know him?"

Loomis shook his head. "I haven't a clue."

"So you've just heard about him, huh?"

"Yes, but not much. The only strange thing I ever

heard about Wild Bill Longley was he got hung once and it didn't take."

"Yeah, I know about that," Sullivan said. "Seems to me it was a pity. Bill only getting half hung, I mean."

"Did you hear how he got the noose off from around his neck? Now there's a strange story. Hamp Dickson, an operator farther down the line told me."

Sullivan shook his head, only mildly interested.

"Well, they say his woman bit through the rope. Fancy that."

Dusk made the gloomy day gloomier as Tam Sullivan left the station and made his way toward the saloon.

For a while a huge coyote, as silver as moonlight, kept pace with him, trotting through the pines like a phantom before vanishing into shadow.

Sullivan thought it strange but dismissed the animal from his mind when he walked in the saloon and stepped to the bar. He ordered a rye and a beer then took a seat at a table, his back against the wall as was the habit of men who made a living by the gun.

Tom Archer strolled over, looking like he'd been through it. "Never saw an Indian. Never saw nothing but snow and ice and mountains."

"You don't say," Sullivan said. "Now that really surprises me."

"I'm glad we didn't get into a scrape. After hours of freezing in the saddle, the expedition was in no shape to take on Utes."

"I reckon not," Sullivan said, looking over the exhausted men at the bar. "Where's Bill Longley?"

"I don't know."

"It's always good to know where Longley is."

Archer shut down for long moments before he spoke again. "Him and Booker Tate left us to scout toward the Cimarron breaks. He said if he ran into trouble he'd fire three shots and that we should come on fast."

"And did you?"

"No. We heard the shots, but by then my men were finished." Archer took a long swig from his whiskey glass. "What did Longley and Tate mean to us? I wouldn't risk the lives of my men to save a couple outlaws."

Sullivan slammed the knuckles of his right hand into the wall behind him. "Archer, you see writing on that? If you don't, I think maybe you should."

"Longley's probably dead by now. If the cold didn't get him, the savages did."

"Don't count on it. He's survived hard times and he's got more lives than a cat. Something else, Archer. Longley was raised to the reckoning and he's an unforgiving man."

His face troubled, the storekeeper turned and stepped back to the bar.

And Sullivan waited for the tragedy he knew must inevitably come.

CHAPTER TWENTY
Judge, Jury, and Executioner

By midnight, only Tom Archer and three of his posse remained in the saloon. Well, them, a saloon girl, and Tam Sullivan.

The girl wasn't Montana Maine and that disappointed him.

The oil lamps that guttered against the gloom cast pools of orange light along the bar and hollowed the faces of the men with dark blue shadows. The raw whiskey had long since lost its soothing magic, and they drank to get drunk in somber, sullen silence.

The girl, bored, stood at the piano and picked out the opening notes of Chopin's Nocturne in F minor. Every time she fingered a wrong key she sighed and started over. Behind the bar, the bartender fed a little calico kitten morsels of cheese and stroked her arched back.

Sullivan stubbed out his cigar in the ashtray. After

two whiskies and three beers, he was about ready to give up his vigil and go to bed.

It seemed that a vengeful Bill Longley was not going to show.

At least not that night.

But no sooner had he risen to his feet than the door slammed open and Longley and Tate barged inside, bringing a gust of wind, snow, and knifing cold with them.

Longley's coat was open and pushed back. His butt-forward revolvers made a belligerent statement. He laid his Henry on the bar then glared at the drinking men. "You three with Archer, I got a dead horse at the hitching rail outside. Bury it."

"Now?" The man who asked was small and wiry with a stubble of gray beard.

"Yeah. Now," Longley said.

"And if we don't?" This came from a bigger, tougher, and more aggressive redhead who was already half drunk.

"Then I'll kill you," Longley's voice was flat. At that moment, he looked like the wrath of God.

"It's time you boys went home, anyway," Archer said. "Just dab a loop on the horse and drag it into the trees somewhere. The coyotes will take care of it."

"I told them to bury it," Longley said.

"The ground is too hard," Archer said.

"Then how are they gonna bury you?" Longley was primed for a killing and there would be no going back from it. "I changed my mind. You three get my saddle off the hoss and take it to the livery. Then haul the carcass up to the graveyard. You'll have some buryin' to do come morning."

The three men carried holstered guns, but they were up against it. No man in his right mind wanted to haul iron on a Texas draw fighter in a tight space . . . not if he wanted to keep on living, he didn't.

The big red-haired man considered his courses of action, didn't find one he liked, and decided to call it a day. "Come on, boys. Let's get the dead horse off of the street."

"And don't forget my saddle and bridle," Longley said.

"I'll go with them," Tom Archer said, stepping away from the bar.

"You stay right where you are." Without turning his head, Longley said, "You aiming to take a hand in this, Sullivan?"

Sullivan shook his head. "Ain't my game. I reckon I'll set here quiet and see how things turn out."

"We didn't mean to leave you in the lurch, Bill. You got it all wrong," Archer said.

"After you heard my shots, how did I get it all wrong?" Longley said.

Archer searched his brain for something, anything. But he was scared, wasn't thinking straight, and couldn't find a way out. "The men were tired. They couldn't make a go of it," he said finally.

"So you left me and Bill to die like dogs?" Tate put in. "Was that the way of it?"

"No, that's not how it was," Archer said. "We . . . the men were in no shape to fight Utes."

"It was Apaches," Longley said. "I killed three or four of them, but they still got lead into me."

"Geez, Bill, I'm sorry," Archer said. "It was just an impossible situation. I mean, we were in the middle of a blizzard. You know how Indians fight. We could've headed right into an ambush."

Longley smiled and nodded his understanding.

And at that moment Tam Sullivan knew Tom Archer was a dead man.

"You a married man, Tom?" Longley asked quietly.

"I sure am. My wife's name is Mary and I have two kids. John is fifteen, Emily a year younger. She wants to be a schoolteacher."

"Nice, very nice. It's tough for a man to put his life on the line when he has a happy little family waiting for him at home," Longley said.

"Then you see how it is with me, Bill," Archer said. "I hoped you would."

"Of course I know how it is with you. Go home now, and no hard feelings. It was all an unfortunate misunderstanding."

Relief showed on Archer's face. He smiled as he walked past Longley and stepped quickly to the door.

"Oh, Tom," Longley called.

Archer turned, still smiling.

The two .44 balls that crashed into his chest removed his smile forever. He was seconds from death when he hit the sawdust.

Sullivan stood and cleared his iron as Longley swung in his direction, just as he knew he would. "Don't try it, Bill. I can drill you right where you stand."

Longley smiled and holstered the Dance. "It was a jest, Sullivan. Just a *bon mot*, you understand."

"Sense of humor like yours will get you killed one day." Keeping Longley in front of him, Sullivan got down on one knee beside Archer. He'd seen a lot of dead men in his day and the storekeeper was one of them.

"Is he gone?" The bartender was a big man, thick across the shoulders and chest. His name was Buck Bowman and he'd been a Texas Ranger for a spell and still carried a Comanche arrowhead deep in his lower back.

"Yeah, he's dead as he's ever gonna be," Sullivan said, getting to his feet.

Bowman, a man with no backup in him, stared at Longley. "Tom Archer has friends in this town."

"Tell them to bury him, or they can let him lie there and rot. I don't give a damn," Longley said.

Bowman eyes moved to Sullivan. "Did you see it as fair play, mister?"

"His wounds are in the front."

"He didn't have a chance," Bowman said.

"No, no he didn't," Sullivan agreed. "Not a hope in hell."

Longley hitched his guns into place and said to Bowman, "Let this be a warning. I'll kill any man in this town who crosses me or does me wrong." His spurs chiming, he walked to the door and a grinning Booker Tate followed him like a trained puppy.

"Why didn't you take a hand?" the bartender asked Sullivan. "You could have made a play."

Gun smoke drifted around the saloon like the ghost of Tom Archer rising from the dead.

"Best advice I ever got was to never interfere with something that ain't bothering me none. It was Archer's fight, not mine."

Bowman let out a drawn-out sigh as he stared at the dead man. "No, I guess it wasn't. But I think I'm going to make it my fight real soon."

CHAPTER TWENTY-ONE
A Hound from Hell

A sleepless man, Bill Longley knew every crack, patch of flaking plaster, and spiderweb on the ceiling and how the silver luster of snow light cast by the window looked like frost in the darkness. He blinked rapidly, his brain working.

So she had come back to claim what was hers by right. His life.

But why here and now? And how had she discovered where he was?

She hadn't, of course.

Clotilde being in Comanche Crossing was just a stroke of bad luck. Or was it fate, fortune, destiny? He could think of a dozen names for it, but not one was adequate.

Damn her to hell!

Longley got out of bed, slid one of his revolvers from the holster, and stepped to the window.

The big grandfather clock in the lobby downstairs chimed one.

She was there. He knew she'd be there.

The woman stood on the boardwalk opposite the hotel, her black cloak and unbound hair streaming in the wind, her eyes fixed on his window.

"Hag," Longley whispered. "You vile English hag." He pulled on his boots, buttoned his fur coat over his long underwear, then shoved the Dance into the pocket.

It was time to have it out with Lady Clotilde Wainright.

He owed her his life, but not his soul. She couldn't force him back into the old ways . . . the ways that had gotten her damned husband killed.

Longley crept downstairs and stepped onto the porch. The night was cold, the color of slate, and snow added its cartwheeling chaos to the carefree wildness of the north wind.

Across the street the boardwalk was deserted.

Everywhere he looked was shadow, deep, black, mysterious, the dark mouths of the alleys brooding like the portals of hell.

He stepped along the boardwalk, eyes restless, gun in hand. . . .

Doctor Allan's Pharmacy . . . The New York Hat Shoppe . . . Sloan's Rod & Gun . . . Archer's General Store . . . Brian T. Grossman, Attorney . . . Brown's Boots and Shoes . . . The storefronts came and went.

Longley reached the end of the timber walk. On the hill, the Wainright mansion was ablaze with light. His mouth suddenly dry, he licked snow off the back of his gun hand and stared at the house. All the curtains were drawn, and he saw nothing of what was happening inside.

But he knew.

It was time he had a plan. He'd kick the door in, find the hag and kill her. Simplicity itself.

Who in this hick town would arrest him for murder? There was no one.

Well, Sullivan maybe. But the bounty hunter was only passing through and didn't care.

Longley grimaced and shook his head. He'd let his anger get the better of him.

It was too damned risky. Cheng was dangerous and so was the grotesque man-thing she kept so well hidden.

And there would be witnesses. That could be awkward. He'd find another way.

Longley turned to walk back the hotel—and then heard the growl.

He peered through the murk at a patch of sagebrush some twenty yards from the end of the boardwalk and caught a glimpse of an animal . . . a coat the color of tarnished silver . . . the gleam of fangs . . . a huge animal.

Warily, he raised his revolver, his heart thudding in his chest.

A minute slid past, the growl seeming to be coming from all around him, a savage, liquid rumble that spoke of hunger—and slavering jaws.

Fearful, he stepped back, holding close to the front of a footwear store. A sign in the window said ALL BOOTS SOLD AT COST.

The growl came again.

Closer.

Longley studied the brush, searching for the animal, hoping for a clean shot.

Tick . . . tick . . . tick . . .

Something dripped on his hat.

He shook. What the hell? Probably drops from melting icicles that hung from the roof of the storefront. Yes, that's what it was, he decided.

A string of something that glistened hung from the brim of his hat. Then another. And another.

He lifted a hand and touched the stuff. It was warm and slimy. Slobber!

Longley jumped back from the store, looked up, and saw the massive head of a dog, saliva stringing from its jaws, staring down at him from the flat store roof.

He brought up his revolver, but the dog was no longer there.

A surge of panic rammed through his gut like a cavalry saber. O sweet Jesu! The animal was stalking him!

Longley shrieked, turned, and sprinted along the boardwalk. Behind him, he heard the heavy thud of clawed paws on the timber and a low predatory snarl.

He yelled and uttered a strangled cry for help.

The animal would soon rend, rip, slash, lacerate, devour him. . . .

"Help me!" he screamed. "Dear God, help me!" Terror lending wings to his feet, Longley reached the hotel door and, gasping, slammed it shut behind him.

A moment later something big, heavy, and demonic slammed against the door and rattled the glass panels. Then . . . silence.

The clock in the lobby sounded. *Tick . . . tick . . . tick* in the quiet.

"What scared you, Bill?"

Longley whirled, gun in hand.

Tam Sullivan stood halfway up the staircase. He wore his long underwear and hat, and held a cocked revolver.

"It's you, Sullivan." Longley was breathing hard and his face was fish-belly white. He holstered his gun.

"As ever was, Bill. I heard boots running on the boardwalk, then the door crashed open and closed. I declare, it shook the hotel to its foundations. I figured it had to be you."

Sullivan grinned. "See a boogeyman out there?"

"It was a dog. Damned thing was stalking me."

"A dog? You mean a little bow-wow dog?"

"Damn you, Sullivan, it was huge. Some kind of mastiff with jaws and teeth like a bear trap."

"Did it bite your butt, Bill? I sure hope it didn't."

"No, it didn't bite me. Damned cur wanted to tear my throat out."

"Why were you out so late?" Sullivan asked. "You know you shouldn't be out in the dark by yourself."

"None of your damned business," Longley gritted out. He began to mount the steps. "Get the hell out of my way."

Sullivan stepped aside, let the gunman pass, and watched him until he went all the way upstairs then returned to his room. He dressed and made his way onto the front porch, quietly closing the door behind him.

Something had badly scared Longley and he needed to know what it was. There was already enough bad stuff going on in Comanche Crossing and a wild animal on the loose was the last thing Sullivan needed.

In his book, anything that had even the potential to delay his departure was a bad thing.

He pulled up his collar and retraced Longley's steps, clearly visible in the half inch of blown snow that had accumulated on the boardwalk. There were also animal tracks, probably from a dog, but they were huge, made by very large animal.

He'd once met an English Mastiff named Bruno in a sporting house in Denver, kept there to protect the girls from aggressive clients. The dog was affable enough, but intensely devoted to his charges. His three hundred pound presence was enough to ensure that even the baddest bad men behaved themselves.

The mastiff that made the tracks on the walk may have been even bigger and a whole lot meaner than Bruno.

Sullivan stopped where Longley had taken shelter against the storefront. With his booted toe, he probed a slimy, damp spot that indeed seem like drool from an animal's jaws.

At the top of the hill across the street, light showed in every room of Lady Wainright's house and a couple of parked carriages stood in the shadows, their teams presumably in the stable.

Sullivan was puzzled. Why would visitors hazard the bad winter weather and the war talk about Utes and Apaches? And from where did they come?

He had no answers, but one thing he did know. Only something mighty important would bring folks out with winter coming down like thunder.

The dog was Lady Wainright's guard mastiff, of that he had no doubt.

Did it sense danger in Bill Longley? Or had the animal known him before and harbored a grudge? Those were more unanswerable questions.

Suddenly chilled, Sullivan made his way back to the hotel, wind and snow driving into his face. He continually glanced over this shoulder, fearing that he might see a massive dog with red eyes and fangs like butcher's knives stalking him.

His imagination working overtime, he was relieved when he stepped into his room and turned the key in the lock.

Happy it actually worked.

CHAPTER TWENTY-TWO
Grave Robbers

No matter the weather, be it the heat of summer or the cold of winter, Miss Angela Davenport made a weekly visit to the grave of her dear mama. Sarah Davenport had died five years before, smitten by a cancer that had ravaged her body and killed her before her time, poor thing.

She had left her hat shop to her daughter and with it an entry into the middle class. Angela enjoyed an income of a full 900 dollars a year as befitted a spinster lady of genteel status.

She was a thin, some would say scrawny, woman in her early forties with brown eyes, brown hair, and a prim mouth. She had never lain with a man and had long since reconciled herself to the fact that she never would.

Donning her coat, hat, woolen gloves, and a stout pair of leather boots, Angela picked up her prayer book and stepped outside into the cold, windy morning. She carefully locked the front door of her house and tested the handle several times before embarking on her journey.

The walk up the slope to the cemetery was always a chore, but she didn't mind, not when Mama expected her weekly visit. Angela bent her head against wind and sleet, and trudged to the cemetery gate.

A previous mayor had encouraged burial in aboveground tombs, but Angela did not approve. It was a foreign concept, begun in New Orleans, and it smacked of popery, a religion of which she vigorously disapproved.

No, her dear mama was buried six feet under as a good Christian should be.

Her mother's grave lay to the right of the gate, under a piñon that marked the spot just as surely as the marble gravestone Angela had set up. She brushed snow off the top of the stone, opened her prayer book, and her lips began to move in a soft whisper.

After ten minutes, she became exceedingly cold as the sleet fell more heavily.

After the murders were discovered, the mayor had ordered proper burials for Sheriff Harm and his helpers. Crow Wallace was also buried properly.

Angela walked to the north end of the cemetery, through a wind that alternately sighed and shrieked like the voices of the damned. A sound she found most distressing. Through the slanting sleet she saw what looked like fresh graves just a few yards in front of her.

Dear Sheriff Harm. She was sure he would appreciate

her prayers. He'd always been such a nice man, a Methodist to be sure, but she never held that against him.

She stepped closer to the graves. . . .

Angela Davenport's eyes almost popped out of her head.

And she screamed . . . and screamed . . . and screamed. . . .

"Doc Harvey gave her a sedative and my daughter is with her," Mayor John York said. "She's had a terrible shock."

"That's why you came to see me, to tell me the graves were empty?" Tam Sullivan asked. "What business is that of mine?"

"No, I came to talk to you about the death of Tom Archer. But don't you think it strange that four recently buried corpses are missing, including that of Crow Wallace? Surely that interests you."

"Coyotes maybe? It's winter. Hard times for coyotes and the like."

"All those men were buried deep," York said. "And there's no trace of the bodies. Coyotes would have scattered their bones all over the place."

"It's strange, Mayor, I'll grant you that. If it isn't coyotes then I don't know what to make of it." Sullivan sat at a table in the restaurant with York.

The mayor was a worried man and it showed in the struggle to get his coffee cup to his mouth without spilling. "Buck Bowman, the bartender, says Tom Archer's death was murder." He set the hopelessly shaking cup back on the table.

"Well, he saw it, just like I did, and he called it," Sullivan said.

"What do you think?" York asked.

"Archer hadn't been notified. So the way things turned out, he'd no chance."

"Then Bill Longley murdered him?"

"Archer was wearing a gun, Mayor."

"Does that make his murder legal?"

"No, I guess not. But a jury would say he had an even chance."

York sighed. "Tom Archer's death, the stolen bodies, all this Indian talk . . . Comanche Creek could soon fall apart."

"Bill Longley is a big part of your problem. And it will get worse. Do you know that Booker Tate plans to marry your daughter?"

York's face registered shock. "Why, that's preposterous! She's never even met the man."

"I think Booker plans on making her acquaintance real soon. He and Longley are set on a Christmas Eve wedding."

"Over my dead body," York said emphatically.

"I'm sure Bill Longley can arrange that," Sullivan said dryly.

York's rugged face seemed to dissolve and his bottom lip trembled. "Oh my God, Sullivan, what can I do?"

"The short answer is to put the run on Longley and Booker." The bounty hunter grabbed the attention of the waitress. "Ida Mae, can I have more coffee here, please."

York waited until she refilled Sullivan's cup then said, "We already have a widow and three orphans. My daughter . . . Lisa . . . says this town can't afford any more."

"Go up against Longley and there will be widows all right. The man's got a yellow streak, but when his back is to the wall, he'll fight. So will Booker Tate."

York shook his head. "I can't take that chance on more deaths. My town is already teetering on the brink. Can I buy them off?"

"Yeah, with every last cent that's in the bank. And maybe that won't be enough."

"A loss like that would ruin practically everybody in this town, including myself," York said.

"Better to be broke than dead."

York's face was stiff. "That was a cold, heartless, uncaring thing to say, Sullivan."

"It's been my experience that this is a cold, heartless, uncaring world. I don't owe this town a damned thing, so it's all up to you. Either gun Longley or you pay him. The choice is simple."

"And what about you? Will you just stand aside like you did in the saloon last night?"

Sullivan didn't like that statement much. "Mayor, I'm only passing through. Get that into your head, huh? I wasn't Tom Archer's nursemaid. He should have gone home when he had the chance."

"Longley would have followed him there," York said, getting to his feet.

Sullivan said nothing, taking time to light a cigar.

"You know, Sullivan, I intended to offer you the sheriff's star."

"Keep it. I'm not a lawman," Sullivan said.

York looked down on him. "Maybe it's time to prove that you're any kind of a man."

CHAPTER TWENTY-THREE
Desperate Encounter

It was, Ebenezer T. Posey decided, terrible weather for travel. But then, alarmed by his treachery, he quickly amended the thought to include *but the business of the Butterfield Stage Company must always take precedence over his own discomfort.*

The temporary inconvenience of a freezing, bumpy stage ride took second place to the greater whole of his employer's well-being and prosperity.

Thus did Posey, huddled into an oversized bearskin coat, journey to Comanche Crossing, a town on the benighted edge of nowhere, to identify the body of Mr. Crow Wallace, recently deceased. And also to make the acquaintance of one Mr. Tam Sullivan, the gent who'd rendered Mr. Wallace that way.

Safely tucked away in Posey's carpetbag were several items. Thirty-six hundred in Yankee dollars, a contract giving Mr. Sullivan ten percent of the monies recovered from the stage robbery, and a wanted poster displaying Mr. Wallace's image and likeness.

Once the body was identified and the transaction completed Posey would waste no time returning to Santa Fe and the bosom of his family.

On that happy thought, he glanced out the jolting window into the gray day. Rank on rank of massive black clouds hung over the mountains to the west and portended nothing but more snow, ice, wind, and suffering. He shivered and drew his coat closer around him. The fare of the last stage station, fried salt pork and beans, had settled in his belly like lead.

The Butterfield coach, a special charter provided for Posey alone, rattled along a rutted wagon road amid lightly falling snow. Buttressing the trail on each side were high, limestone ridges. Their crests were sparsely treed but the bottoms were thick with timber, meadows showing among the pines like green scum ponds.

Posey felt the stage jolt, then clatter to a jangling halt.

The Butterfield stage line did not put much value on the life of a junior clerk, but they set store by the money he carried and the amount he would bring back upon his return. Therefore the stage carried a shotgun guard in addition to the driver.

Big Jim Lloyd's two hundred and fifty pound bulk caused the stage to slant to one side and creak in protest as he climbed down from the seat and stepped to the window.

"Is there something wrong with the coach, Mr. Lloyd?" Posey asked.

"Nothing wrong with the coach, Mr. Posey, but

there's plenty wrong with the landscape. It's got Apaches on it."

Ebenezer Posey, a small, perpetually frightened man, clutched at his throat. "Oh, my poor wife. How will she cope?"

"Worry about your own hair, not hers." Lloyd had heavy features and the broken-veined skin of a drinker.

"Where are the savages? Oh dear me, not too close, I trust."

"Somewhere right ahead of us. Do you have a gun?"

"Oh my, no. Mrs. Posey would never allow a firearm in the house."

"Here, take this." Lloyd pulled a large blue revolver from his waistband.

"How do I shoot it?" Posey held the Colt gingerly, as though it might bite him.

"Just pull back the hammer and squeeze the trigger. Make sure the muzzle—that part right there with the hole in it—is against your temple."

Horrified, Posey said, "My dear sir, are you telling me to shoot myself?"

Lloyd nodded, then put his meaty hand on Posey's thin shoulder. "It may not come to that, Mr. Posey. But don't let yourself get taken alive. The Apaches will kill you, but it will take hours, maybe days."

"You mean torture?" Posey squeaked, his brown eyes wide.

"Like you wouldn't believe," Lloyd said as he stepped away from the stage.

Posey stuck his head out the window and yelled up at the box. "Driver! Mr. Dillard! Kindly turn back now!

I'll come back another day." His voice had the raven croak of a terrified man.

The driver made no answer and Posey felt the stage rock as Lloyd regained his seat.

"Right at 'em, Dillard!" Lloyd yelled. "We'll charge through 'em like Mosby at Fairfax Courthouse."

Posey was thrown hard against the back of the seat as the stage took off, the traces rattling as the six-mule team lurched into a run.

"Oh, God help me," Posey whispered as the first rifle shots roared.

The stage swayed drunkenly as the mules hit their pace.

Posey's already shattered nerves scraped like fingernails on a chalkboard as the firing drew closer and iron wheel rims rumbled on the frozen road.

A bullet splintered into the wood panel above his head and he shrieked as a second hit inches closer.

He heard Dillard's frenzied *"Yeeaah!"* and the *blam-blam* roar of Lloyd's scattergun. A man screamed but Posey didn't know who he was.

The mules stumbled, slowed the stage a little, then the front wheels hit something solid. Suddenly, Posey felt himself go airborne. For long seconds the stage seemed to fly, then the wheels hit the ground with a grinding crash, and Posey was thrown violently to the floor.

He untangled himself from the tentacle folds of his heavy coat, turned on his back . . . and let out an ear-piercing shriek of fright. A painted Indian rode just outside the stage, glaring at him.

The Apache urged his pony to keep pace with the

door, its curtain torn away by a stray bullet, and worked the lever of a new Henry rifle.

Posey thumbed back the hammer of the Colt, shut his eyes, and shoved the big revolver out in front of him, holding the grip with both trembling hands. He fired, a massive explosion in the close confines of the stage.

Stunned, ears ringing, the little man opened his eyes and screeched.

The savage was still there!

But as Posey watched, the Apache slowly bent over, lost ground, and disappeared from view.

In a highly emotional state that went beyond terror, Posey regained his seat and cringed in the corner. Bullets splintered through the stage and up on the box, the driver roared and cursed at his mules as though he was an Apache himself.

Driven to distraction by dread, the little man stuck his head out of the window and yelled, "Mr. Dillard! Surrender at once!"

The wind tore away his words and they went unheard. Ahead of him was a tunnel of cartwheeling snow and behind . . .

"Oh, merciful God!" Posey whispered.

Galloping Apaches fired on the stage. They were all around him, whooping and hollering, demented demons in the wind.

His eyes like dollar coins, Posey clutched at his seat as the stage suddenly rocked. He heard Dillard call out, but because of his gun-deafened ears he didn't catch the words.

An Indian, the lower part of his face painted black, rode close to the stage, but Posey didn't dare shoot again. The noise of the revolver going off was too loud, and why antagonize the savages when they might soon make him their prisoner?

But as the stage rocked wildly again, creaking on its leather through braces, Ebenezer Posey had the feeling that no matter how things turned out, this was going to be a rainy day in his life.

To his shock, a mule, still in remnants of its traces, trotted past his window, heading away from the coach. And then he saw another one on the opposite side, an arrow protruding from its neck.

It all made him more afraid.

For several minutes the stage continued its breakneck pace, but then he heard what sounded like Lloyd's voice yelling the team to a halt.

The coach slowed, stopped, and a man's voice—it was Lloyd's—called out, "You all right down there?"

"I believe so," Posey said, quite shaken. "Where are the savages?"

Lloyd stepped down from the box and stood at the window. "I cut out the pair of lead mules. I guess them Apaches were hungry because they gave up and went after the animals."

"Oh dear, wasn't that terribly dangerous?" Posey asked as he gained some strength.

"Cutting out the mules? Yeah. But not near as dangerous as Apaches. You winged one, you know. Saw it with my own two eyes. Good for you, Mr. Posey. You got sand."

"I discharged the weapon, yes, but—"

"The Butterfield stage line is gonna be right proud of you," Lloyd said. "Hell, man, you're a hero."

Posey saw that the right side of the big man's face

was spattered with blood, and some specks of white that looked like tiny pieces of eggshell. "Mr. Lloyd, you're wounded."

The guard touched his face and his fingertips came away bloody. He stared at them for a long time, surprised, then said, "Nah, this is Deke Dillard's blood. Got his lower jaw blowed off, beard an' all."

"Is he . . . dead?"

"Yup, dead as he's ever gonna be. Lucky fer him. Now help me get him into the coach. We can't leave him up on the box. He ain't a Christian sight, if you catch my drift."

"Oh dear," Posey said, shrinking back. "I don't think I can."

"Sure you can," Lloyd grinned. "A fearless Indian fighter like you."

The little man would have made further objections, but Lloyd grabbed him by the collar of his coat and, none too gently, hauled him out of the door. "There you go, Mr. Posey. You stay right there and I'll lower poor Deke's body to you. Jes' you hold fast to him until I get down. All right?"

To Posey's horror, the stage was splintered by bullets and its rear half bristled with arrows like a porcupine. Fingers of blood, scarlet in the gloom, trickled from the box and drops ticked onto the snow-streaked ground. On all sides of him rose timbered mountains and the ebony sky draped over the entire landscape like a shroud.

Then, for a reason that he would later not fathom, he said, "How many savages did we . . . um . . . kill, Mr. Lloyd?"

"Well, you winged one, I'm sure of that."

"And you?"

Lloyd shook his head. "Apaches know what a scattergun does to a man. They never came close enough for me to get off a decent shot."

"So poor Mr. Dillard was the only fatal casualty?"

"Seems like," Lloyd said. "Now, let's get him down."

"I'll say a prayer for him." Posey bowed his head.

"Sure. Once we get him in the stage, you can do all the prayin' you want."

"Will the savages come back?"

"Hell, no. They'll fill their bellies with mule meat then crawl into a hollow log somewhere an' sleep away the rest of the winter."

"Oh dear," Posey said. "How very uncomfortable."

CHAPTER TWENTY-FOUR
An Unlikely Hero

"The entire lower half of his face was blown away, Mr. Sullivan." Ebenezer Posey shook his head. "It was a terrible sight."

"Sharps .50, I reckon. Apaches are right partial to them, or so I've been told." Sullivan studied the small man. He had narrow shoulders and a tight, clean-shaven face that was as small as a nut. The Butterfield man looked as timid as a house mouse, yet Big Jim Lloyd said he'd shot an Apache, no mean achievement in a running gun battle.

The hour was still early, but Sullivan had insisted that he and Posey repair to the saloon where a brandy would restore the little man to a less nervous state and they could discuss the reward.

Posey sipped his brandy guiltily, like a maiden aunt trying her first sherry at a tin pan cotillion. His eyes moved from side to side as though he feared someone would come up and take his glass away. "Mr. Lloyd assures me that if we can't find a replacement driver he can take the stage back to Santa Fe, leaving first thing tomorrow. My dear wife's business is making . . . ah . . . bloomers for oversized ladies and she does need me to do her daily accounting work. A staff of five and the buying of materials like cotton and lace take a lot of bookkeeping, you understand."

Then, as though the thought troubled him, "Of course I won't leave until after I've identified the late Mr. Crow Wallace's body."

"Well, now, that might be difficult," Sullivan said, selecting a cigar from his silver case. "I mean really difficult."

"On account of how there's no body." Buck Bowman stood behind the bar polishing a glass, a sheriff's star pinned to his vest.

"Oh dear," Posey said. "That is most unfortunate. It's a complication I didn't foresee."

"The body's been stole," Bowman said. "With three others, all recently deceased."

"Oh dear," Posey said again. He looked like a little gray mouse.

"Well, it was Crow all right." Sullivan moved uneasily in his chair.

"Who else saw the deceased?" Posey asked.

"Sheriff Frank Harm," Bowman said, appointing himself as Sullivan's spokesman, much to the bounty hunter's irritation. "But he's dead and one of the missing bodies is his."

"Did you see the late Mr. Wallace?" Posey asked the bartender.

Bowman shook his head. "Saw the body, but I don't

know if it was Crow's. I'd heard of the man but never seen him."

"Damn it. The man I shot was Crow Wallace, and there's an end to it," Sullivan said, talking past the cigar in his teeth.

"I'm afraid not, Mr. Sullivan," Posey said. "Without identifying the body I can't pay the reward. That is the official policy of the Butterfield Stage Company."

Sullivan's temper, always an uncertain thing, flared, but he fought to keep it in check. "Mr. Posey—"

"You may call me Ebenezer."

"I've got six thousand dollars of Butterfield money I recovered from Wallace after I shot him. I can take my reward out of that."

Posey shook his head, his prim lips compressed. "Oh, I'm afraid that won't do. Why . . . why it would be most dishonest."

"Damn right, Ebenezer." Bowman grinned, enjoying Sullivan's discomfort. "Agin' the law as ever was."

"But look on the bright side, Mr. Sullivan," Posey said. "I'm authorized to pay you five hundred dollars for the return of a gold watch I believe is in your possession, along with ten percent of the stolen monies you recovered."

"Yeah, I've got it," Sullivan said, his face glum. The little Butterfield man had him backed into a corner. If he took the reward out of the six thousand, the law, probably the Pinkertons, would come after him. The last thing a professional bounty hunter needed was to get branded by sheriffs and marshals as dishonest on the deal.

"I'll find Crow's body for you," he said finally.

Posey frowned. "By tomorrow morning?"

"Stay in town a day or two," Sullivan said.

"I'm afraid that's impossible." Posey shook his head. "A lady's bloomers wait for no man. A little joke of my wife's there."

A moment later, the impossible became the inevitable.

Jim Lloyd stepped into the saloon and after exchanging a greeting with Buck Bowman, whom he'd known in the past, he stood at the table, a crestfallen look on his florid face. "Bad news, Mr. Posey. When we bumped over the felled tree trunk that time, we damaged all four wheels of the coach."

Posey was alarmed. "What does that mean?"

"Well, the damage to the wheels is bad and the wheelwright tells me he'll need a couple days to repair them."

"This is most distressing." Posey ran his fingers through his thin brown hair. "What will Mrs. Posey think when I'm late? Her nerves are very delicate."

Lloyd grinned. "She'll think you're having a grand old time in Comanche Crossing, wine, women, and song, and all that. You're gonna get blamed for it, so you might as well do it."

"Oh no, I could never do such things. I promised Mrs. Posey on our wedding day that I'd ne'er look at another woman."

"You haven't met Montana Maine yet." Lloyd looked at Bowman. "Is Montana coming in tonight?"

Enjoying Posey's flustered look, the bartender said, "She might well show up. What's this . . . Friday? . . . Yeah, this is usually her red dress night."

Posey said, "I can assure you that my lady wife—"

Lloyd's hearty slap on the back made the little man spill brandy down the front of his fur coat. "Forget the missus for a few days, Ezekiel—"

"It's Ebenezer."

"And have yourself a grand ol' time."

"Well, I don't even know if there's room for me at the hotel," Posey said.

"Room? Room for the Hero of the Cimarron Trail? Of course there's room." Lloyd laughed heartily. "And if there isn't, the Bon-Ton will toss somebody out and make room."

"Damn right," Bowman said. "Nothing is too good for a famous Indian fighter."

"In fact, I'll go over there right now and reserve rooms for both of us. The Bon-Ton will be honored." After another slap on the back for Posey, the big guard stepped to the saloon door.

Bowman's words stopped him in mid-stride. "Jim, Bill Longley's in town. And Booker Tate is with him."

Lloyd's face stiffened. "You think he's still sore at me for putting lead into him that time down to Bastrop County after he shotgunned Wilson Anderson?"

"Jim, Anderson was a boyhood friend of Longley's," Bowman said. "You any idea what he'll do to an enemy?"

"I'll step careful," Lloyd said.

"He's a back shooter, Jim, and he favors his left hand on the draw," Bowman said. "That's all I can tell you."

Lloyd nodded and stepped out of the saloon.

As he crossed the street, his head constantly turned from side to side on his massive shoulders.

CHAPTER TWENTY-FIVE
Of Gunmen and Body Snatchers

Buck Bowman saw a mild questioning look on Sullivan's face. "Big Jim and me were in the Rangers together."

"He got lead into Bill Longley, huh?" Sullivan asked. "That's a powerful claim for a man to make."

"Yeah. Burned him across the shoulder. Jim's shooting was off that day I reckon."

"How did it come up?" Sullivan was taking a professional interest.

"Do we really need to talk about all this violence?" Posey put in. "I'm starting to feel most unwell."

As though he hadn't heard, Bowman said, "Like Jim mentioned, it happened down to Bastrop County, Texas, the summer of seventy-five when Longley got work as a farm laborer."

Sullivan smiled. "Sure don't see ol' Bill as a pumpkin roller."

"Neither did he as it turned out. How it come up, a cousin of his, feller by the name of Cale Longley, Jr., had gotten into it with Wilson Anderson over the affections of a fancy woman.

"From what I heard, Cale called Anderson a sorry piece of white trash and proceeded to read to him from the book. Well, Anderson closed the last chapter of said book with a dose of double-aught from both barrels of his shotgun. Blew Cale's guts out all over a stack of cotton bales sitting outside a Hill City warehouse."

"A testy man, that Anderson feller," Sullivan said.

"Seems like. Ruined about a hundred dollars worth of prime cotton, too, they say."

Ebenezer Posey held up a pleading hand. "Please, gentlemen, no more." He looked about to throw up, like a tiny green frog.

"Well, naturally, Bill heard about the death of his kin and went gunning for Anderson. Mind you, him and Anderson had been close boyhood friends, shared blankets and ate out of the same plate, but in Bill's part of Texas the death of kinfolk has to be avenged. The reckoning, you understand?"

Sullivan nodded. "I've come across the reckoning before."

"Well, Bill saddled up and rode directly to Anderson's farm and caught the man plowing behind an ox team. He blew his belly open with a Greener. An eye for an eye, like." Bowman laid down the glass he'd been polishing. "They say Anderson's wife cut loose with a Springfield rifle as Bill rode away and that it was her, not Lloyd, that winged him. But I don't know about that. Big Jim caught up to Longley a couple days later, took a pot at him, but then lost all trace of the man in the wild hill and oak country down that way. So who knows?"

"You're the new sheriff, Bowman, huh?" Sullivan said.

"As of yesterday. I was appointed by Mayor York."

"Then keep an eye on Lloyd. If he did put lead into Bill, he'll sure enough try to kill him."

"I think I should go to my room and take a nap," Posey said.

"Finish your brandy and I'll escort you across the street," Sullivan said.

"Is my life in danger?" the little man said, panic in his eyes.

"Only from Apaches," Buck Bowman said. "After you shot one of their kin, an' all."

Posey clutched at his throat. "Don't say that, please."

Sullivan said, "You're safe enough in town, Ezra."

"Ebenezer."

"But watch out on the trail back to Santa Fe," Bowman said. "Keep that fast Colt of your'n handy."

"I don't have a fast Colt." Posey looked lost, lonely, and miserable. "I don't even have a slow Colt. I don't have any kind of Colt."

Bowman grinned. "That's all right. You can always buy one before you leave town, Injun fighter," Bowman said.

* * *

After Tam Sullivan warned him that he could sink into the mud of the street and vanish from view, Ebenezer Posey did not think it in the least undignified to be carried across in the bounty hunter's strong arms.

Nor it seemed to Sullivan, when Posey reached his room was he self-conscious about disrobing and changing into a white, ankle-length gown and a nightcap with a tassel.

When he settled himself in the brass bed, a pillow at his back, the little man said, "Mrs. Posey always insists that I dress for bed when I take a nap. She says lying down in my day clothes would not be genteel."

"A refined woman," Sullivan said. "Knows her manners, huh?"

"Indeed she does. Although a lady of somewhat Junoesque proportions, she can fit into any class of society. And, of course, her knowledge of bloomers and female corsetry is quite unparalleled."

"A fascinating woman," Sullivan said, his face empty. "Well, now you're all tucked in, I'll go look for my missing body."

Posey held up a halting hand and didn't speak for long moments, as though marshaling his thoughts. When he did speak again, he baffled Sullivan completely. "Mr. Sullivan, have you heard of William Burke and William Hare?"

"I can't say as I have. Are there dodgers on them?"

Posey smiled slightly. "Oh dear me, no. They were murderous criminals in old Edinburgh town in Scotland some forty or so years ago."

"Ah. Well, that's way off my home range."

"Just so. It is indeed a long way across the Atlantic Ocean. Now let me explain. In Scotland, as in our own country, there was and still is, a chronic short-age of cadavers for the study and teaching of anatomy, so doctors in the Edinburgh medical school turned to grave-robbers to ensure a constant supply."

Sullivan smiled. "I catch your drift, but Comanche Crossing is a long way from Edinburgh."

"The body-snatchers dug up the recently dead, tore them from their coffins and smuggled the corpses to the doctors for payments in cash. As more and more graves were desecrated, you can suppose that this caused a great deal of public anger and outrage."

Sullivan wondered where Posey was headed with this. "Yeah, I can see that. Anger and outrage, I mean."

"The result was that armed guards were placed in graveyards to discourage the Resurrectionists, for that's what the body-snatchers were called, and the supply of bodies to the medical schools dried up."

"Inconvenient for the sawbones, huh? Having nobody to cut into." Sullivan edged toward the door. "Look, it's snowing again outside. I'd better be going."

"Wait, Mr. Sullivan, please," Posey said. "Allow me finish. It won't take long."

Sullivan gave a resigned shrug of the shoulders. "All right, go ahead. I always love to hear about stolen cadavers."

"Burke and Hare, seeing their fun money vanish-ing, had to get fresh bodies from somewhere, so they turned to murder. In all, they killed sixteen men and women and sold their bodies to the doctors before they were caught."

Sullivan tried for a response, but couldn't come up with one and stayed silent.

Posey talked into the quiet. "Bodies are still in huge demand for dissection, Mr. Sullivan. Body-snatching still goes on apace in this country and abroad because it's such a lucrative profession. Is there a doctor in Comanche Crossing?"

"Yeah, I heard the mayor mention a doc. Hardy or a name like that. I don't quite recall."

Posey lifted an eyebrow and stared hard at Sullivan.

"You mean he might buy bodies to cut them up and take a look at their innards?" the bounty hunter asked.

"It's possible. Four bodies are missing and there's a doctor in town. Who else would be interested in buying cadavers of what were young, healthy specimens?"

"Like Crow and them?"

"Exactly."

"Nah, that's dime novel stuff," Sullivan said. "It could never happen in this burg. In Boston or New York maybe, but not in Comanche Crossing."

"I only offer my rather lurid tale as a suggestion, Mr. Sullivan," Posey said. "You want to find Mr. Wallace's body and claim your reward. There is a possibility, remote though it may be, that even as we speak he's lying on a steel autopsy table in the good doctor's back room."

"The doc would be faced with the problem of getting rid of the bodies he'd used," Sullivan said. "Does he bury them in his backyard? A man the size of Frank Harm would need a big hole."

"A physician who's expert with the knife and saw

would have no trouble cutting a body into small pieces and dumping the parts in the woods. Coyotes and carrion birds would do the rest . . . destroying the evidence at it were." Posey yawned. "Well, at least it's an avenue to explore. Now, if you'll excuse me, I really must take my nap."

CHAPTER TWENTY-SIX
Sullivan Draws a Blank

Tam Sullivan stopped at the front desk and got the name of the town doctor.

The clerk said Peter Harvey was a fine doctor, young and eager, and during the war had served as General Braxton Bragg's personal physician. Doc Harvey seemed to have little social life, though he was close with the mayor's family, and most in town believed that his recent marriage was a happy one.

That was as far as the clerk's description of the man went. Apart from his association with the irascible Bragg, he seemed quite ordinary.

Sullivan nodded his thanks to the desk clerk and stepped onto the porch.

Bill Longley was there.

Hatless, the gunman wore black pants and vest and a white shirt open at the neck. He packed both revolvers in their expensive gun belts and was, Sullivan conceded, an intimidating sight.

"Taking the air, Bill? A might cold to go coatless."

"I'm not lingering long. The hotel starts to stink when certain people are in residence."

"Bill, you surely don't mean me?" Sullivan asked.

"If the shoe fits, Sullivan. Hear you carried the new town hero across the street. I heard maybe the brass band will play later if'n the snow quits."

Sullivan glanced at the sky where restless black clouds circled the town like a pack of wild beasts. "Sure don't look like quitting."

"They say the little feller killed himself three or four Apaches. That's what I heard. They're calling him some kind of famous Indian fighter come to visit."

"He winged one, probably by accident," Sullivan said.

"I prefer the other version," Longley said.

Sullivan nodded. "Yeah, well it makes for a better story. It's always a joy to talk with you, Bill, but I got to go."

"Go where?"

"The graveyard."

"Reserving a space, Sullivan?"

"No, but I'll pick out one for you if you like."

"One day that smart mouth of yours will get you killed," Longley said. "You know that, don't you?"

"But not by you, Bill, huh?"

"You figure you're faster than me, Sullivan?"

"Well, I reckon so, but faster or slower, I'm too mean to die easy. I'd get lead into you and you know it. Gives a man a kinda uneasy feeling, don't it, Bill?"

"You got a smart mouth, Sullivan."

"I think you already said that, Bill."

"Ah, the hell with it. This isn't the time for a shooting scrape," Longley said. "Be out here tonight at seven and you'll see Booker goin' a-courtin'."

"A sight not to be missed, I'm sure."

"It ain't, because he'll look mighty fine. One of the store owners donated a new sack coat, vest, and plug hat. Booker's got a bag of molasses candy for his ladylove."

Sullivan smirked. "Donated? Now there's a word you don't hear every day in Comanche Crossing."

"Yeah, well everything in this town is free to me and good ol' Booker. I thought I told you that."

"Must have slipped my mind. What does Buck Bowman over to the saloon think of that arrangement?"

Sullivan touched a nerve, but Longley quickly recovered his poise. "He don't know about it yet."

"I see. Let's set that aside for the moment. Who's the lucky lady?"

"As if you didn't know."

"I hear Miss Montana Maine when she deigns to visit the saloon is a sight to see. It could be her."

Longley frowned. "Yeah, well it ain't her. Tonight Booker is putting Lisa York in the right frame of mind for a wedding."

"And what woman could resist his charms? Is he taking a bath?"

"A bath in the middle of winter? Are you crazy? Booker could catch his death of cold. I know you'd like that, clear your path, like."

"If Booker passed away from the sniffles, he'd be sadly missed by all," Sullivan said.

"You're jealous, Sullivan, huh? That's your problem."

"Well, perhaps just a tad."

"I figured you would be."

Sullivan stepped to the edge of the porch, careful to not turn his back on Longley. "Bill, you're a man of the world. Ever hear of Resurrectionists?"

Longley blinked. "What the hell are those? Some kind of preachers?"

"Body snatchers," Sullivan said. "They dig up fresh corpses and sell them to doctors."

Something dawned in Longley's face. "Oh, now I catch your drift. You're going up to Boot Hill to scout around for the body of Crow Wallace so you can collect your reward. Wherever ol' Crow is hiding, you're gonna dig him up."

Longley slapped his thigh, tilted back his head and guffawed. When he recovered, he wiped tears from his eyes. "Damn it all, Sullivan, even though I'm gonna kill you one day, you make me laugh. You're a Resurrectionist, an' no mistake."

"Wait till you see the funny faces I can make," Sullivan said.

Bill Longley laughed again.

CHAPTER TWENTY-SEVEN
Flying Lead

Driven by a relentless wind, snow swept through the cemetery as Tam Sullivan, bent over against the cold, stepped to a hole in the ground that he figured may have held Crow Wallace's body. The outlaw's rough pine coffin was smashed, long, splintered fragments of the lid lying around with rimes of icy white along their edges.

Whoever had taken Wallace from the grave had transported only the body, probably because it took up less space in a wagon.

The empty graves of Frank Harm and his helpers told the same story, shattered coffin lids hastily tossed aside and the bodies removed.

Where the hell were they? And who took them?

Sullivan shook his head. Maybe it was the ghosts of Burke and Hare come to the Americas to practice their profession.

He scouted around the gravesites but found nothing.

Only his boot tracks marred the spotless virginity of the fallen snow.

It was not yet three, but the ashen-gray sky promised an early dark and a longer banishment of the sun. The air was razor-sharp and smelled of dank earth and rotting things. There were no shadows.

Sullivan began his trudge back to the cemetery gate, feeling helpless. The reward for Crow Wallace was as out of reach as ever. Doc Harvey was his only hope, slim as it was.

Maybe he'd just come straight out with it, state his case. "Excuse me, Doctor, but do you have a body of mine? It originally belonged to a man named Crow Wallace, and now I seem to have mislaid it."

Yeah, good luck with that, Tam, he told himself.

Sullivan was just a few yards from the gate when a bullet knocked him on his back.

For a moment, he thought he was dead.

The bullet hit the left side of his chest with the smashing force of a kick from a Missouri mule. A second, probing round jolted up a V of snow and dirt close to his head and he rolled to his right. A third bullet, scattering twigs and frosted leaves followed him into a clump of boxwood brush.

He looked down at the blood on his coat, pulled his gun, and gave vent to his exploding rage. "Longley, you've done for me!"

The only sound was the mocking moan of the merciless wind.

Sullivan pushed down the boxwood and looked around, seeking a target. Then it dawned on him. . . . He'd heard the flat roars of a mighty big gun, a larger caliber than Longley's .44-40 Henry.

Somebody else was taking pots at him with a damned cannon.

Peering through the brush, he saw nothing but snow sloughing among gravestones and the arched ebony dome of the sky. "Bill Longley! Is that you?" he yelled, knowing it wasn't. "Show yourself like a man and take your medicine."

A bullet crashed terrifyingly close and Sullivan pressed himself into the ground, trying to dig a hole with his face.

He spat out dirt, more scared than angry. The situation was not good. The hidden rifleman had him pegged and it was only a matter of time before his probing shots started hitting.

It was a big gun, all right.

Sullivan swallowed hard. He had it to do. He'd die on his feet.

Then the thought came to him. *I'm shot through and through, so why the hell am I still alive?*

He had no time to ponder the question. He clambered to his feet and thumbed off a shot for no other reason than it made him feel less vulnerable and more in command.

Five running strides took him to the cover of a low, aboveground tomb. He dived for the ground just as a bullet chipped marble from the dome-shaped top and a fragment cut a red gash across his cheek.

Then he did the unexpected.

Anticipating that the bushwhacker would count on him to keep his head down, Sullivan jumped to his feet, his darting eyes seeking a target.

There! Just a glimpse!

A humped back arched above the top of a tombstone, like a fish breaking the surface of a lake.

Sullivan fired from the hip. He heard the angry slam of his gun and a wild shriek at the same instant. He dusted a shot at each side of the stone, then waited.

Just one loaded chamber left.

The windblown snow and late afternoon gloom cut his visibility to about twenty feet. Listening into the quiet, he heard a series of high-pitched yelps, like a cur dog in pain. Then to his left he caught a glimpse of gray moving quickly through a bordering stand of pines.

Walking as fast as his aching wound would allow, Sullivan headed in that direction, his Colt ready.

He saw his assailant.

Dressed in a long greatcoat, the man ran bent over with a strange, limping gait, running close to the ground like an animal.

Sullivan fired and missed by several yards.

He'd known he had no chance of hitting the bushwhacker, but the shot was payback for scaring the hell out of him . . . and for cutting his suspenders.

He took shelter under the skeletal branches of a good-sized tree close to the cemetery gates and opened his coat. His wound was bloody but gave him more numbness than pain.

Then he saw the reason why.

He removed the mangled silver cigar case from his shirt pocket. The rifle bullet had hit the case and deflected, but not before it drove large slivers of silver into his chest. One jagged fragment gleamed in the middle of the wound like a silver tooth in a scarlet mouth, but he kept his gloved fingers away from it.

It looked to be in deep, a job for a doctor.

But he was still alive.

He'd always known that smoking was a healthy habit.

CHAPTER TWENTY-EIGHT
Sullivan Bites the Bullet

Bill Longley, in his usual chair on the porch of the Bon-Ton Hotel, saw Tam Sullivan come down from the cemetery hill with blood on his coat and a face as white as bone. The gunman rose to his feet, stepped onto the boardwalk, and when Sullivan reached the street, he held up a hailing hand. "Howdy, Sullivan, you dead at last?" he yelled, grinning. "You've come over all bloody."

The big bounty hunter stopped, a tall, stooped figure behind the moving veil of the snow. "I got shot, Bill," he yelled back. "Lucky it wasn't a .44-40 or right now you'd be taking your last breath."

"Aw, I figured you were dead. I heard the shots an' all and I was hoping. What a disappointment to hand out to a man."

"Maybe the doc will have good news for you," Sullivan said.

He started to cross the muddy street as Longley

yelled, "Don't forget to come admire Booker tonight, if you're able. Hell, Sullivan, with any kind of luck you might even be dead by then."

Sullivan, uncomfortably aware of the shot-dry gun in his holster, smiled. "I'm going to kill you one day, Bill. Depend on it."

"If you're still around!" Longley laughed.

"You're not able to take your coat off by yourself, Mr. Sullivan. Please, let my nurse do it." Doctor Peter Harvey frowned as Sullivan reluctantly complied.

The nurse was middle-aged and stern. She pointed at his holstered Colt. "Remove that, please."

Again Sullivan did as he was told, but he didn't like the nurse.

The doctor ushered him into a chair and glanced at Sullivan's bloody shirt. "It seems that we've been shot."

"Seems that way to us too, doc," Sullivan said.

"Nurse Fry, please remove the patient's shirt," Harvey said.

"Amazing how a chunk of lead can turn a man from a person into a patient real quick," Sullivan said, smiling at the woman.

"Humph," Nurse Fry said. "That wasn't very funny."

"Let's take a look, shall we?" Doctor Harvey said.

"We shall," Sullivan said.

The physician was an intense young man, somewhere in his middle thirties, with intelligent brown eyes and thinning yellow hair. He was clean-shaven but for a huge pair of frizzy Dundreary side-whiskers popular among medical men.

He examined the wound, and smiled slightly. "Were you shot by a silver bullet, Mr. Sullivan?"

"The answer is in the pocket of my coat, doc," Sullivan said.

"Nurse Fry, if you please," Harvey said.

The nurse, nose wrinkled, reached into the pocket and produced the mangled case.

Harvey studied it closely. "You shouldn't be alive, Mr. Sullivan. You were struck by a large caliber bullet that should have gone right through this cigar case like a hot knife through butter."

"Then I'm lucky, I guess."

"Very lucky. Mind you, strange things do happen with ordnance. During the war, I once saw a ten-pound cannonball deflected by an oak tree twig no thicker than Nurse Fry's little finger."

"Skinny twig." Sullivan kept his face bland. Getting out from under Nurse Fry's glare, he asked the doc, "Can you cut the pieces out of the wound?"

"Yes. Actually, there will be no cutting involved, though the probing might be quite painful."

"However, we can give you ether," Nurse Fry said.

"And put you out," Doctor Harvey said.

"I prefer to stay awake," Sullivan said, feeling contrary. But when the doctor started mining for silver with steel forceps, he regretted those words.

When Sullivan's wound was clean and bandaged, Nurse Fry beamed at him. "What a brave little soldier you were."

He didn't feel brave. It had hurt like hell.

The nurse helped him into his coat and handed over his gun belt. "I'm sure you'll need this," she said, her frown of disapproval back in place. "The surgical fee is five dollars. You can pay at the desk."

"Getting shot is becoming more expensive," Sullivan said.

"Then don't get shot."

"Come back in a couple days so we can check on your wound," Doctor Harvey said. "We don't want gangrene setting in, do we?"

"No, we don't," Sullivan looked him in the eye. "I'd like to ask you a question, doc."

"I welcome questions from my patients," Harvey said, smiling.

The smile fell like a fat man on ice as Sullivan said, "Have you ever heard of Resurrectionists?"

It took the physician a few moments to reply, his eyes troubled. "Yes . . . body snatchers, weren't they? In Scotland, I believe."

"And in this country, from what I've heard."

"I'm afraid surgeons need cadavers for the teaching of anatomy to medical students," Harvey said. "And the great Renaissance artists like Leonardo Da Vinci dissected corpses to study muscles and the like."

"Do doctors still cut into dead bodies?" Sullivan asked.

"Of course, but a steady supply of executed criminals fills that need."

"Nobody's been executed in Comanche Crossing in quite a while, I reckon."

"But then, we don't have a medical school now, do we?" the doctor pointed out.

"Doctor, I think he's talking about the missing bodies at the graveyard," Nurse Fry said.

"Ah, yes, yes of course," Harvey said. "That is unfortunate, I might say macabre, indeed." He smiled, staring at Sullivan like a philosopher who's just discovered the answer to a great mystery. "I don't think there's anything sinister in it, though. It's alarming, yes. Dangerous, possibly, if it's the mischief of Indians. But it's not the handiwork of Resurrectionists."

"Then who?" Sullivan asked.

"Then *whom.*" Nurse Fry corrected, her face stern.

Doctor Harvey stepped to the window. "Look out there, Mr. Sullivan. From what I've been told, Apaches infest every hill and valley, eager to kill white men. What better way to plunge Comanche Crossing into a panic than to steal bodies from the cemetery? Terrorize a community sufficiently, and it loses the will to fight and becomes easy prey." He turned and stared into Sullivan's eyes. "Apaches are the answer to the missing bodies."

"Doc, in enemy territory, Apaches scalp the dead and later throw the hair into a tree to keep the deceased warrior's vengeful spirit at bay," Sullivan said. "They don't carry away the bodies of their enemies."

"Then this town is an exception, Mr. Sullivan. The savages are trying to instill fear in us, and as far as I can tell, they're succeeding. Nurse, do we have a patient waiting?"

"Yes, doctor. Mrs. Lucas is here. Her husband is down with the ague again, I'm afraid."

"Then, if you'll excuse me, Mr. Sullivan?" Harvey left the room.

A couple of minutes later, Tam Sullivan found himself back in the street, five dollars poorer, his shoulder punishing him. He suspected Dr. Harvey knew more than he was telling. It was obvious he'd made up the Apache story on the spur of the moment.

Sullivan nodded to himself, his face grim. There was only one way to find out.

CHAPTER TWENTY-NINE
Two More Notches for Bill Longley

Tam Sullivan returned to the hotel, reloaded his Colt, then lay on the bed, tired from the events of the day.

A *tap-tap* came to the door, and with an effort, he rose to a sitting position and slid his revolver out of the holster. "It's unlocked. Come in real sociable, like."

Ebenezer Posey opened the door and stuck his head inside, as fearful as a mouse approaching the cheese in a trap. "Are you alone?" His eyes darted around the room.

Sullivan nodded. "Seems like."

Posey stepped into the room and quietly closed the door behind him. "I heard you got shot." He was fully dressed.

"Damn, word travels fast in this town," Sullivan complained.

"I suspect Mr. Longley spread the news abroad," Posey said. "Dear me, what happened?"

Sullivan told him.

Posey looked even paler than usual. "This is most distressing. I fear your life is in the greatest danger, Mr. Sullivan."

"And yours, Elijah."

"Ebenezer. Why would someone harm me?"

"The body snatchers know that it's because of you I'm forced to look for Crow Wallace and by doing so, I've upset their applecart. You've become a pest and a target."

Posey gave a little start of alarm. "I never thought of that. Are we really in the midst of Resurrectionists, Mr. Sullivan?"

"Doc Harvey says Apaches dug up them bodies, to scare the town."

"Is that possible?" Posey asked, eagerly anticipating the *Yes* that would ease his fears.

"No," Sullivan said. "Or at least, very unlikely."

Feeling faint, the Butterfield man sat on a corner of the bed and tried to disappear inside his fur coat. "Oh, what do we do, Mr. Sullivan? My poor lady wife would be so upset if she knew my life is in such peril."

"Here's what we do . . . . um . . . ."

"Ebenezer."

"Yeah, now listen up."

Sullivan told him.

For long moments, Posey sat stunned, then he let out a sharp cry of anguish and shook his head vigorously.

"I won't do it, Mr. Sullivan. "I-will-not-do-it."

"Suit yourself. Make yourself a target."

"Suppose I'm slain? I won't even be able to rest easy in my grave," the little man wailed.

Sullivan disagreed. "Not if we catch the body snatchers. Then, if you get shot, you'll sleep like a baby."

It was Longley's decision that Booker Tate would be too nervous to properly go a-courtin' until he had imbibed a few drinks.

Tate, though not a man known for his high-strung nature, readily agreed. The thought of facing pretty Miss Lisa York with molasses candy in hand and his heart on his sleeve did make him feel a little uneasy.

He didn't want to scare the girl . . . at least not until their wedding night.

With two hours to go before Tate needed to get gussied up, he and Longley crossed the street to the saloon. For the moment, the snow had stopped, but the wind was bitter cold. Apart from the lighted saloon and restaurant the buildings were lost in darkness, the stores shuttered early for lack of hardy customers.

Longley, a swaggering man made even more arrogant by the town's lack of action following his killing of Tom Archer, stepped up to the bar on the brag. After ordering whiskey, he turned to the patrons and slapped Tate on the back. "Boys, meet the future husband of Miss Lisa York. We're doing a little celebrating this evening."

If Longley expected a cheer, he didn't get it.

The dozen or so men in the saloon sat in stony silence. Behind the bar, Buck Bowman scowled and slammed down a polished glass with considerable force.

Longley smiled. "Booker, it seems that these gentlemen don't think you're a fit match for the mayor's daughter."

"Who cares what they think." Tate looked around with lowered brows like a great, shaggy buffalo bull. He smelled like one, too. "Anybody says Lisa York ain't gonna be my bride, step right up here and say it to my face." He swept his mackinaw away from his gun. "I got an answer for ye right here."

"There will be no gunplay in here tonight." Bowman put a shotgun on the bar. "Here are my bona fides."

Longley smiled and decided to smooth things over. "Booker is just a little overexcited about his courtship, Sheriff. He means no harm."

"Then rein in your dog, Longley," Bowman said, a tough, unyielding man. "Don't make me do it for you."

"Drink up, Booker," Longley said, grinning. "I don't think we're among friends this evening."

"I'm not your friend, Longley and never was."

That came from a tall, lanky man who stood at the table where he and another fellow, just as tall and even lankier, were nursing five-cent beers.

Longley turned from the bar and looked the standing man over. He and his companion were obviously punchers, laid off by the winter and riding the grub line. Both wore threadbare mackinaws and scuffed shotgun chaps. They were gaunt and needed a shave and their last six meals.

Longley shrugged out of his coat and let it puddle on the ground around his feet. His guns bulged under his black frockcoat. "When riffraff and low persons address me, they call me, sir."

"Easy, boys," Bowman said. "I told you, I want no trouble here."

"There will be none, Sheriff," Longley said. "Unless these men call it."

As though he hadn't heard, the lanky puncher said, "I recognize you, Longley. You got a two thousand dollar reward on you for a scattergun killing down to Bastrop County, Texas."

Longley didn't move. "And? State your intentions and make them plain."

"We're taking you back. Is that plain enough?"

As the other man at the table got to his feet, a chair scraped on the timber floor, a significant sound in the silence.

Longley shook his head as though more in sorrow than anger. A pair of starving, fifty cents a day punchers determined to make a score were almost beneath his dignity. Idiots. They hadn't even cleared their guns. Just a couple of bounty hunter wannabes on a short trail to nowhere.

"Longley," Bowman said. "Back away from this. You men sit down, finish your beer, and then ride. You're overmatched here."

The lanky man, driven by desperation and a desire to get it over with now that he'd opened the ball, made the worst and last mistake of his life.

He went for his gun.

Longley drew in an easy, almost languid motion and put a bullet into the puncher's belly.

Despite a death wound, the lanky man had sand. He took the hit and staggered back. As his back hit the wall, he raised his revolver and pulled the trigger.

Click.

As Longley had half-expected, damp powder and

an ancient cap refused to ignite. Professional gunmen took exquisite care of their weapons. Cowpunchers seldom did.

Longley fired again and the puncher dropped.

The other man, younger and scared, yelled, "I'm out of it!"

"No, you ain't." Taking a split second longer than he normally would in a gunfight, Longley raised his Colt to eye level and shot the youngster smack in the middle of his forehead.

Spinning on Bowman, Longley didn't watch the man fall. "Don't try it!" he yelled. "I can drop you."

Buck Bowman was game but didn't dare make a try for the shotgun.

"Get the scattergun, Booker," Longley said.

Grinning, Booker lifted the gun from the bar.

"Damn you, Longley," Bowman said. "I'm sick of burying your dead."

"Then give your damned star back."

Bowman shook his head. "You murdered those men. You knew they'd no chance with you."

"Pity *they* didn't know it, huh, Buck?"

Bowman was beside himself with anger. He couldn't pin the killing of the older puncher on Longley. The man had drawn down on him first, or tried to. The second man said he was out of it, but he wore a gun and a smart lawyer could convince a jury that he was still a danger.

"You planning to arrest me, Sheriff?" Longley hadn't holstered his gun.

Bowman felt a sense of defeat and a gut-sick weariness.

"Get the hell out of here, Longley. And leave the shotgun."

"We're going, Buck. Me and Booker won't stay where we're not wanted. Oh, and you can have the Greener back. Give it to him, Booker."

Longley waited until Tate put the scattergun on the bar, then reached into his pocket and threw a handful of coins onto the floor. "Bury them, Bowman."

CHAPTER THIRTY
"Bill Longley, I Presume?"

"Oh, my God! Where is the shooting?" Ebenezer Posey stared at Tam Sullivan in alarm.

"Over to the saloon, sounds like. And I'm willing to bet Bill Longley is involved."

"More bodies to steal." Posey's little head poking out of his coat collar made him look like a turtle.

"What did you say, Ephraim?" Sullivan asked.

"Ebenezer. I said, 'more bodies to steal.'"

"Damn. You're right." Sullivan was lost in thought for a moment. "Come on. We'll head over to the saloon and see what happened."

"Not me. I'll stay right here."

"Yes, you. The Hero of Comanche Crossing Trail can't hide in his hotel room when he might be needed to grab his gun and get his work in."

"I don't have a gun and I'm not a hero."

"Sure you are . . . um . . . Ebenezer. Now help me into my coat."

Sullivan buckled on his gun belt and Posey helped him into his coat.

"This garment is bloody," the little man said.

"That's what happens when a man gets shot in the shoulder." Sullivan smiled. "Damn, if everything pans out the way I figure it will, I think we might have a way of getting closer to ol' Crow's body."

"Mr. Sullivan, I hope you're not thinking what I think you're thinking," Posey said.

"I probably am. Now let's go see who got himself shot. Hell, it might be ol' Bill himself. There's a prime body for cutting up if ever I saw one."

The bodies of the two dead men were being carried out of the saloon when Sullivan and Posey arrived. They stood back to let the sad procession pass.

Inside, a swamper mopped up blood, staring intently at his pink-stained mop as though it was a job that required all of his concentration. There was no sign of Montana Maine and Sullivan felt oddly disappointed.

Buck Bowman stood behind the bar, his earlier anger replaced by a look of unease and apprehension, like a man staring at a passing rattlesnake. He looked at Sullivan, then at the bloodstain on his coat, but said nothing.

"Bill Longley, I presume?" the bounty hunter asked.

Bowman nodded. "You presume right."

"Fair fight?"

"Longley's lawyer would sum it up that way."

"What happened?" Sullivan asked.

Posey sat in a chair, his face ashen.

"Two broke punchers recognized Longley and figured it would be a good idea to collect the two thousand reward on his head," Bowman said.

"Two thousand, they said?" Sullivan asked, interested. He might be able to turn a profit on this trip after all.

"Yeah, that's what they said, a couple drovers who probably only used the barrels of their guns to string fence wire and never shot at a man in their lives." Bowman set a couple of glasses on the bar and poured whiskey into each. As he recorked the bottle, he said, "The older of the two drew down on Longley, or tried to. His gun never cleared leather. Longley gut shot him, then put a second ball between his eyes."

"And the younger one, what was he doing all that time?"

"He said he was out of it, but Longley shot him anyhow . . . in keeping with the merry spirit of the evening, like."

"Was the man armed?"

"Yup. He wore a gun."

Sullivan shrugged. "Self-defense. Not guilty and ol' Bill walks free as a bird."

Bowman nodded in agreement. "That's how I see it."

"Blood and guts everywhere, Buck," the swamper said, pausing in his work. He was a small, narrow man with mean eyes.

"Do what you can, Lem," Bowman said. "Then spread fresh sawdust all over that area."

The swamper nodded and went back to his task.

Only a few men remained in the saloon. One of them sat close to the cherry-red, potbellied stove. "It was murder pure and simple. If I was on a jury, I wouldn't let that damned killer walk. He shot down a couple rubes."

"A rube with a gun can still kill you," Sullivan said. "Look what happened to Hickok."

"Well, mister, you're right about that I suppose," the man said. "But I still call it murder."

Sullivan picked up one of the whiskey glasses and handed it to Posey.

"I just couldn't. I feel sick. I can smell blood. It's like iodine and raw iron all mixed together."

"Drink it, Ebenezer. It will do you good. Calm your nerves. You'll be fighting fit in a moment." Sullivan shoved the glass into Posey's trembling hand despite the little man's further protestations.

The bounty hunter stepped back to the bar. "Bowman, you've been around. I got a question about that time Bill got himself half-hung."

"Yeah, what about it."

"The story is that his rescuer bit off the rope around his neck."

"It's a big windy," the big barman said. "Longley wanted his rescue to sound more—what do you call it?—yeah, glamorous. He made up a yarn that his sweetheart did it, that she was so devoted to him she chewed the hemp apart. The truth is the vigilantes bungled the job. After they left, his friends cut him down with a knife. That half-hanging damn near killed Longley, but there are a lot of lively lads who'd still be above ground today if it had took, including them two he just done for."

"You think a woman could have been involved?" Sullivan wondered.

"Why not? Longley has a lot of kin down Karnes

County, Texas, way." Bowman raised an eyebrow. "Why are you so interested in a woman being there?"

"No reason." Sullivan shrugged. "Idle curiosity, I guess." It was much more than that, but he didn't see any purpose in tipping his hand.

"Who shot you, Sullivan?" Bowman pointed to his own shoulder. "There."

"I don't know."

"Longley?"

"I don't think so. I got hit by a big gun, not a .44-40."

Bowman looked at the position of the bloodstain. "I'm surprised you're able to walk."

"Bullet hit my cigar case," Sullivan said. "Saved my life."

"Good excuse to keep up the smoking habit." Bowman smiled.

"Ain't it, though?"

"I'll look into it," the sheriff said. "The attempted murder, I mean."

Sullivan nodded. "And so will I."

CHAPTER THIRTY-ONE
Search for a Cadaver

When Tam Sullivan and Ebenezer Posey left the saloon, snow was falling again. The night was dank, dark, and smelled of the dead. It was not yet seven, so Booker Tate wasn't on the porch dressed in his new finery.

"Well, I'm to bed," Posey said. "It's been a long, wearisome day."

Sullivan grabbed the little man's arm. "You're staying with me. I may need you to identify Crow's remains."

Posey jerked his arm away. "I've seen enough of bodies tonight, thank you, Mr. Sullivan."

"We'll stroll to the end of the boardwalk. First, I want to take a look at Lady Wainright's house."

"Without me, I do assure you," Posey said. "My adventures are—"

Sullivan grabbed Posey by the back of his coat and marched him along the boards without saying a word.

"I must protest, Mr. Sullivan. This is an outrage."

"Shh. Lady Wainright has a guard dog the size of a mountain lion, only with bigger teeth."

"You'll get me killed, Mr. Sullivan, and Mrs. Posey will never forgive you."

"I'm sure she will in time," Sullivan said facetiously.

Posey let out a thin, terrified wail.

To Sullivan's surprise, the house was in darkness but for one light in the upper story, a bedroom presumably. There were no mud-splattered carriages at the door. The place looked oddly forlorn, as though it shrank away from the assault of the wind and snow.

"Well?" Posey stood stock-still. "What now?"

"Now we go to the doctor's office," Sullivan replied.

"Why?" The Butterfield man was thoroughly alarmed.

"See if we run into Crow Wallace."

"But he's dead, or so you say," Posey argued.

"There may be enough of him left for you to identify," Sullivan pointed out.

"No, I'm going back to the hotel. Now unhand me this instant."

"You're staying with me." Sullivan shook the little man like a terrier with a rat. "The damned body snatching idea was all yours in the first place." He all but dragged Posey away from Lady Wainright's house and to Doctor Harvey's office.

It was a narrow storefront office wedged between a greengrocer and saddle shop. It's only claim to grandeur was the gold lettered sign on the blacked-out window.

PETER HARVEY, M.D.
General Physician

Sullivan had already learned that Harvey had a gingerbread house on the hill that he shared with his bride of just six months.

"Pretty girl," the man who'd sold him cigars and a new case had said. "If you like 'em small."

"I like them in all sizes," Sullivan had answered.

The man had grinned. "Then you obviously haven't seen Montana Maine yet."

As Posey shivered on the boardwalk, Sullivan tried the office door. As he'd expected, it was locked. "We'll go around the back, Ebenezer. Take a look-see."

"And get shot as burglars. I know we'll get shot," Posey whined.

"The only people who do any shooting around Comanche Crossing are me and Bill Longley, and he's otherwise engaged tonight." Sullivan dragged the protesting Posey into the pitch-black depths of the narrow alley next to the saddle store.

Ahead of them a bottle clinked. Sullivan froze and Posey bumped into him, crying out in alarm.

"Shh." Sullivan said. "I swear, you're loud enough to be heard in the next county."

"What was that?" In the gloom, Posey's eyes were round as coins.

"Kitty cat," Sullivan whispered.

A moment later, a tiny calico strolled past and ignored them with practiced feline aloofness.

"Damned cat," Sullivan muttered as his heartbeat returned to normal.

"We should go back." Posey grasped at straws. "It's bad luck when a cat crosses your path."

"Nah, it has to be a black cat. That was a . . . some other kind of cat."

The alley opened up into a storage area, swept by wind gusts and a ragged lace of snow. Behind the saddle shop, the Butterfield stage was propped up on timbers, its front wheels missing.

"That's my stage," Posey whispered. "Oh dear. It's got no wheels."

"Seems like," Sullivan said.

"I wish the wheels were repaired and I was on it, driving away from here," Posey said.

"You'll get your wish, soon enough." Sullivan tried the back door, turning the handle. Locked. Stepping back, he studied the two rear windows and attempted to open them. They were shut tight.

"Mr. Sullivan, look there." Posey pointed upward. Snow crusted his fur coat and he looked like a diminutive polar bear.

Sullivan followed his pointing finger and saw that the skylight above the door was open a crack. "We can push that open then you can climb through."

Posey shook his head. "Not me. It's so dark back here, and I'm afraid."

"Hell, I'm too big to climb through there," Sullivan grumbled. "Get your coat off."

"I'll freeze," Posey wailed. "It's cold."

"No, you won't freeze. You'll keep warm climbing through the skylight."

Despite the little man's protests, Sullivan tugged off the coat and tossed it onto the ground. "Now, come on. I'll give you a boost."

Posey, shaking like a willow in a whirlwind, stamped his foot. "No, you will not. This is far too dangerous. Suppose there's a body snatcher back there, lying in wait?"

"Who would want your body?" Sullivan sighed. "Oh, all right. Just open the skylight and I'll do the rest."

Posey turned distrustful eyes toward the bounty hunter.

"Honest," Sullivan said. "Open the window then I'll climb up there and get inside."

"Very well, then," Posey said, his voice shaking. "The sooner you get in there, the sooner I can get back to my room."

"That's a good way to think, Ebenezer. It's a crackerjack take on things."

Posey stepped into Sullivan's cupped hands, weighing not much more than a hundred pounds. He was pushed up but not close enough to reach the window. "A bit higher." he said.

Sullivan, a big and strong man, had no trouble boosting him higher. He watched Posey push on the window. It creaked, then fell inward.

"Ebenezer, stick your head in there," Sullivan said in a coarse whisper. "Tell me what you see."

When it came to dealing with professional bounty hunters, among the most ruthless men on the frontier, Ebenezer Posey was way out of his depth.

To Sullivan's joy the little man stuck his head and shoulders inside.

"I can't see a thing," Posey said, his voice muffled. "It's dark as night."

"Look closer. Let your eyes get accustomed." Sullivan heaved upward on Posey's foot with all his strength.

As though he'd been shot out of a cannon, the

little man went through the open skylight headfirst, and vanished from view.

A despairing wail was followed by a reverberating crash that sounded like a shelf of tin pans collapsing onto a stone floor.

"Damn!" Sullivan muttered. "Posey, you clumsy—" He stepped quickly from the yard, ran through the alley and into the street. Surely somebody had heard the clanging, clamoring racket.

But to Sullivan's relief, the town remained dark and quiet and no curious passerby was in sight.

He quickly returned to the back of the doctor's office and stepped to the door. "Ebenezer . . . open up."

Sullivan was answered by a groan from the other side that only served to irritate him.

"Damn it, man, open the door."

"I'm trying Mr. Sullivan. I'm very much bruised," Posey said, his voice trembling

Sullivan heard shuffling feet, then the *click-click* of a turning key, and the door slowly opened. Rushing inside, he said, "You see any sign of Crow?"

"I've hurt my head," Posey said. "I feel very dizzy."

As his eyes became accustomed to the gloom, Sullivan looked around him. "Wait. This is a storeroom. They wouldn't keep Crow here."

A bucket and mop stood in a corner and the surrounding shelves were stocked with bottles and jars of all shapes, sizes, and colors, except for the one Posey had knocked down during his fall.

Metal bedpans, basins, and small pails were also scattered all over the floor.

"Damned careless of you, Ebenezer," Sullivan chided, irritated again.

"I think I'm badly hurt, Mr. Sullivan," Posey complained. "I took a terrible tumble."

"Let's explore the rest of the office, see if the doc has Crow stashed away someplace else." Sullivan grabbed Posey's arm.

"I-I don't think I can manage. I want to go to bed."

"Follow me." Sullivan headed out of the storage room.

But a further search proved fruitless. There was no sign of Wallace's body or any other.

"Damn it, we've hit a brick wall," Sullivan said.

"Can I go to bed now?" Posey whined. "I hurt all over, Mr. Sullivan."

"Bodies don't just disappear," Sullivan said, scowling in thought. "Crow's got to be somewhere." He stared through the darkness at Posey. The little man looked worn out, like a scarecrow that had been left in the cornfield for too long. Sullivan frowned. "Did you get hurt?"

"Well, I—"

"Good, glad to hear it," Sullivan interrupted. "Now let's get the hell out of here." He glared at Posey. "I swear I never met a man who could make as much noise as you."

CHAPTER THIRTY-TWO
Booker Tate Goes A-Courtin'

Bill Longley knocked on Mayor York's door, then turned to Tate. "You look good, Booker. All gussied up and cutting a dash like a big city dude."

"I'm nervous," Tate said. "I've never gone a-courtin' afore, Bill."

"Don't be. Remember, you're trying to impress the girl now, but she's a throwaway later." Longley knocked again. Louder.

They stood on the porch and behind them a heavy snow drove past the house like a herd of spotted ponies.

The door opened. York saw who it was and stepped outside, his face stiff. "What can I do for you gents?"

"My friend Booker has come, in all his courting finery, to talk with Miss Lisa," Longley said importantly. "Please invite us inside so he can fairly state his romantic intentions."

"My daughter is not entertaining callers at this time," York said stiffly. "Now be off with both of you."

"Mr. Tate has molasses candy for Miss Lisa and he wishes to present it to her personally, like," Longley continued.

York said nothing. He stepped inside and tried to close the door behind him.

Longley held it open with his foot and his big Dance revolver came up fast, the muzzle under York's chin. He smiled. "I said, personally."

"John, let him pass."

This from Buck Bowman who stood in the shadowed hallway.

York wavered, but Bowman said, "He's a mad dog and cold-blooded killer."

Longley's smile widened. "Why bartender—or should I say *Sheriff*? How very clever of you to sum up my personality so perfectly."

"Don't push me, Longley," Bowman said, stepping forward.

"I wouldn't dream of it. Now, may we come in? It's cold standing here."

"This is my home," York said. "When I say leave, you leave."

"Mr. Tate would never dream of quarreling with his future father-in-law over such a trivial matter." Longley pushed past York and said to Bowman, "Will you give us the road?"

"The parlor is straight ahead of you." York pointed. "I want no violence here."

"Of course you don't," Longley said, his voice silky. "My associate has come to court Miss Lisa York, not to shoot someone, for heaven's sake."

"Wait." York stopped them. "Leave your guns on the table in the hallway there."

Longley nodded. "Booker, do as the gentleman says. As for me, my revolvers are both wife and child to me, and I never part with them." He glanced at Bowman. "I see Mr. Bowman is wearing his gun."

"He's the sheriff," York said. "He's entitled to wear a revolver."

Longley watched Tate drop his gun belt onto the table. "We were kept waiting on the porch. Now do we have to do the same in the hallway?"

"Longley, you pointed a gun at the mayor," Bowman said.

"A harmless prank, bartender. I'm just a little overly excited about Booker's upcoming nuptials."

"Let it go, Buck." York turned to Tate, "You will never marry my daughter."

"Let's hear what the little lady has to say about it," Tate said.

York was silent for a few moments then seemed to make up his mind about something. "Very well. Follow me."

Apart from Bowman and York and his daughter, there were two other people in the parlor—Perry Cox the banker, looking well fed and prosperous and a slim, middle-aged woman that Longley took to be the girl's mother.

To say that Lisa York was ravishingly beautiful that night would be an exaggeration, but her cornflower blue eyes, wide full mouth, and the curled yellow hair piled up on the top of her head added up to a wholesome prettiness. Her firm, shapely body promised much to a man.

Tate raked her with hot eyes. "I brung you candy, Miss Lisa," he said, extending a red and white striped paper sack to her.

"Your hat, Mr. Tate," Longley said.

"Oh yeah." Tate removed his plug hat revealing a tangled mat of red hair, lank because he was sweating profusely.

"Thank you," Lisa said, forcing a smile. "How thoughtful of you." She took the sack and, without looking inside, laid it on the table beside her.

"It's molasses taffy," Tate said.

"Very sweet of you," Lisa said, her face expressionless.

"Well, is no one going to offer us a chair? A drink?" Longley asked.

"No. You've given my daughter the candy and now it's time to leave," York said.

"A cold reception," Longley said. "Not what we'd expected."

"It's the only kind you'll get here," the mayor said.

Longley turned to Tate, his face furious. "Say your piece, Booker."

The man's dim brain worked, then he said, "About what, Bill?"

"Your proposal of marriage, stupid."

Tate's brutish face lit up. "Oh yeah." He coughed. "Miss Lisa, will you—"

"Don't ask. Tell her!" Longley ordered.

Tate was momentarily flustered. His hat dropped

from his hands and he bent and picked it up before he spoke again. "Miss Lisa, you will be my wife."

"Tell her when the nuptials will take place, Booker," Longley went on.

"Yeah. On Christmas Eve."

"Tell her where, Booker," Longley continued.

"Um . . ."

"Right here. Now tell the little lady the rest," Longley said.

Tate's face became animated again. "Yeah, right here in this parlor. How do you like that idea, Miss Lisa?"

The girl's eyes flew wide open and it took her a while to find words. "Are you stark raving mad? I'm not going to marry you."

"Sure you will, Miss Lisa," Tate said. "Me and Bill are gonna make you marry me." He frowned, trying to remember, then smiled. "Bill says you're a bride first and a throwaway later."

The girl's mother rose to her feet. Polly York was normally a quiet, even-tempered woman, but her face was flushed with anger. "Get out of my house, you pair of scoundrels, and don't ever come back. Get out now!"

"Unfriendly words from a future mother-in-law," Longley said, his thin mouth twisting into a sneer.

"I said get out!" Polly cried and did something that surprised everybody.

She stepped quickly to the piano stool, opened it, and came up with a massive Colt Dragoon revolver. She thumbed back the hammer, two-handed the revolver to eye-level, and pointed the unwavering muzzle at Longley. "Leave, trash. Or as God's my witness, I'll shoot you."

Longley wavered, enraged at the woman's presumption.

But like a tigress protecting her cub, Polly York would not yield an inch. "Out!" she yelled.

"Longley, make a move for those pistols and I'll drop you right where you stand." Buck Bowman had his Colt in hand and his eyes glittered like a hoar frost. That night the Texas Ranger in him was not hard to find.

Bill Longley thought about it. A fast grab for both guns, shoot Bowman, step quickly to his left and kill the woman. Then another ball for the sheriff if he needed it.

But as soon as he considered it, he dismissed the idea entirely. Buck Bowman was a big man. He would take his hits and shoot back . . . and wouldn't miss at the close range, damn him. Longley considered his skin too precious to attempt a risky double play.

It was a tense situation, stretching taut as a fiddle string, ready to break at any moment.

Booker Tate's thick wits ended it. "Well, Miss Lisa, what do you think about our wedding day?"

"Shut your trap, Booker," Longley spat out. "Mrs. York, we're leaving, but Booker will wed and bed your daughter on Christmas Eve. And do you know why?"

He answered his own question in the silence that followed. "Because I wish it so. It amuses me."

"Longley, I should kill you right now," Bowman said.

"Sure, bartender. And see how many shots I get into the two ladies present before I go down."

"You're a murdering, yellow dog, Longley," Bowman said. "And I plan to be at the gallows to see you hang."

John York took the Dragoon from his wife. "Get out."

Longley smiled. "Sure thing, Mayor. But you'll rue this day. Every damned one of you will regret every moment of it." He moved his attention to the banker. "Mr. Cox, you and I will do business real soon."

"Not with the First Bank of Comanche Crossing, you won't," Cox said.

Longley grinned, enjoying himself. "Oh, but we will, Mr. Cox. Depend on it."

CHAPTER THIRTY-THREE
Terrible News

Ebenezer Posey was in such a low state, battered, bruised, and woebegone, that Tam Sullivan felt a twinge of conscience. "We'll stop at the saloon and I'll buy you a brandy."

Posey shook his head. "I'd rather go straight to bed, thank you, Mr. Sullivan. I feel most unwell."

"A brandy will do you good, Ebenezer. Hell, we might even see Montana Maine."

"I don't think so. I—"

"Doctor's orders," Sullivan said. "Besides, we've got to make future plans."

"My only future plan is to return to the bosom of Mrs. Posey."

"And you will, just as soon as we find Crow Wallace." Sullivan settled the agitated Posey in a chair then stepped to the bar. "Where's Bowman?"

"He went to visit the mayor," the gray-haired man behind the bar said. "I'm filling in until he gets back."

"That's odd, Bill Longley and Booker Tate are doing the same thing," Sullivan said. "Except Booker is there to spark Miss Lisa."

"I wouldn't know anything about that, mister," the bartender said. "I'm only here to serve the drinks."

Sullivan ordered two brandies and took them back to the table.

"Mr. Sullivan, I fear I have broken bones," Posey said.

Lost in thought, it took Sullivan a while to say anything. "Huh?"

"I think I have broken bones. Both my wrists hurt and my back is very sore."

"Listen, Ebenezer, let's take a shortcut. When you get back to Santa Fe, all you have to say is that you saw and identified Crow's body. You hand over the reward to me tonight and then get back to your Mrs. Posey and her bloomers."

"Oh, I couldn't do that, Mr. Sullivan. I would betray the sacred trust placed in me by the Butterfield company."

"Hell, they'll be so glad to get money back from the stage robbery, they won't even question you."

Posey shook his head. Swaddled in his fur coat, he looked like a little bird poking its head out of a nest. "No, no, Mr. Sullivan, that would never do. Ebenezer Posey's honesty is a byword among the stage line fraternity."

Sullivan leaned back in his chair and sighed. "It would be so easy."

"Easy, yes. But a dead weight on our consciences."

"Not on mine. My conscience isn't inclined in that direction."

The saloon door opened and Buck Bowman stepped inside, wafting snow following him. A usually affable man, the big sheriff's face was bleak, as though his smile had been crumpled like a piece of paper and tossed away. He nodded to Sullivan then stepped behind the bar. "Everything all right, Joe?"

The relief bartender nodded. "It's been quiet. Maybe six customers since you left and now only those two gents."

"Montana Maine make an appearance?"

The man called Joe shook his head.

"She won't come in on a quiet night like this. It ain't worth her while."

Bowman nodded. "All right." He called across the room, "Sullivan, you and Posey drink up. It's time to close the place."

"How did it go at the mayor's house?" Sullivan asked.

"Bad. How else would it go?"

"Want to tell me about it?"

"Why would you care?" Bowman frowned.

Sullivan shrugged. "Suit yourself."

Bowman seemed to reconsider his testy remark. "Longley aims to see Mayor York's daughter wed to his friend Tate. And he pretty much laid it on the line that he plans to rob the bank."

"That's nothing new," Sullivan said. "He's made no secret of those things."

"There is one thing new—I'm going to stop him."

"You can't, Bowman. I know you were a Texas Ranger an' all, but you're hardly in Bill Longley's class. Not even close."

"Then I can outlast him."

"A couple of .44 balls in the belly can change a man's mind about that real quick."

"And what about you, Sullivan? I hear plenty of talk from you but see mighty little action. Can you shade Longley? I've heard he may have killed as many as sixty, seventy men."

"It's Comanche Crossing's fight, not mine."

Bowman got testy again. "Answer the question. Can you shade Longley?"

"On a good day, yes I can."

"But you won't."

Sullivan shook his head. "Not unless he does me some personal harm."

"He'll step around you, Sullivan, and then shoot you in the back," Bowman said. "Take my advice. Get out of this town."

"Sure, when I find Crow Wallace's body." Sullivan glared at Posey, "This man here won't fake it for me."

"I safeguard my integrity at all times," Posey said, feeling the brandy.

"Sometimes a lie greases the wheels," Bowman said.

"Not from these lips," Posey said firmly.

Sullivan was about to say something further when the door opened . . . and he knew he was about to hear more bad news.

Big Jim Lloyd, the shotgun guard, walked into the saloon. His entire posture was tense and stiff, a man with a story to tell. He ignored Sullivan and Posey, stepped right to Buck Bowman. "You're the new sheriff?"

"That's what they call me."

"Then let loose the bloodhounds. Deke Dillard is gone."

"Mr. Dillard, the Butterfield driver? But he's dead," Posey said.

"Yeah, he's dead, but you'll have a hard time proving it. His body's been stole."

"Not another one," Bowman said, his face ashen.

"Seems that dead folks can't stay dead around here," Lloyd said.

"How did that happen, and when?" Sullivan asked.

"When? Sometime earlier this evening," Lloyd said. "How? Hogan Strike, the undertaker, says he was embalming Dillard for a trip back to Santa Fe so he could be planted by his family. He went out front to lock his door and that's when the body was stolen from his back shop."

"Did he see anything, hear anything?" Sullivan questioned.

Lloyd shook his head. "Not a damned thing. Dead men don't walk by themselves. Gimme a whiskey."

"Drink up, Ebenezer, I want to take a look at the undertaker's place," Sullivan said. "All these body-snatchings are linked and Crow Wallace is in the mix somewhere."

"Hogan Strike is still there," Lloyd said. "I'm sure he'll be glad of company. He lives at the back of his shop."

"I'm going to bed," Posey insisted. "I feel so ill."

"Damn, but you're a complaining man, Ebenezer." Sullivan hauled him up. "Get on your feet."

"Sullivan, if you find anything let me know," Bowman said.

"You'll be the first to hear, Sheriff."

CHAPTER THIRTY-FOUR
Sullivan Turns His Back on Danger

"Quit whining, Ebenezer," Tam Sullivan said. "Like I told you already, you began the whole damned thing with your talk of Burke and Hare, and body snatchers."

"And now I rue it very much, Mr. Sullivan. My words were spoken in an ill-considered moment."

Their feet thudded on the boardwalk like dim drums as they walked toward the undertaker's premises. Snow plastered their fronts, driven by a frigid, scudding wind, and the unseen cloud-deck had dropped lower, shrouding the town in Stygian darkness.

"My feet are freezing," Posey complained. "I can't feel them anymore."

"Ah, here's the place." Sullivan rapped on the door.

A wide alley separated the undertaker's from the rest of the stores, as though they wished to put distance between themselves and a business that dealt in death.

Posey was uneasy and tried to withdraw into his

coat as the door opened a crack and a man's unsteady voice said, "Yes?"

"We're here about the missing body," Sullivan said.

It seemed that Hogan Strike was either a trusting man or badly shaken because he didn't ask for Sullivan's bona fides. "Come in." He opened the door wide. "And welcome."

After they introduced themselves, Strike led Sullivan and Posey along a narrow hallway lit by a single, guttering oil lamp. As befitted his profession, the undertaker was a thin man, pale as a cadaver. Blue shadows pooled in his sunken cheeks and temples.

He spoke with an echoing, booming voice as though he was talking from within a marble sepulcher. "The deceased was resting in the slumber room you see at the end of the hallway . . . before . . . before this terrible thing happened."

"An unhappy business, Mr. Strike," Posey said. "One senses an evil hand at work."

"Ah, yes indeed, one does," Strike agreed, sensing in Posey a fellow traveler. "The trials and tribulations of the undertaking profession are many, but this is beyond even my experience."

"Smells mighty strange in here," Sullivan said as he reached the door.

"That's the embalming fluid," Strike said.

"Very necessary in your profession, I'm sure, Mr. Strike," Posey added.

"Yes, a valuable tool of the trade, Mr. Posey. And, as you will appreciate, a vital one. I always keep an adequate supply on hand to cater to the demands of the dear departed."

"Very commendable, Mr. Strike," Posey said. "My

dear wife says something similar about the demands of the bloomer manufacturing profession."

Sullivan stood next to a steel table surrounded by glass vessels and coils of rubber tubing. "The stiff was lying here, Strike?"

"Yes. This is where Mr. Dillard slumbered," the undertaker said.

"Was that window shut and locked?" Sullivan pointed to a large one, cut into the far wall.

"Apparently not," Strike said. "When I got back from securing the front door, it was wide open."

"These days one can't be too careful, Mr. Strike," Posey said.

"Yes, indeed, Mr. Posey. Not fastening the window was—if you'll forgive a little undertaker humor at this sad time—a *grave* omission on my part."

"A little joke helps one bear up in times of stress, Mr. Strike," Posey said.

"Indeed it does, Mr. Posey. That's exactly what I tell my bereaved. I say, what is Mr. Sullivan doing?"

"Searching for clues, I suspect, Mr. Strike," Posey said.

Sullivan had opened the window and climbed outside. The distance of the windowsill from the ground was only about three feet. The body could have been shoved, dragged, or even carried through comparatively easily.

He kneeled and examined the muddy ground just under the window. As he'd expected, tracks led from the window and disappeared around a gable wall of a timber shed with a tarpaper roof about ten feet behind the building. The area between was sheltered from the worst of the snow.

The boot prints were huge and the soles seem to be studded.

Sullivan whistled through his teeth. A mighty big feller had left those tracks, judging by their size and depth. The bounty hunter placed his boot in one of the prints and it looked like a canoe in a barge.

Whoever he was, the body snatcher was a giant. Sullivan had seen no one answering that description in Comanche Crossing.

He tensed.

He'd heard a whisper of sound . . . like the rustle of a dead leaf across cobbles.

Looking around him, his eyes searched the darkness, the hair on the back of his neck standing on end. Without thinking about it, he opened his coat and dropped his hand to his gun.

Posey's frightened face appeared at the window. "Mr. Sullivan, are you all right?" he whispered.

"Shh. There's something out here."

"Then come in at once." Hogan Strike sounded scared.

Sullivan ignored the man and listened into the black tunnel of the night. He heard it then, a low, primitive growl from somewhere to his right, in the direction of the alley. Then a whisper of stealthy movement, padded paws on giving ground.

Something wicked this way comes. Where had he heard that? Sullivan swallowed hard.

Yeah, he remembered. Pa reading Shakespeare aloud to Ma by the midnight firelight. Macbeth. The Scottish play. The bad luck play.

Drawing his Colt, Sullivan backed toward the window, staring wide-eyed into the menacing darkness. Fear grabbed at his gut, twisting, spiking, giving him no peace.

He backed up slowly, followed by the snarl that seemed to come from everywhere, a malevolent presence hovering the air around him. He reached the window, a step away from safety.

It was shut!

"Let me in, damn it!"

His wild plea unheeded, Sullivan did what a man who lives by the gun learns to never do—he turned his back on danger. He frantically tried the window. It was locked.

Behind him came a frightening rush of sound.

He caught a glimpse of something gray. Something huge. Something terrifying. He fired. Fired again. His shots scarred the darkness with dazzling flashes of scarlet light, then he heard a piercing whistle in the distance.

Silence.

His ears ringing, half-blind from muzzle flare, Sullivan stood in a drift of gun smoke and waited for what was to come.

The wind sighed, snow flurried, and the night, shattered like a mirror by gunfire, slowly pieced itself together again.

Booted feet pounded on the boardwalk and a man's voice yelled, "Who's there? Identify yourself or take the consequences."

"It's me, Bowman. Tam Sullivan."

A few moments past as the sheriff seemed to absorb this information. Then he roared his exasperation. "Git the hell out here!"

CHAPTER THIRTY-FIVE
Death by the Sword

Buck Bowman stood on the boardwalk, gun in hand, as Tam Sullivan stepped out of the alley. Before the bounty hunter could say a word, the sheriff demanded, "Are you drunk?"

"No," Sullivan answered.

"Then you got no excuse for your behavior. Explain yourself." Bowman looked mean as a curly wolf. He kept his Colt in his fist.

"You ain't going to believe this," Sullivan said.

"If you and Posey are involved, I'll believe anything." Bowman stepped closer to Sullivan, almost to kinfolk distance. "Doc Harvey came to see me tonight. He said he'd gone back to his surgery to mix a powder for old Mrs. Clark who's down with the rheumatisms and found his place ransacked."

"It wasn't ransacked—" Sullivan realized his slip and stopped. "Oh, hell."

Bowman waited.

"I was looking for Crow Wallace's body."

"You thought Dr. Harvey had it."

"Yeah. I thought that."

"But you didn't find it?"

Sullivan shook his head. "Not a trace."

"We'll go into Strike's store, or whatever the hell it's called," Bowman said. "I don't want to hear the rest of your story in a blizzard. But first hand over your gun, Sullivan, real slow and easy, like."

The bounty hunter smiled, snow on his mustache. "I must be a real desperate character, Bowman."

"Yeah, I came to that decision a while ago." The sheriff shoved Sullivan's Colt into the pocket of his sheepskin. "Now get inside and don't make any fancy moves."

They walked into the undertaker's place. The lamp in the hallway glowed with feeble light, but it was bright enough to reveal the blood splashes on the walls and floor and the mangled bodies of Ebenezer Posey and Hogan Strike.

Sullivan rushed to Posey's inert form and took a knee beside him. He held the little man's shoulders in his arm and looked up at Bowman. "He's still alive. He's breathing."

The sheriff looked closely at Strike and shook his head. "This one's done for. All cut to pieces."

"Ebenezer, can you hear me?" Sullivan said, bringing Posey's face close to his own.

The little man's eyes fluttered open. "If it's all right with you, I want to go to bed now, Mr. Sullivan."

"What happened, Ebenezer?"

"So tired now. Time for bed." Posey's voice was as weak as the mew of a newborn kitten.

"Bowman, don't just stand there, get the doc."
Sullivan held Posey closer to him. "Damn it, Ebenezer.
Don't die on me just as I got to liking you. Talk to me."

The little man's fur coat was matted with blood and
his hands, small as a child's, were badly slashed.

Sullivan frowned, suddenly angry. Someone had
used an axe on Posey or a heavy knife and his tiny
body had suffered terrible wounds.

Gray shadows gathered in the little man's face,
something Sullivan did not want to see.

"Damn you, Ebenezer. If you let yourself die I'll put
a bullet in you, I swear I will," Sullivan said.

Posey was silent. He still breathed, but barely.

Suddenly Sullivan was angry with himself for caring
about the little man. "Damn it, Ebenezer. I don't need
this. I don't want to grieve for somebody." To prove to
himself that he was only person on earth he was concerned about, Sullivan said, "I need you to identify
Crow Wallace's body, you hear? Don't die on me."

If Posey heard he made no sign.

"Don't die on me, Ebenezer," Sullivan whispered
again.

"I give him maybe a one in ten chance of pulling
through this," Doctor Harvey said. "He's badly in-
jured."

"What do the injuries to Posey and Hogan Strike
tell you, doc?" Bowman asked. He and Tam Sullivan
stood in the physician's spare bedroom.

Ebenezer lay in the bed, his head and hands visible,
swathed in bandages.

"That someone tried to kill them both," Harvey said.

"With a knife or an axe?" Sullivan questioned.

"Neither, I think," the doctor said. "I saw wounds like these during the war, usually on cavalrymen. They were inflicted by a saber."

"You mean somebody used a saber on Posey and the undertaker?" Bowman was astonished.

Harvey nodded. "Yes, an edged weapon of some kind. A sword in my estimation."

Sullivan and Bowman exchanged glances. Guns they knew . . . but swords?

"That's hard to believe," Sullivan said. "Nobody carries a sword in Comanche Crossing."

"Nonetheless, it's a fact," Harvey said. "Now, if you will excuse me, gentlemen. Mr. Posey must rest. He's very weak."

"Take care of the little runt, doc," Sullivan said. "I kinda like him. His wife makes bloomers for ladies, you know."

CHAPTER THIRTY-SIX
A Deal with the Devil

Bill Longley sat in his dark hotel room, his chair pushed by the window. The boardwalk opposite was deserted. No sign of the woman, damn her.

He didn't regret shooting up the Negro street dance that time, but it began his association with Clotilde Wainright and her husband. That, Longley knew, was an ill-fated day.

Of course, no one blamed him for killing the blacks, except the Yankee law. But the white people understood all too well why he did it.

As old Colonel Thaddeus Walker, the Tiger of Kennesaw Mountain, told him, "By what God-given right do the sons and grandsons of slaves dance in the street while the South lies bleeding?"

Longley nodded to himself, remembering . . .

He and Johnson McKowen, as fine a man and as true a patriot as ever lived, were returning from a horse race down

Lexington, Texas way when they saw a swarm of Negroes drinking and dancing in the street.

They were celebrating victory day, they said.

Longley's eyes glittered in the darkness. Yes, the blacks had been whooping it up over the defeat of the South, the deaths of so many fine men and the end of the Noble Cause.

"Such deviltry could not stand," Longley whispered to himself. "I could not let it stand."

He and McKowen rode their horses off a ways and then drew their revolvers.

"We'll make but one pass, so shoot to kill, Johnson," Longley said.

The other man nodded and set spurs to his mount.

Guns blazing, hollering the grand old Rebel yell, the galloping horsemen crashed into the packed ranks of the celebrating crowd. Men and women went down under the blazing guns and blood stained the dusty street.

The Yankee law tried to play down the incident, saying it was the deed of desperadoes acting alone and did not reflect any hatred between black and white.

Longley closed his pale eyes. Two dead and three wounded, the authorities had said. That ridiculous figure made him smile. His Dance revolvers had claimed at least eight blacks, all head or belly shots, and McKowen had downed close to that number.

Longley figured in those few moments of hell-firing

glory fifteen or sixteen Negroes had bitten the dust. They'd never celebrate their victory day again, damn them.

Shots hammering into the night roused him from his reverie. That was strange. The only man allowed to shoot a gun in Comanche Crossing was him.

He listened, his face intent, ready to catch any sound.

He heard nothing but the wind.

Sullivan?

No. Why would he shoot at anybody? The only outlaws in town were Longley and Booker. Sullivan didn't have the sand to brace either one.

Longley sat back in his chair and dismissed the gunshots from his mind. It was probably some scared housewife taking pots at a scavenging coyote.

He rose to his feet and stretched. Ah well, time he was in bed.

Someone tapped on the door.

Longley's gun came up fast. "Who's there?" He stood still, rigid as a steel rod.

"Clotilde."

A jolt of surprise almost staggered him. "What do you want?"

"We must talk."

"Who's with you?"

"Only Dr. Cheng."

Longley turned the key in the lock, then stepped back, the big Dance up and ready.

"May we come in?" Lady Wainright asked. "Or are you planning to shoot us both?"

"Sit in the chair, Clotilde," Longley said. "Cheng, get into the corner." He stepped to the lamp.

"No, please, no light," Clotilde said.

The bed creaked as Longley sat on the edge of the mattress.

The woman composed her slim hands on her lap and stared through the gloom at the gunman. Fat snowflakes rambled past the window. "I have a proposition. I very much hope you will take it."

"I can guess what it is and the answer is no," Longley said. "It's a dirty business and I got sick of it."

"You didn't used to think that, Bill," Clotilde said. "I mean, when you were happy to take my money."

"The British hung your husband for it. Isn't that enough for you?"

"Anglo-Saxon barbarians. Arthur should have been made a Knight of the Garter, not executed."

"The Chinese killed for the old man. Ain't that right, Cheng?" Longley smirked.

The Oriental's eyes were on fire. "You did your own share of killing in Louisiana," Cheng said. "And you made money."

"I killed only blacks and swamp Indians," Longley pointed out righteously. "Their lives came cheap. Nobody cared about their loss."

"Professor Joran Van Dorn is in Santa Fe," Clotilde said, changing the subject abruptly.

Longley shook his head. "Never heard of him. Yet another of your fine doctor friends, Clotilde?"

"He's probably the most skilled surgeon in the country. His knowledge of the human anatomy is second to none."

"And you've been supplying him with cadavers," Longley said, figuring it out.

"Professor Van Dorn and others." Clotilde's smile

was cold enough to freeze the air around her. "Santa
Fe has recently become quite a center for Boston and
New York medical men."

"Because of you and Cheng, huh? Comanche Crossing's resident Resurrectionists."

"You choose to be flippant, Bill," the woman said.
"Please don't continue in that vein. Flippancy doesn't
become you."

Longley thought he heard Cheng growl, but he
could not be certain.

"I would also like to remind you that I saved your
life once," Clotilde said. "Or Dr. Cheng did. He
brought you back from the dead."

"I was only half-hung, remember? I was still alive
when he cut me down."

"He brought you back from the dead, Bill. And
please put that revolver down. It's making Dr. Cheng
nervous and I don't want bad things to happen."

Longley laid the Dance on the bedside table, the
walnut handle facing him.

"What do you want from me, Clotilde? I never did
find sleeping with you much of a pleasure, you know.
A cold woman brings little comfort to a man."

"And you always smelled like the grave, Bill. We
were quite a pairing, were we not? Death and the Ice
Queen, *n'est-ce pas?*"

"I'll ask again, Clotilde, why are you here?" Longley
was getting tired of the conversation.

"Professor Van Dorn needs a body, a young woman
of child-bearing age, the younger, the better. Such
women are hard to find and their bodies are usually
jealously guarded by their relatives until enough time
passes for corruption to take place."

"There are no Resurrectionists in Boston?" Longley asked.

"Some, no doubt. But the law cracks down hard on doctors and body snatchers in that benighted town." Clotilde leaned forward in her chair, her face bladed by hard shadows. "This icy weather helps keep cadavers in reasonable condition, but Professor Van Dorn wants the girl's body to be as fresh as possible. As soon as I have her, she'll be transported to Santa Fe by carriage."

"That's a stupid arrangement," Longley said. "Yeah, sure, put her in a carriage, but alive, then kill her in Santa Fe."

"As ruthless as ever, Bill. It's one of your traits I've always admired," Clotilde said.

Longley's brain ticked over. "How much?"

"Five hundred dollars for an unmarked cadaver."

"That ain't much. Black, Indian, Mexican . . . make any difference?"

"No. The female anatomy is the same, no matter the race. But being pretty helps. The medical students like that." Clotilde smiled again, narrow, pinched, humorless. "Can you do it, Bill? You've worked for a lot less than five hundred in the past."

"I wasn't famous then. But give me a moment. I'm studying on it."

"I don't want to know the details," Clotilde said. "But your idea of taking the girl to Santa Fe and ending her existence there is an excellent one."

"If I take the job, how much time do I have?" Longley asked, considering it.

"Professor Van Dorn, two other doctors, and several students are booked into the Excelsior Hotel near the San Miguel Mission. They will remain for a week. The hotel staff has already been bribed and they'll turn a blind eye. You understand?" Clotilde raised a pale, warning hand that could have been sculpted by Michelangelo. "You will not be questioned as to the origin of the body, but it's best you do not volunteer any information. Just be sure you kill the girl before you drive into town."

"I've done this before, Clotilde." Longley stared hard at the woman. "What's in this for you?"

"I'm advancing medical science. What does the life of one girl matter, or two or ten, or how many you care to mention, when the study of her body may help ensure mankind's future? No sacrifice is too much to advance the knowledge of medical science." She turned to Cheng who'd been intently listening. "Is that not so, Dr. Cheng?"

"It is indeed, my lady. The needs of the many must take precedence over the sacrifice of a nameless few. One day, they will make you a saint, Lady Wainright."

"Hardly a saint, but perhaps a baroness. Well, Bill, will you take part in this endeavor?"

"Yeah, but on one condition."

"Name it."

"I plan to rob the Comanche Crossing bank and everything else I can grab in this town. If I skip across the border into Louisiana until the heat dies down, I'd like to use your place on the Sabine."

"Why of course you can," Clotilde said. "I have an old caretaker living there, a Mrs. Guthrie. She keeps her mouth shut."

"Yeah, I remember her," Longley said. "She'll be no trouble."

Clotilde rose to her feet. "Then it's settled."

"Not quite. I want to take the girl to your place after I grab her."

Looking troubled, Clotilde said, "Is there no other way?"

"Hell, I can't stash her in my hotel room."

After she thought about that the woman nodded. "Very well. She won't be in my house for long. As soon as you've acquired the subject, you will head south for Las Vegas, then swing west to Santa Fe. That's the route my medical guests take. It's a two day journey, but Dr. Cheng will give you something to keep the girl sedated."

"Two days? More like three and that's if the snow lets up. You ain't giving me much time, Clotilde," Longley said.

"No, I'm not, am I? If you can't handle it, we can postpone the affair to another time. The three physicians will have wasted a trip, that's all."

"I can do it. Me and Booker will have to push our plans ahead, that's all."

"Then do what you have to do, Bill. But get it done."

CHAPTER THIRTY-SEVEN
Questions Without Answers

Buck Bowman took the opportunity to bend the doctor's ear about his recurring lower back problems as Tam Sullivan left the house and made his way to the boardwalk. The clock in the church bell tower struck midnight, but its hands claimed twelve-fifteen. Over the years, no one had been able to fix the clock though many had tried.

Despite his gloves, Sullivan's hands chilled in the cold wind and he shoved them deep into his pockets. He stepped along the walk, head bent against the oncoming snow, looking forward to his bed and a good night's sleep. Ahead of him, he saw two figures cross the street from the hotel. One of them, a woman, had hiked up her skirts to clear the churned up mud, the other was a small compact man wearing a heavy black coat.

Sullivan stepped into a storefront and stood in shadow, watching.

The woman's cape billowed in the wind as a huge dog appeared from an alley and trotted beside her. She patted the dog's anvil of a head as she and her male companion hurried on.

Sullivan recognized Clotilde Wainright by her tall, elegant form and fluent walk. The man with her was the Chinese man she called Cheng. What were they doing at this time of night and in a snowstorm?

There was only one answer—visiting Bill Longley.

Rubbing his chin with a gloved hand, Sullivan tried to fathom the why of the thing, but he had no answer.

Unless . . . Longley and Lady Wainright were somehow involved in the body snatching business. And was Cheng, no doubt trained in the use of a sword, responsible for the death of the undertaker and the terrible injuries to Ebenezer Posey?

It was a stretch, Sullivan knew.

Then he remembered the mud-stained carriages that often stood outside Clotilde's front door. Who were the passengers and where did they come from? Their purpose seemed to be much more than mere social calls to a beautiful woman.

Stepping out of the doorway, Sullivan was determined to find answers to the questions he'd asked himself. The savage attack on Posey had made things personal.

And Sullivan suddenly felt mad as hell. From past experience he knew that his anger was not a good omen . . . for somebody.

When he reached the hotel, he climbed the stairs. When he reached the landing, he drew his gun. Still not wearing spurs because of the mud, he walked on cat feet in the direction of Bill Longley's door.

A murmur of voices from within stopped him in his tracks.

He recognized Booker Tate's rough whisper and Longley's high-pitched, giggling laugh. Apparently, something about Clotilde Wainright's visit had amused him.

It had been Sullivan's intention to burst the door open, catch Longley in bed, and ask him at gunpoint what he knew about the missing bodies and the attack on Posey. It was not much of a plan to begin with, and probably a good way to get himself killed, but slamming open the door and wading into the fast guns of Longley and Tate while they were both wide-awake would be pushing his luck a tad too far.

Unwilling to trust the creaking floor any further, Sullivan backed off, walked down the stairs, and entered his own room. He turned the key in the lock and holstered his Colt. Bone tired, he unbuckled his gun belt and threw himself on the bed.

All he could do was wait and see what the morning would bring.

CHAPTER THIRTY-EIGHT
A Conspiracy of Evil

A restless man, Bill Longley had grown tired of Comanche Crossing. The experience had not been what he'd expected and he had not taken over the town in any significant way. The presence of Tam Sullivan, a man of reputation and good with a gun, had derailed him. And tough Buck Bowman, a former Texas Ranger, also stood in his way.

"That's why we're taking Clotilde Wainright's offer," Longley told Tate as they huddled in a secluded corner of the restaurant, drinking coffee.

"What about the girl?" Tate asked.

"The wedding's off." Longley smiled. "She's worth more to us dead than alive."

"I meant, when do we grab her?"

"Tonight. We'll take her to Clotilde's house and rob the bank early tomorrow morning." Longley grinned. "Then we'll head for Santa Fe, kill Miss High-and-Mighty Lisa York, and ride for the Louisiana border after the job is done."

"Bill, I can still get a taste, huh?" Tate begged. "I'm right partial to that little gal."

"Sure you can, Booker. She'll be on the trail with us two, three days. Time enough for both of us to enjoy her."

"Bill, she'll have to be ready to go after we take the bank," Tate said.

"I'll arrange that with Clotilde today. We'll need a mount for the girl and a packhorse with some kind of shelter and supplies for three days. The rubes might chase after us, but when I threaten to scatter pretty Miss Lisa's brains, they'll keep their distance."

Tate's thinking was slow, but he spotted a flaw. "It's thin, Bill, mighty thin. When the rubes see us pick up the girl at Lady Wainright's place, they'll burn her house down."

"That's her problem, not mine," Longley said.

Tate shook his head, worried. "I don't like it, Bill. There's too much can go wrong. Your plan is tight, like a hangman's noose."

Longley was irritated at Tate's reference to hanging, a sore spot with him, but there was some logic in what the man said. "We got five days to get the girl to Santa Fe. Of course it's close. It has to be."

"Then forget the girl," Tate said. "We'll have the money from the bank so we don't need the lousy five hunnerd."

Longley glanced out the window. The snow had stopped. "I owe Clotilde a favor. I must repay it. It's a reckoning."

"Hell, Bill, she cut you down because you were supplying her with dead Mexicans and blacks.

Back then, she was making a fortune jamming stiffs

in packing cases and shipping them off on the Southern Pacific Railroad."

"Clotilde didn't make a pile of money, Booker," Longley said. "She was trying to save the world. She still is."

"Hell, the world ain't worth saving," Tate said.

Longley smiled. "You got that right." He was silent for a while, thinking.

Breakfasters came and went. He didn't notice them. Finally, he said, "All right, here's what we do." He leaned closer to Tate. "We grab Lisa York tonight and take her to Clotilde's place where we pick up the packhorse and another mount. You understand me, Booker?"

"Yup, I got it so far, Bill."

"Then we take her out of town and stash her someplace with the horses. Tomorrow morning after we clean out the bank, we can pick her up on the trail. The girl will be drugged, so she'll give us no trouble."

"She could freeze to death out there," Booker said.

"So? All the doctors want is her body. If she freezes, she'll be that much fresher."

Tate's laugh was so loud heads turned his direction. "Damn it, Bill, but you're a smart one," he said, dropping his voice to a whisper. "The plan ain't too tight anymore."

"And it's payback time," Longley said. "John York and his wife made us unwelcome in their home and subjected us to the greatest humiliation." He grinned. "Just wait until their precious little daughter disappears."

* * *

After Bill Longley returned to the hotel, he sat at the table in his room and composed a note. Reading it over a few times, he was satisfied it was the bait he needed to catch Lisa York.

Dear Miss York,
    Your father's life is in the greatest danger. Meet me tonight at seven o'clock outside the footwear store at the end of the boardwalk and I will tell you what I know. Show this note to no one and come alone. My life is also imperiled.

            —CMW

The initials meant nothing of course, but Longley thought them a nice touch. He stuck the note in an envelope, sealed it shut, and addressed it to Miss York.

He left the room and went down to the boardwalk. Half-grown boys were always hanging around the rod and gun store across the street and he spoke to a gangly towhead who looked fairly intelligent. "Boy, do you know Miss Lisa York?

"I'll say I do. She's a real pretty lady." The youth was spotted all over with freckles, like a bird's egg.

Longley produced the letter and held up a silver dollar. "Deliver this letter into Miss York's hand and I'll give you this."

"You're Wild Bill Longley, ain't you?" the boy said.

"Yeah, that's me."

"They say you've killed fifty men."

The other boys gathered around, their eyes big.

"People say a lot of things," Longley said. "Now, will you deliver this note like I asked you?"

"Sure thing, Mr. Longley," the boy said. "I'll tell her it's from you."

"No, don't tell her that," Longley said hurriedly. "I'm planning a birthday party for Miss York and if she knows I sent her the note, it will spoil the surprise."

One of the other boys frowned. He was a small creature with the face of a ferret. "Here, what's the deal? Miss York's birthday party was a month ago. I know because my ma was invited."

Longley badly wanted to put a bullet into the little creep, but he smiled. "It's a late birthday party. That's why it's a big surprise."

"I wish I could have two birthdays a year," the ferret said.

Longley smiled and nodded. *If it were up to me you'd never have another one.*

"I'll deliver the note, Mr. Longley," the towhead said, grabbing the envelope and the dollar.

"Remember, when Miss York asks who gave it to you, just say a man you don't know. Got that?"

"Sure do, Mr. Longley."

"Then get going."

Longley watched the boy hurry along the board-walk, then made his way back to the hotel. Tate was concerned about weak links. Trusting the boy to keep his mouth shut was yet another, but Longley figured he had no other choice since he couldn't very well hand the note to the girl personally.

Well, if it didn't pan out, he'd need to take more drastic measures, was all.

He stood on the porch and studied the sky. Black and iron gray clouds building from there to the mountains threatened cold and sleet and the death of the sun.

It seemed that little Miss York would spend an uncomfortable night out in the wilderness where the hunting wolves howled.

CHAPTER THIRTY-NINE
Book of the Dead

"A feller asked me to give you this, Miss York. Happy birthday!" The boy turned and ran from the door.

"Wait!" Lisa York cried.

But the youth had already vanished.

"Who is it, Lisa?" Polly York called from the parlor.

"It was the McLean boy delivering a letter."

"We're not expecting mail delivery," Polly said.

"It's for me, Mother. It's not mail." Lisa closed the door and stepped into the parlor where her mother sat by the fire, knitting in her lap.

Lisa turned the envelope in her hand. "Whomever in the world could it be from?"

"There's only way to find out. Open it."

The girl tore the envelope open and read the enclosed note.

Polly York saw the color drain from her daughter's face and rose from the chair. She lay down her knitting and rustled to Lisa's side.

Without saying a word the girl handed over the note.

Polly read it and let out a little gasp of concern. "What in the world? This is most singular."

"Dare we choose to ignore it?" Lisa asked.

"With all the terrible things that have been happening in this town? I think not. The danger to your father's life may be of the greatest moment."

"Who is CMW, I wonder," Lisa said. "I don't recognize the initials."

"I have no idea," Polly said. "Perhaps a stranger in town, even a law officer."

"Then I must go, Mother. I can't ignore this missive."

"Then your father will accompany you with his revolver."

Lisa shook her head. "The note says to come alone."

"No, it's far too dangerous."

"Mother, we're to meet at seven o'clock on the boardwalk, not midnight. How dangerous can it be?"

"The night is winter dark at that time and most, if not all, of the stores shutter early because of the snow," Polly said. "You could find yourself quite alone."

"There will still be people around, and the saloon doesn't close, remember?"

"We'll let your father decide."

"No, don't tell him. I've no wish to worry him unnecessarily. This could be nothing, perhaps even a prank. Besides, I have the brand new Remington derringer Father gave me for my birthday. I can take care of myself."

"Lisa, I just don't like the idea of you going alone," Polly said, her face creased in worry. "And those two

dreadful men who came to the house last night are
still in town. They could—"

"If Father's life is really in danger, it's worth the
risk, any risk." Lisa insisted. She frowned and her chin
was determined, signs her mother knew only too well.

"I'll worry about you the whole time you're gone,"
Polly said.

Lisa smiled. "Mother, I'm a big girl now. Trust me,
I'll be just fine."

Fortified with a couple of shots of brandy from the
bottle in his room, Bill Longley climbed the hill to
Clotilde Wainright's mansion. As the sky had pre-
dicted, icy sleet slanted in a slashing wind and the way
underfoot was slick, muddy, and treacherous.

Cheng opened the door to Longley's knock and
with a noticeable lack of enthusiasm ushered the
gunman into the parlor where he was joined a couple
of minutes later by Clotilde.

"Not bad news, I hope." Her beautiful eyes searched
Longley's face. "Take a seat by the fire."

"A change of plan," the gunman said. "That's all."

"I don't like changes of plan, Bill."

"For your own protection, Clotilde. All I need from
you is a horse for the girl to ride and another with supplies for three days, including a shelter."

"Cheng will supply you with a canvas tarp and whatever else you need for the trail. I also have a horse
for the girl." The woman's eyes burned with green
fire. "Your change of plan is for my own protection? I
hardly knew you cared, Bill."

"It's too risky to pick up the girl here," Longley

said. "There will be a hue and cry and if they see that you're involved . . . well, you know what might happen. Remember after the vigilantes hung me? Well, the Comanche Crossing vigilantes could come after you with a rope."

"I remember the day you were hanged very well, Bill. Now tell me of your new plan."

Irritated at the woman's memory for things he'd rather forget, Longley told her.

"You'll be busy tonight and tomorrow," Clotilde said. "First a kidnapping and then a bank robbery. My, my."

"Booker and me can handle it," Longley said.

The woman handed him a glass of brandy. "Who is the girl? Or dare I ask?"

"Lisa York."

"The mayor's pretty little daughter?"

"None other."

Clotilde jolted back in her chair, surprised. After a few moments, she clapped her hands and then held them clasped to her breast. "Brava!" she exclaimed. "How perfectly, wonderfully droll."

Longley grinned. "I thought you might like that, Clotilde."

"Oh, I do! The little stuck-up baggage is an excellent subject, such a young, nubile body. Professor Van Dorn will be so pleased."

"Clotilde, I plan to knock her out with one of Cheng's potions and hide her on the trail until we pick her up tomorrow morning. She could freeze to death overnight."

"No matter. A little frost will keep the body fresher longer." Clotilde nodded her permission for Longley's cigar and then she said, "This matter is of the utmost importance, Bill. I'm doing it for Professor as a personal favor."

"You sold stiffs to him in the past?"

"A few, but none of yours. Dr. Cheng used most of those for his own study. No need to explain away the bullet holes, you see."

"I didn't know Cheng was a real pill roller," Longley said. "I thought you just called him Doc for some strange reason."

"He was a quite famous surgeon in his native China. My husband and I helped Dr. Cheng obtain bodies which led to our . . . ah . . . difficulties."

"Your husband's hanging among others," Longley said.

"Quite," Clotilde said, icing the word. She picked up the brandy by her chair and refilled Longley's glass.

The wind drove sleet past the windows and the ravaged morning was gloomy as night. A withered leaf fluttered against a pane like a trapped brown bird.

"Professor Van Dorn is currently writing a book that his publisher believes will be the definitive work on the female anatomy and will make him famous in this country and abroad. As part of the illustrations for his work, he will dissect the York girl's body and make a series of painstakingly *accurate* drawing of its various parts, internal and external." Clotilde's face took on a serious expression. "Note my emphasis on the word *accurate*. To achieve such results the subject's carcass must bear not even a hint of corruption."

Longley smiled. "So the professor is an artist as well as a doctor."

"Is not any fine surgeon an artist? Why should you sound so surprised?"

Longley smiled. "How much artistry does it take to saw a man's leg off?"

"Bill," Clotilde said, "how little you know."

"Well, to sum it up—I rob the bank, take the girl to Santa Fe, and then head for your place on the Sabine." Longley grinned. "We had good times there, Clotilde."

"No, we didn't." The woman rose to her feet. "I'll wrap up my business here and join you in Louisiana as soon as I can."

"Maybe we can get back into the business again, Clotilde," Longley said. "I can provide plenty of bodies over that way."

"No, I'm done. Lisa York is the last and then I'll return to my fight to preserve our American Indian culture."

"Do you think anyone will thank you for that?"

"Perhaps not. The Indians are ungrateful children, I know. But I will persevere in my endeavors. And there's one more thing before you leave."

Longley drained his glass then stood.

Clotilde answered the question on his face. "That man Sullivan is getting way too close, as I feared he might. Hong-li tried to kill him twice and failed each time."

Startled, Longley said, "Hong-li? Is that . . . thing still alive?"

"He's not a thing. He's a human being who left the womb not yet fully formed and, for some reason known only to the gods, grew to a monstrous size. You heard what happened in the night?"

"I heard shots. Figured somebody was taking pots at a coyote."

"Sullivan fired those shots. My dog got too close to him. There's more."

"Then tell it," Longley said.

"Dr. Cheng wanted the stage coach driver's body for his own research, but he and Ransom ran into trouble. The undertaker and another man came into the office and Hong-li killed them both with the Japanese sword he carries."

"And what does this have to do with Sullivan?"

"He was also nosing around the undertaker's place. He wants to find the body of an outlaw he killed and I believe he thinks I had something to do with its disappearance."

Longley smiled. "And you did, Clotilde. You and Cheng did some grave robbing on your own and Crow Wallace was among them."

"The men were dead. That's not a crime, or at least it shouldn't be. The bodies advanced Dr. Cheng's knowledge by leaps and bounds and he will use that knowledge for the good of everyone. Frank Harm, the sheriff, had a cancer in his belly and Dr. Cheng removed it. He told me if the subject had been still alive he would have survived the surgery and lived on for many years."

"Why don't you give Crow Wallace's body to Sullivan, Clotilde?" Longley suggested.

"It's cut up and buried, like the others. Wallace, if that was the outlaw's name, would be unrecognizable by now."

"Tam Sullivan is a bounty hunter who doesn't give

a damn about anybody or anything. You've nothing to fear from him. He'll drift soon."

"Perhaps I am overreacting, but I think you should kill him before you leave just to make sure," Clotilde said.

Longley nodded. "I'll see what I can do. Anything else?"

"No, I think we've covered it. Just get that girl and don't fail me."

Longley grinned. "Trust me, Clotilde. Lisa York's female parts are as good as in the professor's book already."

"Then I'll see you in Louisiana."

"Just like old times, huh?"

Clotilde smiled but said nothing.

CHAPTER FORTY
Sullivan's Temptation

"He's not going to pull through, Mr. Sullivan. The punishment he took was just too severe for such a frail little body." Dr. Peter Harvey put his hand on Sullivan's shoulder and looked into his eyes. "I'm real sorry."

Sullivan wanted to say that the little runt meant nothing to him and that all Posey had ever done was to deny him his reward money. But he couldn't say those things, not with any sincerity. Instead, he found himself saying, "He's a Butterfield man, you know."

Harvey nodded. "Yes, he is, and a genuine frontier hero. The whole town will mourn his passing."

"Can I see him?" Sullivan asked.

"Yes, you can. But he won't know you're there."

Sullivan stepped into the bedroom.

Because of the somberness of the morning, a single oil lamp burned and cast shadows, as deep and dark as those that pooled in Ebenezer Posey's face. The little man's breathing was so quiet it was lost in the greater sound of the lamenting wind.

"Ebenezer, can you hear me? It's Sullivan."

Posey lay still, his face like chiseled stone.

"He's far gone," Harvey said. "He's probably already made the acquaintance of the death angel."

Sullivan turned and looked at the doc. "How long?"

"He'll be dead before sundown."

Sullivan smiled slightly. "There's no sun to go down, Doc." He took off his glove and laid the backs of his fingers on Posey's forehead. "He's cold."

"Yes. It's a step along his way," Harvey said.

Sullivan stood in silence for a few moments, staring down at Posey. "I'll come back." Then, after thinking about it, added, "Before sundown."

On Sullivan's way out the door, Dr. Harvey stopped him and dropped the key of Posey's hotel room into his hand. "You'll need that. He has no kin or friends in town."

"I'll take care of his stuff." Sullivan thought about the money. There was a lot of it.

"My wife said Ebenezer cried out last night," Harvey said. "I didn't hear him, but she told me he clearly said the word *monstrous*. What on earth did he mean?"

"I guess it was his opinion on what happened to him," Sullivan said. "Posey used words like that. Hell, maybe he was talking about me."

Harvey didn't contradict that last. "I suppose such could be the case. But it's strange all the same."

Sullivan nodded. "Sometimes I think the whole world is strange and getting stranger all the time, Doc."

Tam Sullivan returned to the hotel and went directly

to Posey's room. The maid had neatly folded the little man's nightgown and sleeping cap and laid them at the bottom of the bed. The gloomy morning cast feeble light into the room, but the air was chilly and damp, and smelled musty, a cold welcome for any visitor.

Sullivan picked up Posey's carpetbag and returned to his own room. As he'd expected, his thirty-six hundred dollar reward was there, stuffed under a clean shirt, socks, and underwear. The stack of bills was bound with a paper band that bore the Butterfield Stage Co. stamp.

Sullivan riffled through the bills, money that was rightfully his. He could take it and the money left from the stage robbery and hell, even the gold watch.

"You've earned it, Tam," whispered the devil on his shoulder. "Let Posey take the blame. He's a dead man, anyway."

Sullivan let the money drop into the bag. He'd pushed Ebenezer beyond his limits and in the end was responsible for his death.

He thought about destroying the man's memory, leaving his wife only a legacy of shame. Once the word got around that her husband was a thief, how many pairs of bloomers would she sell?

Sullivan shook his head. There was only one trail to take. "Damn it, Ebenezer, you've destroyed me. I'll never be the same man again."

He took what was left of the stage robbery money and the gold watch from his saddlebags, put them in the carpetbag, and buckled the straps, vowing to himself that he wouldn't see it open again until he carried it into the Butterfield stage office in Santa Fe.

CHAPTER FORTY-ONE
A Favor Asked— and Refused

As he toed the carpetbag under the bed, a timid knock on his door startled Sullivan. His hand instinctively dropped to his gun. "Who is it?"

A slight pause for breath, then, "It's Polly York. The mayor's wife."

Sullivan opened the door. "Come in . . . if you don't mind entering a gentleman's quarters unaccompanied."

Polly's face was cool and composed. "I'm sure I will face no impropriety, Mr. Sullivan." The woman walked past him into the room. Her bonnet and cape were damp from sleet and her ankle boots left traces of mud on the floor.

Sullivan saw concern in her eyes as he provided her with a chair. He sat on the corner of the bed and waited for her to speak.

When she did, her voice was firm and calm, but the

fingers of the gloved hands on her lap tied themselves in knots. "Earlier this morning, a most singular event disturbed the tranquility of my home, Mr. Sullivan, when my daughter received a most alarming communication. This was no *billet-doux*, but a warning that the life of my husband was in the greatest danger."

"Who sent it?" Sullivan asked immediately.

"We don't know. It came from a gentleman, the delivery boy told Lisa, and it was signed CMW."

Sullivan shook his head. "Doesn't strike a chord with me," he said, wondering why the hell the woman had come to see him, of all people.

Polly untangled her fingers and opened her purse. She passed a piece of folded paper to him. "Please read it."

He scanned the note, meticulously penned in schoolboy copperplate, nodded and passed it back to the woman. "Mrs. York, I don't see—"

"What you can do to help me?"

"Yes, exactly."

"Lisa insists on meeting CMW alone," Polly said. "She doesn't want to unnecessarily alarm her father, and as for Sheriff Bowman, well . . . his very, dare I say, *large* presence might scare off the informant."

"So what do you want me to do?" Sullivan questioned, surprised.

"Guard my daughter with your gun, at a discreet distance of course."

Sullivan smiled, genuinely puzzled. "I don't get it, Mrs. York. Why me?"

"Because you have the reputation of being a skilled and experienced gunman and as far as I can tell you have a trustworthy face."

Sullivan took the double-barreled compliment in silence. Then he said, "Mrs. York, do you figure I owe you a favor?"

"You owe me nothing, Mr. Sullivan. Or my daughter."

"So why ask me?"

"Because you are the only one who can change what this town has become. Men murdered, bodies ripped from their graves, notorious outlaws pressing their suit on my daughter, and talk of murderous savages in the hills." Mrs. York composed herself. "Comanche Crossing used to be a nice place to live, Mr. Sullivan. No longer. My daughter can't go alone to that meeting tonight. It's just not safe."

"If he choses, Buck Bowman can be discreet, I fancy," Sullivan said.

Polly York rose to her feet. "I'm sorry I wasted your time, Mr. Sullivan."

Sullivan opened the door for the woman and she left, stiff-backed as she stepped into the hallway.

Closing the door, he stepped to the window and stared into the day, stores, houses, and the surrounding hills shadowed as though draped in mourning for the death of the light.

Ebenezer Posey was dead when Tam Sullivan returned at the noon hour to the doctor's office.

"He took his last breath ten minutes ago," Dr. Peter Harvey said. "To the very end, he fought a gallant fight."

"I hardly knew him." Sullivan pulled up the sheet over the little man's head and smiled. "I liked him though."

"He's in a better place."

"No, he isn't. His place was beside his wife in Santa Fe." Sullivan stared into the physician's eyes. "The dead are quiet, aren't they? Look at him lying there, very still, very silent, like he's in a deep sleep."

"I've stood in the presence of the dead many times, Mr. Sullivan," Harvey said. "Yet I still can't find the words."

"Not much to say, is there?"

"I guess not."

"I'll take his body back to Santa Fe," Sullivan said. "The dead don't rest easy in this town. His wife should bury him."

Harvey's face took on a stricken look, like a man who's suddenly remembered a mortal sin from his past. "Come into the parlor, Mr. Sullivan. I'd like to talk to you."

"Seems like everybody wants to talk to me this morning. I guess I'm a real popular feller, huh?"

A faint smiled touched the doctor's lips. "I wouldn't say that, Mr. Sullivan."

CHAPTER FORTY-TWO
Trigger Control

"Drink, Mr. Sullivan?" Dr. Peter Harvey asked.

"I could use one," Tam Sullivan acknowledged.

"Hennessey brandy to your taste? A gift from a patient."

"Suits me just fine."

After Sullivan and the physician were settled, glasses in hand, on either side of the parlor fire, Harvey said, "I need to get something off my chest. It troubles me."

"I love listening to other people's troubles, Doc," Sullivan said with a straight face. "Lay it on me."

"Let me say this first. You understand the need for ongoing medical research? The study of the human anatomy and the brain in particular?"

Sullivan quickly jumped to a conclusion. "Are you talking about body snatching?"

Harvey nodded. "There is a particular shortage of available bodies, and it's been going on since the 1830s when a great many people of all ages were executed for petty crimes. You have, of course, heard of Burke and Hare who supplied bodies to physicians in Scotland?"

"Ebenezer mentioned them, then wished he hadn't."

"At first, Burke and Hare were grave robbers, but when the bodies of executed criminals became harder to find, they turned to murder."

"Ebenezer told me that, too."

"After committing eighteen murders Burke was hanged and Hare died in poverty, a hopeless drunk."

"I'm not catching your drift, Doc," Sullivan said.

"I don't condone what they did, but I don't condemn the doctors who accepted the bodies for study, either. Who knows? A hundred years from now, Burke and Hare might be hailed as heroes."

"Is that what you wanted to get off your chest, Doc?"

"No. But I wanted you to know that I have dissected cadavers myself."

"Here? In Comanche Crossing?"

"Yes. I was present at Lady Wainright's home the night Crow Wallace's body was opened."

"Where is it?" Sullivan asked quickly.

"Buried where you'll never find it. By this time, nothing human of Crow Wallace will remain or be recognizable."

"You cost me twenty-five hundred dollars," Sullivan said.

"And I may have helped cause the death of Ebenezer Posey," Harvey said.

Tam Sullivan looked like he'd just been punched in the gut.

"You know, I've never shot a doctor before, but there's a first time for everything." He carefully laid the brandy glass at his feet. "If I was you, I'd choose my next words very carefully."

If Harvey was scared, he didn't let it show. "I made the decision to never attend another autopsy after that one. The way so many graves are being desecrated and bodies stolen repels me. I begged the doctor to stop, but he is a man obsessed. I had nothing to do with what happened last night at the undertakers when Ebenezer was wounded."

"Who is the doctor?" Sullivan gritted out.

Harvey saw a hundred different kinds of hell in the big man's eyes.

"His motives are pure, even honorable, but his methods are reprehensible. He believes the scalpel can cure a tumor of the brain, but the problem is to remove the tumor while leaving the brain undamaged. Given our present state of medical knowledge, it's an almost impossible feat." Harvey picked up Sullivan's glass and handed it back to him. "Of necessity, the doctor disposes of many cadavers until he finds one with a tumor advanced enough to hone his skill with the knife and improve his surgical technique."

For a moment Harvey watched scarlet and yellow flames blossom between the logs in the fire. Then he continued. "Once the doctor believes he's skilled enough to operate on any cancer, in any part of the body but especially the brain, only then will he feel qualified to treat living patients."

Sullivan rose to his feet. "I won't ask this a third time. Who is he?" His gun was level with Harvey's eyes.

The doctor saw the gleam of blued steel, the brassy glint of percussion caps, the beautiful sweep of the walnut handle. He knew little of guns and Texas draw fighters but had no doubt that Tam Sullivan was prepared to use the revolver. "Dr. Cheng Lian," he said in a whisper.

"Clotilde Wainright's hired man?" Sullivan frowned.

"Her husband," Harvey said.

Sullivan was surprised. "Since when?"

"As far as I know, since soon after the death of her first husband."

"Who killed Ebenezer and Hogan Strike?"

"I don't know."

"Why did Ebenezer say *monstrous?*"

"I don't know."

"I think you know more than you're telling me, Doc." Tall, grim-faced, and angry, Tam Sullivan was an intimidating figure.

"I don't know," Harvey said, slanting his eyes away from him. "You said he was outraged over what happened to him and we agreed on that, didn't we?"

"That's what I thought, but I don't think it any longer. I know Ebenezer was trying to tell me something."

"He was in pain and he wasn't thinking straight," Harvey explained.

"No, Peter, that's not true, and you know it. Now tell him. If you won't, I will." The doctor's wife stood in the doorway. Her face was pale but set in a stubborn expression.

"Jane, I don't know what to think," Harvey said.

"Yes, you do, Peter. Tell Mr. Sullivan about Hong-li."

"You've been listening, Jane," Harvey accused.

"I couldn't help but overhear. Now tell him."

"I think . . . God, I told you, I don't know what to think," Harvey said, a man in pain.

"Tell him," his wife said.

"Hong-li was probably the—I can't call him a man—the creature who murdered Ebenezer Posey and Hogan Strike."

"There is no *probably* about it, Mr. Sullivan," Jane Harvey said.

"How can you say that with so much certainty, Mrs. Harvey?" Sullivan asked.

"Peter said you were at the undertaker's place the night Ebenezer was killed. Did you see a dog?"

"I didn't see it, but I heard it snarling. I fired a couple shots but don't think I hit it." Sullivan tried a wan smile. "I was too scared I guess."

"And with good reason, Mr. Sullivan," Jane said. "The dog is evil because Hong-li made it that way. He himself is as evil as he is deformed. To this day, the slaughter of the White family has never been explained."

Sullivan directed his attention to her husband.

"The Whites had a cabin to the west of town on La Jara Creek," the physician explained. "Abe White lost a leg at Gettysburg and was trying to make a living as a trapper. His wife was called Martha and they had three kids, all of them girls. Daisy, the oldest, was about sixteen and a tomboy. I once treated her for a broken arm after she fell out of a wild oak. She was real pretty. All three White girls were real pretty."

"The family was slaughtered," Jane said. "Sheriff Harm said it looked like they'd been hacked to death with a bladed weapon, maybe an axe."

"Their killer was never found," Dr. Harvey said.

"That was just a month after Lady Clotilde Wainright moved into Comanche Crossing and brought Hong-li with her," Jane said. "Coincidence? I think not."

"Mrs. Harvey, are you aware that your husband cut apart cadavers at Clotilde Wainright's house?" Sullivan asked.

"Only once, Mr. Sullivan. After that, Dr. Cheng was out of control, demanding more and more bodies. His wish is to return to China as a famous brain surgeon."

"Did you know that Cheng and Clotilde are man and wife?" Sullivan asked.

Jane looked genuinely surprised. "I had no idea. Did you, Peter?"

"Yes. I knew."

"Why didn't you tell me?"

"My dear, I don't traffic in idle gossip."

"Only in bodies, huh?" Sullivan stepped to the door and stopped. "I'm going to end this. I aim to kill the man, or whatever it is, that murdered Ebenezer Posey and if Clotilde Wainright and her husband were involved, well, I'll deal with them, too."

"More killing and violence never solved anything, Mr. Sullivan," Dr. Harvey said.

"Maybe not, but it's my way. It's the only way I know." Sullivan hesitated at the door, his expression hard and inflexible. "Was Bill Longley involved in Ebenezer's death?"

Harvey shook his head. "Not as far as I know."

"You, Mrs. Harvey?"

"I know nothing of the man except that he's a killer

and that everyone in this town is afraid of him," Jane said. "But Longley kills with a gun, not a sword."

"One more thing before I go, Doc," Sullivan said. "Think yourself damned lucky you're still alive. When I lose control of myself bad things happen and I came real close to losing it this morning."

Peter Harvey said nothing, but his face was ashen. He knew.

CHAPTER FORTY-THREE
Booker Tate
Makes a Decision

"Your money is no good here, Longley. Go elsewhere." Perry Cox stood behind the bank counter next to a frightened clerk who looked like he was about to puke.

"You're refusing my hundred dollar deposit, Cox?" Longley asked.

"If it comes from your pocket, it's bound to be tainted money," the banker said. "I want no part of you or your deposit."

"Uppity this morning, ain't you?" Longley's eyes looked like they'd been chipped from flint.

But, like many heavy, big-bellied men, Cox was not easily intimidated. "Longley, Tom Archer was a respected man in this town and that's why we want you out of it."

Longley's smile was thin as the edge of a knife. "I'll go when I'm ready, Cox. Not a minute before."

"Don't count on it," Cox said. "We have a noose all ready for you."

"That's been tried before. And the men who tried it are all dead." Longley picked up his money, smirked at Cox, and barged out the door into the street.

He had no wish to pick a fight with Cox. But maybe he'd get a chance to gun the banker later. As it happened, all he'd wanted to do was scout the layout of the bank, hence the ruse of the hundred-dollar deposit.

The counter had a brass grill, but there was a door at the end of the counter that another pale clerk had opened and closed without the use of a key. That made things a lot easier.

The First Commercial Bank of Comanche Crossing was a ripe plum ready for the picking . . . and come tomorrow morning, Bill Longley intended to pick it clean.

Booker Tate had plans of his own.

He'd had women before, hog ranch whores for the most part. No decent woman would have anything to do with him and he'd forced a few to show the little gals what they were missing.

But Lisa York was in class by herself.

Since he and Bill had gone courting to the girl's house, Tate dreamed of making Lisa his wife . . . to have and to hold until death do them part.

His old idea of using the girl before she was gutted in Santa Fe was gone. He'd never cottoned to the plan anyway.

Love—starry-eyed, head-over-heels love, had taken its place—suddenly, like a thief in the night.

Standing at his hotel room window in his underwear, Tate scratched his belly and stared out at the dark, dismal street. Sleet hurtled past his window and the wind screeched like fingernails scarring the blackboard of the morning. People scurried on the boardwalks, bent over against the cold, barely taking time to greet each other.

He let out a little sigh, imagining beautiful Lisa out there, shopping basket over her arm, braving the elements to get the grub she needed for her man's supper.

He smiled. The joyful image made him very happy.

But then another vision . . . darker, bloodstained, terrifying. He saw Lisa York on a steel table, cut open and her intestines spilled over the floor. Her pretty face still and white, blue eyes wide but staring into nothingness.

Anguished, Tate plunged his face into his hands. "Make it go away," he whispered. "Please make it go away."

Then a great truth came to Booker Tate.

Pretty little Lisa shopping was a fantasy. But the image of Lisa lying butchered on a table was reality . . . Bill Longley and Clotilde Wainright's reality.

Tate would not allow it to happen. The girl was his and he'd let no one harm her.

He knew he couldn't face Longley's guns, but there had to be another way.

And he'd find it.

The *rap-rap* on the door made Tate reach for his gun. "Who's there?"

"It's me, Booker. Open up."

Tate unlocked the door and opened it wide.

Bill Longley stepped inside. "Get dressed. You've got something important to do this morning."

Tate gave the other man a blank stare.

Longley scowled.

"Damn it, man, what's wrong with you? Wake the hell up."

Tate shook his head as though trying to clear the cobwebs. "Sorry, Bill. What is it you want?"

"That's better," Longley said. "I want you to ride up to Lady Wainright's house and pick up the packhorse and Lisa York's mount. Then head south into the mesa country, maybe a ten-mile, and hide the animals somewhere. Make sure you pick out a landmark so you know where the hell you left them."

"Miss Lisa won't have a horse when you grab her tonight?"

"No, she'll ride with me. She'll need the horse on the trail to Santa Fe, that's all." Longley stepped to the window. "As to whether she'll ride the horse or be tied to it, I don't know. Have you seen the weather out there?"

Tate laid his revolver on the bedside table. "Bill, maybe we should rethink this. About Miss Lisa, I mean."

Longley's face settled into a scowl. "It's a done deal. What is there to rethink?"

"I don't know. It just doesn't seem right to leave Miss Pretty out there to die of cold or get eaten by a wolf."

"Listen, set your mind at rest. You can have the girl all to yourself on the trail," Longley said. "I won't touch her. I guarantee you'll be tired of her by the time we reach Santa Fe."

"You reckon so?" Tate asked, his bovine brain struggling with the implications of that.

"Sure you will and there will be plenty of women in Louisiana. Hell, I heard they swim naked in the Sabine, summer or winter."

"Well, whatever you say, Bill," Tate said. But he had no intention of letting Miss Lisa get anywhere near Louisiana, or Santa Fe for that matter.

"Good. Now get dressed," Longley said. "Do what I told you and make sure you get back here before seven. I'm counting on you, Booker."

"You can depend on me, Bill." Tate knew then that he'd have to kill Bill Longley.

At seven o'clock.

CHAPTER FORTY-FOUR
Sullivan Sees the Light

"She might come in around seven o'clock," Buck Bowman said. "But Montana Maine does what she pleases."

"She got a special feller?" Tam Sullivan asked, making conversation.

"Naw. She plays the field. It would be impossible for just one man to pin down Montana Maine to a life of domestic bliss."

"She must be quite a woman."

"She is. Believe me, you haven't seen a real woman until you set eyes on Montana Maine."

Sullivan stood at the bar eating an early lunch of crackers and blue-veined cheese.

Bowman topped off his beer. "I heard about Posey, poor little feller. I liked him."

"So did I," Sullivan said. "I liked him a lot."

"I'll find out who murdered him and Hogan Strike,

depend on it," Bowman said. "And I'll arrest those responsible for the stolen bodies."

Sullivan smiled. "You're not a detective, Buck."

"I was a Texas Ranger. That's enough."

"Have you ever dealt with evil before?" Sullivan asked.

"Sure. Wasn't I the Ranger who gunned White River Vic Polson? Vic was a half-breed Apache and real evil."

"Hey, Buck, I didn't know you killed Vic Polson," said a man standing at the far end of the bar. "I seen his body in the window of Steve Yates's hardware store down Amarillo way. He was shot all to pieces."

"Took two loads of double-aught buck to stop him," Bowman said. "As I recollect, Vic had a simple brother who got hung. But none of that Polson clan ever came to any good."

The two men talked more about the Polsons, and when the conversation petered out, Sullivan said to Bowman, "Cutting a breed in half with a scattergun ain't detective work."

Bowman shook his head, smiling. "Hell, Sullivan, I'm not catching your drift. You're not a Pinkerton yourself."

"I know, but the killing, the stolen bodies, the evil that's descended on this town, it all ends tonight," Sullivan said pointedly.

Bowman's face hardened, and he gave the younger man a long, stern look. "I'm the law in this town, Sullivan. If there's a summing-up to be done with a gun, I'll do it. You see how it is with me."

"It's a reckoning, long overdue. I'll handle it."

"You'd better tell me about it," Bowman said.

Sullivan took a drink of his beer. "If tonight pans out like I think it will, you'll know soon enough."

"I don't like this. I don't like this at all," the sheriff said. "If I'm pushed to it, I'll lock you up to keep you off the street."

"No, Buck, you're not locking me up. Not today or on any other day."

Until that moment, Bowman had considered Tam Sullivan a bumbling fool, a wannabe hardcase obsessed by a dead man, boasting an inflated reputation he knew the man didn't deserve.

But when he looked into the sky blue hell of Sullivan's eyes he knew he was wrong.

The man was a killer.

He was another Bill Longley, saved only by a thin veneer of humanity and a respect for the law that the gunman did not possess.

Sullivan brushed away a cracker crumb from his great cavalry mustache and pushed himself away from the bar. "You still got that scattergun, Buck?"

"Sure do and she's loaded for bear."

"Then I'll come for you when I need you," Sullivan said.

Bowman said, "Wait. Let's talk about this."

But Sullivan stepped toward the door and for the first time in days the spurs on his heels chimed.

Half-a-dozen men were in the saloon, but the one at the end of the bar was the most talkative. As Sullivan passed him, he said, "Hey, mister, is there really evil in Comanche Crossing, devils and ha'nts an' sich?"

"More than you know," Sullivan answered.

He returned to his hotel room and, using .36 caliber

paper cartridges, loaded the 1861 Colt Navy he'd taken from his saddlebags. He laid the revolver beside his gun belt on the bed then pulled a chair to the window.

For a while, he gazed into the storm-torn street.

On the opposite boardwalk, a plump matron wrapped in a hooded cape dragged along a small, reluctant dog. A youth stepped out of the general store holding a pair of new boots tied together by the laces. A mule-drawn wagon passed, its precious cargo of swaying Ceylon tea chests covered by a canvas tarp.

Sullivan saw but paid little heed, his mind working. He was convinced the pale, distorted face he'd glimpsed at an upper window following his visit to Clotilde Wainright was Hong-li. Man, beast, or whatever species, he was Clotilde Davenport's creature, and she knew he was likely to kill anyone who got in his way.

Maybe she didn't sanction the murders of Ebenezer Posey and Hogan Strike but she was responsible.

Sullivan was sure Hong-li had taken that pot at him on his way to the railroad station and his was the grotesque, hunchbacked form of the bushwhacker he'd winged in the graveyard. His bullet had stung the man and he would still bear a scar.

And what of Bill Longley?

He'd made his reputation as a Texas bad man by killing blacks and terrified rubes. Seemed he'd be in way over his head dealing with a cold, calculating woman like Clotilde Wainright. Unless . . . it was her . . . or one of her associates . . . who'd saved his life when he got half hung down to Karnes County.

Almost as soon as Sullivan thought it, he dismissed

that possibility. Bill had been strung up for killing a black soldier and horse theft.

Sullivan continued thinking, trying to connect Longley and Lady Wainright. Why would she, an English aristocrat, go out of her way to save the life of a common criminal?

Suddenly, the answer was obvious. Because she needed him.

But not for herself. For her husband. For Dr. Cheng.

Musing on that possibility, Sullivan remembered what Buck Bowman had said about Bill Longley killing sixty or seventy men. He'd dismissed that figure as typical saloon gossip exaggeration, but suppose it was true—which raised another question . . . or two. In the past, had Longley provided freshly murdered bodies for Cheng's research . . . and was he still supplying them from the town graveyard?

Sullivan knew he was close to the answer.

A man like Longley, if he'd run out of bodies, could easily kill scores of unarmed blacks, blanket Indians, and Mexicans to supply Cheng's endless need for fresh cadavers.

That was why Clotilde Wainright had saved Longley's life—to ensure that her husband's research would not be interrupted, an activity she considered vital to the advancement of medical science.

Sullivan realized his own obsessed hunt for the last remains of Crow Wallace had blinded him to the reality of what was happening in Comanche Crossing. Unfortunately, it had taken the death of Ebenezer Posey to open his eyes.

He mentally flagellated himself for that.

Right there and then, he vowed to make amends

and save what little was left of his integrity . . . and his manhood.

He shook his head and focused on the street. Still daylight.

Seven o'clock, after darkness fell.

That's when Tam Sullivan would bring about the reckoning.

CHAPTER FORTY-FIVE
Tate's Fatal Decision

Booker Tate left the packhorse and spare mount in an arroyo close to Black Mesa, the country around him wild, windswept, and achingly lonely.

He made his way back to Comanche Crossing, riding through driving snow and a day as gray as mist on a lake. Chilled to the bone, the lean cloth of his mackinaw giving him little protection, Tate thought of Miss Pretty.

She was a delicate little thing, unused to rough men and savage weather, and her chances of living through just one night on the trail were slim.

He had done what Bill had asked, he'd stashed the horses, but Lisa York would not leave Comanche Crossing, at least not that night.

His snow-spattered face grim, he knew he would have it out with Bill.

But Bill is a reasonable man. Certainly—Tate didn't finish that thought.

Bill Longley was not a reasonable man. He was a stone cold killer and unbending. As surely as night follows day, Miss Pretty's fate would be decided by the gun.

Tate accepted that fact and understood its implications.

"Who rides out on a day like this?" Clem Weaver said, his face sour.

"I do." Tate dismounted. "You got coffee in the pot?"

The livery man nodded. "It's on the bile. I'll get you a cup."

"Rub down my hoss and feed him some oats as soon as I've had coffee," Tate ordered. "And don't skimp. I want him ready to ride again in a couple hours."

Weaver poured a smoking cup and handed it to Tate. He waited a few moments until the big man had swallowed some and thawed out a little before saying, "Your friend Longley bought Crow Wallace's hoss, paid cash on the barrelhead, too. Says he's riding tonight."

Tate shrugged. "Bill has some strange notions sometimes and I follow along."

"Well, rather him than me," Weaver said. "A man could freeze to death out there on the trail, if'n the Apaches don't get him first." The liveryman's smile was wicked. "Then a man could roast to death instead, huh?"

Tate drained his coffee cup and made no answer, his face strained and solemn.

Since the red-haired gunman seemed in no mood for small talk, Weaver said, "I'll see to your hoss."

Still silent, Tate rose to his feet and walked out of the stable.

Two prosperous-looking men in greatcoats and mufflers stood on the boardwalk and discussed the sluggish, muddy river that was the street. As Tate passed he heard one of the men say, "Shell rock won't work."

"Then what will?" his plump companion asked.

"I don't know. But I told the mayor we can't ever go through this again."

"There has to be a solution."

"Drain it like a swamp, I reckon."

Both men laughed and walked on their separate ways.

Booker Tate heard and was deeply envious. Instead of facing death when the clock struck seven, he could be like those men, prosperous burghers discussing nothing more urgent than mud in the street. He mulled that over, his feeble brain working hard. Once he wed Miss Pretty, he could leave the violent, hunted outlaw life behind and settle down right in Comanche Crossing and perhaps turn his hand to trade. He figured he might prosper in the construction business, since even as a boy he'd been good with his hands, building things, like.

Smiling to himself, Tate considered that an excellent plan. He'd build a nice little house where Miss Pretty would be happy. It would have extry rooms for the young'uns and maybe a guest cottage for Mr. and Mrs. York when they came to visit.

The mind pictures Tate saw, all with Lisa York center stage, were bathed in a golden glow—a heavenly light that would always, miraculously, be there after he and Miss Pretty got hitched.

As he entered the hotel and his muddy boots left stains on the stair carpet, Booker Tate was madly in love, his Miss Pretty the entire focus of his being.

"So if she dies, she dies. All we have to do is deliver a body to Santa Fe. Dead or alive, it makes no difference." Longley stared ice-hard at Tate. "Not going soft on me, are you? It's too late at this stage of the game."

Tate was silent for a while, dredging for the right words. "Bill, I want to marry Miss Pretty."

"Marry her! Why, she'd leave you the first chance she got, or kill you in your sleep. A girl like that isn't for a wild animal like you, Booker."

"But you said you wanted us to get hitched, Bill. You told me that."

"Because the thought of it amused me. Well, it doesn't amuse me any longer. We grab the York girl tonight and there's an end to it."

"I could become a carpenter," Tate said. "Keep Miss Pretty at home."

"Yeah, until the night you get drunk and kill a man. Then it's all over." Longley smirked. "Booker, you're an idiot."

Tate's face was set and stubborn, enamored of his impossible dream.

Longley read the expression. "All right, Booker. We'll talk about this after we grab the girl. Hell, take her to Louisiana with you, marry her there."

Tate's face brightened and he smiled. "Do you mean that, Bill?"

"Sure I mean it. I'm not going to break your heart, Booker." *But I'm going to kill you.*

"Bill, you're true blue and a white man," Tate said.

"Hey, that's what friends are for, Booker. We'll build the girl a nice big fire in a sheltered spot come tomorrow morning, then go rob the bank. After that, we're Louisiana bound, all three of us."

"She'll need plenty of wood if we're gone for a few hours," Tate said.

Longley played along. "Yeah, we'll leave her a woodpile real close."

"Dry, Bill. It's got to be dry."

"Uh-huh. Dry wood it is." Longley rose and stepped to the window.

The day had fled. The long night and darkness lay on Comanche Crossing. The snow had stopped, and the lighted stores on both sides of the street angled rectangles of amber light onto the boardwalks.

That was not entirely to his liking. What had to be done would be better accomplished in gloom.

But there were still two hours until seven. Many of the stores would close by then for lack of customers, especially when the snow started again as the somber night promised.

"Me and Miss Pretty could build a house right on the Sabine," Tate said.

Without turning, Longley nodded again. "Sure thing, Booker. You and Lady Wainright could be neighbors. Lisa York would like that."

"Lisa *Tate*, Bill. She'd be my wife by then."

"Oh yeah. I plumb forgot." Longley simply smiled.

CHAPTER FORTY-SIX
Night Riders

"Seems like everybody is riding this evening." Clem Weaver shook his head. "It's a mystery to me."

"Besides myself, who else?" Tam Sullivan asked.

"Well, that Booker Tate feller came in on a played out hoss, said he was just riding but will go out again. Then Bill Longley wants his mount saddled and ready before seven. And now you. All you Texans hauling your freight at the same time, huh?"

"I don't know about them other two, but I plan to stay close to town," Sullivan said. Alarm bells rang in his head. He was sure it was Longley who'd sent the note to Lisa York. He hadn't yet figured the why of it, unless it was a clear-cut case of abduction followed by a ransom demand.

By the standards of Comanche Crossing, the mayor was a wealthy man and he'd pay a pile of money to get his daughter back unharmed.

It was Bill Longley's kind of business. He was real good at it.

"If'n you're staying close to town, then why do you need your hoss?" Weaver questioned.

"Don't ask questions, Clem. You might get answers you don't want to hear."

The liveryman hunched his shoulders and shook his hands in the air. "You're right. Don't tell me nothing. I don't want to meddle in the affairs of Texas draw fighters. It ain't healthy."

"Don't tell Longley I was here, understand?" Sullivan said.

"Hell, I can't see you. Are you here?" Weaver said, looking around him in the exaggerated manner of a blind man.

Sullivan smiled. "You got it, Clem." He thought for a few moments. "Longley lost his buckskin. You loaning him a horse?"

"Naw. I sold him Crow's mount. The gray you brung in."

Sullivan was instantly suspicious. "How much did you get for it?"

"Two hunnerd, cash."

"You only gave me a hundred," Sullivan admonished.

Weaver's smile was sly. "It's called business, young feller. Profit and loss. Your loss, my profit."

"You'll get hung fer a horse thief one day, depend on it," Sullivan said.

"Naw, Bill Longley will. I sold the gray to him too cheap."

* * *

"Where is Lisa?" John York asked as he entered the parlor of his home.

His wife looked up from her knitting. She'd expected the question. "She decided to take a stroll in the snow." Her reply was at least a half-truth, she told herself.

York poured himself a brandy and sat by the fire. "Odd. She's never done that before."

"Young people do get restless when they're stuck inside by weather. She may visit a friend."

"Did she wrap up warm? It's freezing cold out," York said.

"Yes. She's wearing her furred cloak." Polly smiled at her husband. "Don't worry, John. She'll be all right."

But Polly was worried.

She was worried sick.

"I'm real worried about Miss Pretty," Tate said. "It's cold tonight."

Longley turned from the window. "She'll be just fine, Booker. You can hug her close when we get on the trail. Keep her cozy, like."

Tate smiled.

"I'm gonna enjoy that, Bill. Me and Miss Pretty snugglin' up by the campfire and talking about out future plans an' all."

"You're a real romantic, Booker," Longley said. "You remind me of Bill Scrier, the feller I killed down to Bell County that time. We'd a running horseback fight and he took thirteen rifle and pistol shots before he went down."

"How come I remind you of him?" Tate asked.

"Because he was a romantic like you. He wanted to live real bad so he could marry a gal he was soft on. Damn him, he was a hard man to kill." Longley shouldered into his fur coat and grinned.

"You're a lover, Booker, just like Scrier."

"I sure hope Miss Pretty thinks so," Tate said.

"Well, I reckon you are," Longley said. "Just like Bill Scrier."

CHAPTER FORTY-SEVEN
Miss Pretty's Deadly Mistake

It was fifteen minutes till seven when Tam Sullivan tied his horse to the handle of an outhouse behind the general store, locked and shuttered since Tom Archer's death. He stepped along a close passageway too narrow to be an alley between the store and another, and standing in shadow, looked into the street.

Snow fell under the vast, black dome of the night and the street reminded him of a bog, moving in the wind as though infested by crawling, grinning things. The air smelled of open coffins.

His view was where the opposite boardwalk ended. As yet there was no sign of Longley or Lisa York.

Sullivan opened his coat, clearing the gun on his hip and the .36 in his waistband. The German prince's yellow muffler hung loosely around his neck.

Time ticked past as he slowly numbed in the cold.

Five minutes later, he thought he saw a shadow of movement on the boardwalk. A snow flurry momentarily obscured his view, but when it cleared, he saw Longley, clad in his ankle-length fur coat, step to the edge of the walk and look around him. Tate joined him after a few moments, but Longley irritably waved him back into the darkness.

The perverse north wind chose to blow full force down the passageway. It chilled Sullivan to the bone and his wounded shoulder ached. He removed the glove from his frozen gun hand. Once in the flannel-lined pocket of his coat, he worked his fingers, trying to keep stiffness at bay.

His plan was to watch for Lisa York and grab her before she crossed the street.

Longley might shoot or he might not. Either way, Sullivan was mentally prepared for a gunfight, though exchanging revolver shots across the breadth of the street in darkness would be a mighty uncertain undertaking.

He and Longley were up close and personal duelists . . . not long-distance marksmen.

The *click-click-click* of a woman's high-heeled boots rose above the sigh of the wind.

Sullivan braced himself. As soon as the girl was close enough, he'd leap out and seize her. He figured she would scream blue murder, of course, and bring folks running, but at least Longley's plan would be foiled.

Or so Sullivan thought.

The trouble was, Lisa stepped along on the opposite boardwalk.

Sullivan cursed under his breath. Why had she gone and done that?

Actually, he knew why. Some of the storeowners had placed wooden boards across the mud as makeshift street bridges for the convenience of their customers. Most had sunk without a trace, but Lisa had taken one that still floated.

Her female sensitivities had ruined Sullivan's plans.

Reluctant to wade across the street into Longley's gun, he turned and went back for his horse.

And missed the action across the street.

Lisa slowed down as she recognized the man in the long coat. "It's you," Her face registered shock and fear.

Tall and terrible amid a shifting coil of snow, Longley grinned. "And who did you expect?"

The furred hood of the girl's cloak blew off in the gusting wind and flakes of snow studded her hair. "What about my father?"

"Worry about your ownself, girlie." Longley lunged for her.

Lisa took a step back and eluded the gunman's grasp. Her hand dived inside her cloak and she reached into the pocket of her woolen dress. Her derringer came up fast and she fired.

Longley yelped as the bullet burned across the meat of his left bicep. But he recovered quickly and backhanded the girl across the face.

She dropped like a stone.

"Leave her alone, Bill," Tate yelled. Furious, he

stepped between Longley and the girl. "You've hurt her. Don't slap Miss Pretty again."

The shot would bring the curious, Longley knew, but he had no time to waste. He reached inside his coat, drew, and fired.

Hit hard, Tate staggered back, sudden blood staining the chest of his mackinaw. "Bill?" Hurt and wonder filled his eyes. "Why . . ."

"Git the hell away from me," Longley snarled. He pushed Tate hard and the big man crashed onto his back on the boardwalk.

Effortlessly, Longley picked up the unconscious girl and carried her into the waste ground where his horse was waiting.

"Damn you, Longley!" Tam Sullivan yelled, urging his horse through the fetlock-high mud of the street. "Leave that girl be!"

A voice came from the darkness. "Keep away, Sullivan or I'll scatter her brains!"

Two shots followed. One plucked at the turned up collar of Sullivan's coat. The next sang its death song close to his ear.

He drew rein, shaken. Damn, Longley was good.

At a distance of twenty-five yards in almost pitch blackness both balls had come within inches of ending the life and times of Tam Sullivan.

"That was close," he told himself. "Way too close." Warily, he urged his high-stepping horse across the street.

Booker Tate was up on one elbow, staring at him, his face a tangle of emotions.

His Navy Colt leveled at Tate, Sullivan said, "I can kill you from here."

"You can't kill a dead man, Sullivan. I'm done for."

"Where is Longley taking Lisa York?" Sullivan demanded.

Full of blood, Tate's mouth oozed dark scarlet in the gloom, stringing pink saliva. "Tell Miss Pretty I love her."

"Damn you, Tate. Where?" Sullivan cried. "Dead man or no, I'll put a ball into you."

"South . . . Black . . . Mesa . . ." His fading eyes already dead, Tate managed three more words, "Oh my God," and was gone.

"Sullivan, git off that hoss or I'll blow you off it."

The bounty hunter looked into the cold, close-set stare of Buck Bowman's scattergun. "Longley took Lisa York. I'm going after her."

Bowman motioned with the shogun. "Him?"

"Longley done for him. Not me."

A deliberate-thinking man, the sheriff said nothing. Footfalls sounded on the boardwalk behind him. John York, his wife, and several other people were running toward him.

"Buck, guard Clotilde Wainright's house," Sullivan said. "Don't let her or anyone else leave. I'll explain it later."

"Wait. I'm still thinking about killing you, Sullivan," Bowman said.

John York was within shouting distance. Sullivan said, urgently, "For God's sake, Buck, do as I told you. Give me the road or I'll lose Longley in the snow. The girl's life is in danger."

"Damn you fer a smooth-talking scoundrel, Sullivan.

Get the hell out of here and bring back Lisa York alive," Bowman shouted.

Polly York heard that and screamed.

"Don't forget what I told you, Buck." Sullivan kneed his horse into motion.

Then he was gone, galloping into the murk of the merciless night.

CHAPTER FORTY-EIGHT
Storm of Lead

Sullivan's American stud was a much better horse than the one Bill Longley rode. It was strong and would run all night and into the next day without tiring, but the darkness of the night, scoured by wind and snow, forced the bounty hunter to slow down and walk the horse in places where there was no visible trail.

Of course, Longley faced the same difficulties and he was riding two-up on a Texas-bred mare with no liking for brutal cold.

Sullivan rode into flat country tufted with coarse grass. Here and there, dark junipers shivered in the wind. The darkness was all encompassing, raked with freezing sleet, and the only sound was the wail of the wind.

Ahead of him, he saw no sign of Longley and the girl.

Despite the conditions, now and then a horse track

showed in the muddy ground and Sullivan was assured that he was headed in the right direction. He was certain Longley knew he was being shadowed, and an ambush was an ever present danger.

After thirty minutes of watchful misery, Sullivan caught a break. From somewhere ahead of him, he heard the thin whinny of a horse and wondered, had the gray mare caught the scent of his stud?

He drew rein and his frost-rimmed eyes searched into the ragged distance of the shredding night. About sixty yards away, barely visible in the gloom, was a limestone ridge about as tall as a man on a horse. The south face of the rise went straight up from the flat as though it had been sliced by a knife and it ran west to east, providing shelter from the wind.

Its head erect, ears pricked, Sullivan's horse snorted and tossed its head, the bit jangling.

The big bounty hunter slid the Henry from the boot under his knee. He'd never been great shakes with a long gun, but in the dark at middle distance the rifle held the edge over his revolvers.

A moment later, Bill Longley surprised the hell out of him. "Sullivan!"

"Yeah, it's me, Bill." Sullivan swung out of the saddle and yelled, "What can I do for you, Bill?"

"A feller who hunts men for a living should never ride a stud. But then, you ain't too bright, are you, Sullivan?"

"Bright enough to kill you, Bill, unless you let Lisa York go."

"And if I don't?"

"I'll keep coming after you, Bill."

"You're low down," Longley called, a voice in the darkness.

"Seems like," Sullivan answered. "Now, give me the girl."

"Come and take her, Sullivan."

"You got your rifle, Bill?"

"Sure do. Right here in my hands."

"Then step out where I can see you and we'll settle this *de hombre a hombre.*"

"Ain't my style, Sullivan. I ain't gunfighting in a damned blizzard."

Sullivan stepped away from his horse. "Then I'm coming after you, Bill." His rifle ready at waist level, the bounty hunter stepped toward the ridge, sleet raking him with icy spurs and cutting his visibility to ten yards.

If it hadn't been for the girl he would have dusted a few shots into the shadows where Longley lurked. But he couldn't take the chance of hitting Lisa.

Then Longley cut loose, firing a shot from under the ridge.

Sullivan dived for the muddy ground just as the gunman rode from the darkness at a gallop.

Longley fired a couple of shots that kept Sullivan's head down. Then he screamed, "Damn you, Sullivan. Take her. She's all yours!"

Sullivan scrambled to his feet and fired at the fast, fleeting shadow that was the departing Bill Longley. Fired again. And a third time.

But Tam Sullivan knew he'd scored no hits. He was not a rifleman and on his best day, he couldn't make such a shot.

Half-blinded by muzzle flare, he gathered up the reins of his horse and called, "Miss York, are you all right?"

No answer.

Was the girl still unconscious?

Torn between riding after Longley or checking on Lisa York, Sullivan chose the latter. He told himself that the girl's welfare came first, but he knew in his heart that was only an excuse. The truth was he didn't want to ride into Longley's rifle. Unlike himself, the man was real good with a Henry.

"Miss York," Sullivan called again as he led his horse toward the ridge. "You can come out now. Longley's gone."

The north wind mourned noisily among the pines and the frigid air was thick with splinters of slicing sleet.

Sullivan stepped into the lee of the ridge, spotting a dark mound at the bottom of the wall. Something flapped around it.

Stepping closer, he made out the still form of Lisa York, her cloak lifting in the wind. "Are you all right, Miss York?"

His words fell on dead ears. The girl had been shot once in the chest and the blood around the wound looked like a scarlet corsage.

But Lisa York was not going to the ball.

CHAPTER FORTY-NINE
Sullivan Calls the Shots

Tam Sullivan rode into Comanche Crossing holding the dead girl in his arms. His horse stepped fastidiously through the mud of the street toward the gathering of people who stood on the boardwalk outside the town hall.

The clock struck ten and did its best to cover Polly York's screams.

He drew rein and passed Lisa's body into the outstretched arms of her father.

"She's dead," John York said. "Oh my God, my daughter is dead."

Mrs. York screamed and screamed, her tears falling on Lisa's white, upturned face.

Clem Weaver was among the crowd and Sullivan said to him, "Bill Longley."

Weaver's weathered face was shocked. He managed only one word. "Why?"

"I don't know why," Sullivan said. "I can't think like Longley thinks."

Drawn by the screams of Mrs. York and other women, more people showed up, among them Dr. Harvey.

Polly saw him and shrieked, "Doctor, save my child! Save her!"

The physician's practiced eye told him the girl was dead. With a question on his face, he stared up at Sullivan who was still mounted.

"Bill Longley," Sullivan answered the unspoken question.

"Doctor!" Polly York shrieked.

Harvey put his arm around the woman's trembling shoulders. "She's gone, Polly."

In a state of profound shock, John York held his daughter in his arms and said nothing. But Mrs. York gave way to profound grief.

Amid the hysterical woman's wails and shrieks, Harvey said, "John, let's get them inside."

Stiff-legged, walking like an automaton, John York let the doctor usher him along the boardwalk, followed by his wife and a group of sobbing women.

Sullivan's throat worked as he swallowed hard. "Damn." Seeing the grief of parents over the death of their beautiful child was hard to take. He stepped out of the saddle onto the walk and tossed the reins to Weaver. "You know what to do, Clem. Where is Buck Bowman?"

"I talked to him just after Longley killed Booker Tate an' took pots at you. He said he was headed for the Wainright place," Weaver said. "I heard shootin' from up that way and decided to march right into the saloon and stay there."

"Anybody else head up the hill?" Sullivan asked.

"There was some talk about it, but everybody decided to let the sheriff handle it. Buck Bowman was a Ranger, you know."

The few men remaining on the boardwalk listened to what Weaver said.

"You going up there?" one of them asked Sullivan. "If you want company, you can count me in."

"Yeah, I'm going up there, but I'll do it alone."

The man persisted. He wanted to do something, anything. "Should we organize a posse, go after Longley?"

Sullivan raised his eyebrows. "In this weather?" He shook his head. "You'll never find him."

"Then Longley goes free?"

"No, he doesn't go free. One day I'll find him and I'll kill him." The bounty hunter felt empathy for the young man eager to avenge Lisa York's murder. It was an emotion new to him.

Talking to all three of the men who stood watching him, Sullivan said, "If you boys hear a heap of shooting going on up at the Wainright house, grab your rifles and come a-running. It means I'm in trouble and so is Sheriff Bowman."

"We got you covered." The earnest young man turned to his companions. "Let's get our guns and meet back here." He turned back to Sullivan. "At the first sign of trouble, we'll be right behind you . . . Mr. Sullivan, isn't it?"

"You can call me Tam. And you are?"

"Hank. Hank Lively."

Sullivan put his hand on the young man's shoulder. "I know I can count on you." He felt something strange slam inside him—like a kicked open door. Had he really said that?

I know I can count on you.

The old Tam Sullivan didn't count on anybody. He didn't need anybody. Even in bed with a woman, he took refuge behind an impenetrable wall and always felt the better for it.

As he watched Lively leave with his friends, Sullivan shook his head. "Ebenezer, what the hell have you done to me?"

He left the boardwalk and took to the dubious path that led up the hill to the Wainright house. The place was lit up, its windows glowing gold through the ashy mass of the riven night. The dragon wind vane hissed in the north wind and the air was thick with ice crystals.

Ahead of him, lying across the walk, sprawled an enormous carcass.

Sullivan stopped and drew his Colt from the holster. He walked on slowly, warily, afraid that the great beast was sleeping . . . or worse, wounded and enraged.

But the massive dog was dead.

A shotgun blast had torn great holes in its shaggy coat just under the high shoulder hump formed by a mass of powerful muscles that had driven the animal's front legs. Its great yellow fangs were bared in death, black eyes open, glittering as though it was still alive.

Sullivan shuddered and stepped around the creature . . . and his boot hit an even greater horror . . . a round thing that rolled.

Buck Bowman's body lay close to its severed head, stiff and ungainly in death.

The sheriff's face was upturned, crusted sleet on his hair, eyebrows, and mustache giving him the look of an old man. He had no serenity in his expression, only transfixed horror at the manner of his death . . . frozen during the split second before his brain had ceased to function.

Bowman's death didn't affect Sullivan as deeply as the murder of Lisa York. The man was a lawman and had taken his chances. But it had been Sullivan who'd sent Bowman to his death.

And it wasn't a peace officer's death. Beheading was foreign, vile, unnatural—savage in the extreme.

Bowman's soul must be crying out for revenge.

Sullivan stared at the house, shining brightly in the night as though for a Christmas imagined by Mr. Dickens. He used the back of his gloved gun hand to wipe sleet from his eyes, his gaze fixed on the house door where the restless dead beckoned to him.

Ebenezer Posey . . . Lisa York . . . Buck Bowman . . . big Frank Harm . . . and all the others . . . each demanding justice, standing in the light of Clotilde Wainright's windows, each dead face as white as a skull.

Rage beyond rage ravaged Tam Sullivan. He roared his terrible fury and ran for the door, its polished brass gleaming in the light. He roared still as the door splintered and crashed open under his kick. Still roaring, he charged inside.

CHAPTER FIFTY
The Reckoning

His gun up and ready, Tam Sullivan's reception was not what he'd anticipated—the hallway was empty. Recalling that the parlor lay to his right, he stepped quietly . . . and warily . . . to the open doorway that allowed a rectangle of light into the hall.

Lady Clotilde sat in a leather chair by the fire, licking blood from the blade of a great curved scimitar. Her mouth scarlet, she said, "Ah, Mr. Sullivan, how nice to see you again."

Sullivan stood fixed in place, overcome by horror.

The fire crackled in the hearth and the close air smelled of incense and burning pine.

"Surprised?" Clotilde said. "You shouldn't be. Fresh blood is good for a woman." She smiled, raised the blade, and her pink tongue slid along its gory edge, making her mouth bloodier.

Sullivan found his voice. "Lisa York is dead."

"Really? How unfortunate. But hers was such a little life it hardly matters."

"It mattered to Lisa," Sullivan said.

Clotilde laid the sword at her feet and dabbed her mouth with a dainty lace handkerchief that turned red. "How remiss of me. May I fetch you a brandy?"

"Where are Cheng and Hong-li?"

"Dr. Cheng is probably in his office, and I'm sure that Hong-li is fast asleep. Because of his infirmities, he goes to bed early, you see."

"Did you order him to kill Ebenezer Posey and Hogan Strike?"

"Who?"

"The two men Hong-li murdered at the undertaker's office."

"Oh that. I can't recall, nor do I care. Does the butcher remember all the rabbits he ever hung in his shop window?"

"Ebenezer was my friend." Sullivan's anger was cold as steel.

Clotilde rose to her feet, her face twisted. "He was nothing, a nonentity who stood in the way of a great man."

"You mean your husband?"

"Yes. I mean Dr. Cheng, the surgeon who will one day remove cancerous tumors and leave the host brain intact. He will pass his knowledge on to others, and tens of thousands of lives will be saved . . . because of him." Clotilde's expression changed to one of pure hatred. "And you, you uneducated dancehall lout, won't stand in his way, either. Do you think I care a fig for that little slut Lisa York? Medical science needed her carcass and now its been wasted."

"Your boy Bill Longley killed her," Sullivan said.

"Is he still alive?"

"As far as I know."

"Then we'll meet again and I'll square accounts with him."

"Get Cheng and Hong-li down here," Sullivan ordered. "I've accounts of my own to settle."

"As you wish," Clotilde said.

Sullivan caught a slight flicker of the woman's eyelids and moved toward her, avoiding the worst of the two-fisted blow to the back of his neck that would have shattered his spine. The huge, meaty fists hit between his shoulder blades, but the blow was powerful enough to send him sprawling to the floor.

Dazed and hurting badly, the instincts of the trained Texas draw fighter cast Sullivan, the man, aside and Sullivan, the skilled killer, took his place. He rolled on his back, raising his Colt . . . and beheld a creature from the lowest pit of hell coming at him.

A hunchbacked, monstrous white thing, vast rolls of fat overlying a seven-foot frame, advanced on him, its clawed hands the size of steam shovels ready to tear him apart.

The man, for that's what nature had intended him to be, was completely hairless. His piggy eyes seethed with black intensity and the desire to maim and kill.

"Destroy him, Hong-li!" Clotilde shrieked.

Sullivan fired. One shot at a distance of six feet. He aimed for the head, afraid that the man's mass of blubbery body fat might stop a ball. But the .44 shot true. The ball smacked the monster right between the eyes.

No matter how big and tough he was, a man could not survive a hit like that.

Despite his enormous body size, Hong-li's head was small. The ball plowed though his brain and erupted from the back of his skull in a halo of blood and bone.

His eyes rolled up in their sockets and the monster staggered . . . then fell forward.

Sullivan tried to roll out of the way, but the man's body crashed on top of him, a mountain of fat, sweat, blood, and stink.

No matter how he struggled, Sullivan couldn't get out from under Hong-li's vast bulk. Worse, his gun hand was pinned between his chest and the man's body.

"No, Clotilde, not the head!" Cheng's voice, a frantic yell at the top of his lungs. "The brain! Save the brain!"

Gasping for breath, crushed under Hong-li's weight, Sullivan twisted his head and saw Clotilde lower the bloodstained scimitar.

"Where's his gun?" she yelled.

"It's under him." Cheng grabbed a pillow from the back of Clotilde's chair and kneeled next to Sullivan. His face in an evil grimace, he shoved the pillow over the bounty hunter's face.

Helpless, Sullivan tried moving his head, but Cheng was a man of great strength, and he was relentless.

Desperately trying to wrench his gun free, Sullivan felt his hand move perhaps an inch—no more than that—across Hong-li's sweaty chest. The big Colt was trapped as though in a vat of hardened concrete. As was Sullivan. He couldn't catch a breath, feeling as though his lungs would explode.

As sudden darkness overtook him, his movements slowed, and he knew he was seconds away from death.

BLAAAM!

The rifle shot hammered loud in the close confines of the parlor.

Immediately, the pressure on the pillow stopped, and Sullivan felt Cheng fall away from him.

Someone pulled away the pillow, then a man's voice said, "Mr. Sullivan, are you all right?"

Sullivan looked into the concerned face of young Hank Lively and gasped, "Get . . . him . . . off . . . me."

"Deke, Les, help me here," Lively said.

It took the strength of three men to roll Hong-li off Sullivan. He didn't get up immediately but lay there, breathing heavily, until Lively helped him to his feet. Cheng lay in front of him, a bullet hole in his temple.

Like a female cougar at bay, Clotilde shrank against the fireplace, her green eyes fixed on Sullivan, aglow with hatred. "You stupid, miserable wretch. This night you killed a better man than yourself. My husband could have saved the world from a great scourge and you destroyed him."

Sullivan glanced at Cheng's slender body. "Seems like." His voice was level, cold.

"You haven't beaten me, Sullivan." Hatred and anger had transformed Clotilde's beautiful face, twisted it grotesquely like a gargoyle as she spewed her venom. "Bill Longley will find you and kill you, and I'll go on. There will other towns, big cities, free from savages like you, and I'll find other doctors to carry on my husband's work."

"No, you won't, Clotilde, You're done," Sullivan said. "When you killed Ebenezer Posey, you stepped over the line I'd drawn in the sand."

"You won't stop me, Sullivan. You're a midget among giants and you know it. Now, get out of my house, all of you."

Sullivan, chilled to the bone, thumbed back the hammer of his Colt.

Clotilde smiled. "You won't kill me, Sullivan. You don't have the nerve."

Sullivan fired and his ball crashed into her chest.

She slid slowly downward to a sitting position beside the fireplace. "You shot me . . ." she said, the light dying in her eyes. "You . . . killed me."

Sullivan stared at her. "Yeah, I did. Now you know how Lisa York felt."

CHAPTER FIFTY-ONE
A Sad Burden

Tam Sullivan answered the knock on his hotel room door.

Isaac Loomis stood there excitedly waving a piece of paper in his hand. "You got an answer to your wire, young feller."

"Come in," Sullivan said, stepping aside. He took the paper and read it.

RE WALLACE REWARD STOP BUTTERFIELD AGENT ON
WAY TO VERIFY REMAINS STOP HE WILL CONTACT
YOU STOP

"A bit late, ain't it?" Sullivan said.

"Yup," Loomis agreed. "Delayed going and coming. Bad snowstorms and the like."

Sullivan lifted Posey's carpetbag onto the bed. "You heard anything along the line about Bill Longley?"

"Sure did, and no later than this morning. Seems

he killed a man down Jasper, Texas, way then skipped across the Sabine into Louisiana."

"We sure it was him?"

"Yeah, it was ol' Bill all right. The Rangers put his name out." Loomis was quiet for a few moments. Then, his eyes probing, he said, "Heard about what happened up at the Wainright house."

Sullivan threw his saddlebags over his shoulder. "Seems like everybody has."

"Hard thing to kill a woman."

"No, it wasn't. Not hard at all."

"Everybody in town understood, depend on that." Loomis looked tentative, like a barefoot man picking his way through a nettle patch.

"You trying to make me feel better, Loomis?" Sullivan asked.

The stationmaster smiled shyly. "Why, yes. I guess I am."

Sullivan returned his smile. "Then I feel just fine." He picked up his key from the desk, looked around the room one last time, and stepped to the door. "Will you give me the road, Loomis?"

The stationmaster stepped aside, smiling. "Sullivan, you sure livened things up around here."

"Does that include the dead men?"

"And women," Loomis said.

The big bounty hunter nodded. "Yeah, and the women."

The slender little body, wrapped like an ancient mummy, lay on the examination table.

"I've done what I can to preserve him," Dr. Peter Harvey said. "The cold weather will help."

"He sure looks small, all wrapped up like that," Sullivan said.

Harvey nodded, said nothing.

"Ebenezer had sand though."

"Yes, he did," the doctor said. "He fought for life very hard."

"The town bought the buckboard and horse for you from Clem Weaver," John York said. "It's outside. And there's a . . . coffin."

"I appreciate it," Sullivan said. "How is your wife?"

"Montana Maine is with her. That helps."

"Yeah, I'm sure it does."

"Montana Maine says there's another angel in heaven, and her name is Lisa," York said.

Sullivan nodded. "I'm sure she's right about that."

"And she says there are three new demons in hell."

"She's right again," Sullivan agreed.

Head down, York was silent for a while, composing his thoughts. He looked up at the bounty hunter. "Clotilde Wainright had to die, right Mr. Sullivan?"

"The woman that was Clotilde Wainright died a long time ago," Sullivan answered. "Back in China, I'd say."

York visibly bit the good Christian bullet. "Then may God finally give her peace," he said, the words brittle on his tongue.

Sullivan ignored that. "I guess Ebenezer and me better go. We got a long trail ahead of us." He passed his saddlebags and the carpetbag to Harvey. "Take these. I'll carry Ebenezer."

"I'll help you," York said.

"No. I'll do it myself." Sullivan lifted the light burden of Ebenezer Posey from the table, carried him outside, and placed him in the coffin. He roped it down in the middle of the buckboard, next to his saddle.

York had already tied Sullivan's stud to the back of the wagon and the stone-faced Harvey handed him his bags. He placed them on the seat beside him, slapped the reins, and the buckboard trundled through the mud of the street, sleet borne by the north wind spinning around him.

A dog ran out from an alley and trotted alongside the passing wagon, barking furiously. It was the only farewell Tam Sullivan received from the town of Comanche Crossing.

CHAPTER FIFTY-TWO
A Curse on Bill Longley

Driving through snow that fell slowly in large flakes, Tam Sullivan was five miles west of the old Santa Fe Trail when he came upon Black Mesa and the dead packhorse. The carcass lay at the mouth of a narrow arroyo and the animal had been shot and its pack rifled.

Before he'd died, Booker Tate had stashed horses there and Bill Longley had already taken what he needed. Judging by the trampled mud and horse droppings, two animals had been there, the other probably a riding horse intended for Lisa York.

It was likely that Longley had left nothing in the pack, but to his joy Sullivan found a sack of Arbuckle, a round loaf of bread hollowed out and stuffed with sliced ham, and a paper package secured with a rubber band. Inside the package were four prime cigars. He smiled for the first time since leaving town and embarking on his high lonesome.

It seemed that Longley, fearing a posse, had been in a big hurry and overlooked some valuable items.

Sullivan raised his eyes to the iron-gray sky and said, "Thankee."

In his eagerness to leave Comanche Crossing, he'd laid in no grub but some hardtack and beef jerky. This find was a heavenly bounty, indeed.

He walked back to the buckboard. "Lookee what we got, Ebenezer. Coffee, grub, and cigars. What do you think of them beans?"

The wrapped body lay perfectly still. Perfectly quiet.

Sullivan's gloved hand brushed snow off Ebenezer's chest. "You can't hear me, can you old fellow? Well, maybe you can see me. I sure hope so."

The wagon creaked as Sullivan regained his seat and the floor under his boots immediately shed a long slat of rotted pine. "Damn you, Clem. Remind me to shoot you fer a hoss thief the next time I see you."

The morning gave way to afternoon, but the snow didn't let up and the Santa Fe Mountains to the west were almost hidden behind a hard, ashy light.

Sullivan's breath smoked as he crossed the Mora River at a point where there were rocky, flat-water shallows. He swung due south into broken, desolate country, pine and aspen growing on the higher rises.

As the day began its shade into evening, he peered through the snowfall and saw the faint glow of a campfire. At first, he thought it was his imagination, a trick of the fading light, but after he drove closer he realized it was no mistake.

Odd though it was, someone had a fire going. Sullivan could even smell the wood smoke.

The glow came from a small, horseshoe-shaped ridge, its top crested by snow-capped pines. Since the fire was situated in the curve of the shoe, he saw only its glimmer and no sign of the builder.

When he was within hailing distance, Sullivan drew rein. "Hello, the camp!" he yelled.

In answer, a man's voice, roughened by age and living, called out, "You got coffee?"

"I got coffee, but no pot," Sullivan said.

"I got a pot, but no coffee," the man yelled.

"Then we're a good match," Sullivan said.

"Come on in, an' welcome to ye." A short, stocky man dressed in buckskin and furs stepped to the opening of the rise. He cradled a Henry in his arms. "Name's Faith Butler, an' if you say Faith is a gal's name I'll plug ya."

"I have no such intention. Name's Tam Sullivan."

"What you got in the wagon, hoss?" Butler asked.

"A dead man, friend of mine. I'm taking him to Santa Fe for burial."

"Well, I got nothing agin' the dead, you understand, but I'd appreciate it if you don't bring him into camp. Might make me think about death and Judgment Day, like."

"I'll leave the wagon right here in the shelter of the rise," Sullivan said. "He'll be all right."

"Put your animals back with my mule over there." Butler pointed in the general direction of his animal. "I cleared away the snow and ice and there's good grass underneath."

Sullivan did what he could for the horses then

stepped to the hearty blaze of the fire, warming immediately. "How'd you find dry wood, Faith?"

"See the hole in the rock by the dead piñon
yonder? I found plenty of wood stacked in there.
Probably left by Apaches, but I'd like to think it was a
white man done it." The oldster's eyebrow lifted. "You
said you'd coffee in your poke?"

"Sure do." Sullivan reached into his pocket and
produced the sack of Arbuckle, then from under the
coat the bread and ham.

"Well, that's just top hole," Butler said. "I'll get the
coffee onto bile and then we'll have us a feast. Got
me a chunk of salt pork I'll fry up. Ran out of coffee
three days ago after I had to hole up because of the
damned weather. A coffee-drinking man sure pines
for it when he don't have none."

He stared at Sullivan from under bushy white eyebrows. "Son, don't talk to me again until I got my first
cup down me. That square with you?"

Sullivan nodded.

Pleased, Butler said, "Good. You catch on fast."

After his first cup of coffee had gone down the
hatch and he'd declared it, "Crackerjack!" Butler
sliced and fried the salt pork, added the ham from the
loaf, fried that, and then restuffed the sandwich after
cutting it neatly in half.

"Good eating, Faith," Sullivan said as he chewed.

The old man nodded. "I was tole that the salt pork
came from a Kentucky hog. That's how come it tastes
so succulent. Them hogs feed on nothing but corn
an' beer, or so they say."

"What brings you to this neck of the woods?" Sullivan asked, making conversation.

"Huntin', trappin', an' tracer gold. That is, when the Apaches let me be, which is most of the time." Butler's shrewd glance fell on the younger man. "You'd be Tam Sullivan the bounty hunter, ain't you? One of them Texas draw fighters that gets his name in all the newspapers. You kilt Crow Wallace a spell back. That ain't him in the back of the wagon is it?"

"No. It ain't Crow."

"Crow needed killin'. I'd have done it myself if he'd bothered me any."

"You hear anything of Bill Longley?" Sullivan asked, no longer simply making conversation.

"He's in Louisiana, last I heard. They say the Texas Rangers are after him for a killing down in Bastrop County when he gunned some poor sodbuster that was staring at a mule's ass and pushing a plow. But I don't know the truth of any o' that. Folks talk."

Sullivan reached into his saddlebags and produced a pint of whiskey, then the cigars.

Butler's face lit up and he grinned. "Hell, boy, are you some kind of angel come to visit old sinners like me? Pour a couple fingers of the who-hit-john into my coffee. Yeah, that's it. You're a white man an' true blue. An' here's to your very good health." The old man lifted his cup and Sullivan did likewise.

They lit their cigars from a brand Butler took from the fire. "Heard a thing about Bill Longley that could be true."

"I'd like to hear it," Sullivan said. "If it ain't just loose talk."

"Well, one of them Jesuit preachers tole it to me

over to Las Vegas way right there in the plaza. He saw I was readin' the newspaper with the bit about Bill and the Texas Rangers in it."

"He'd have pretty good bona fides I'd say."

"Sure did, an' he was a real smart feller. Frenchman he was, and we had a nice parley, *puisque je parle très bien le francais.*"

Sullivan didn't raise an eyebrow over an old mountain man like Faith Butler speaking French. Some of the fur traders spoke nothing else.

"Anyhoo," Butler said, "the Jesuit tole me that Bill Longley was cursed by a Louisiana bayou witch on account of how her nephew had been shot down by Longley at a street dance in Texas. Now the witch is a voodoo queen, and the preacher said they're the worst kind."

Sullivan said nothing, his eyes glittering as he stared across the scarlet campfire flames at Butler.

"The swamp witch cursed Bill to be hung three times for his crimes," the old man continued.

"He's already been half hung once," Sullivan said.

"Then he's got two more times to go, ain't he?" Butler smiled, then said behind a veil of cigar smoke, "I kin see you don't set store by curses an' sich, huh?"

Sullivan shrugged. "Until recent I didn't. Now I'm not so sure anymore."

"You mind Handsome Jules Villemont, the gambler? Worked the Mississippi riverboats?"

"Can't say as I do," Sullivan said.

"Before your time, I guess. Well, Jules trifled with the affections of a Creole gal and then left her with a broken heart and a big belly. Her mama didn't like it."

"And she was a swamp witch," Sullivan guessed. His front was toasty warm and his back was freezing.

"Damn right she was, and she laid a terrible curse on his man parts."

"Inconsiderate of her," Sullivan said, pushing his knees together.

"The curse took, an' ol' Jules wandered the streets of New Orleans for nigh on three years, wailing for his lost manhood. He tried everything of course, including powdered monkey bone, but nothing worked. He stayed limp as the little finger of an empty glove."

"Poor feller. So what happened to him?" Sullivan asked.

"Jules begged the witch to raise her curse, but she refused. 'Serves you right,' she said. Well, then he blew his brains out."

"At least he went out with a bang."

"Uh-huh. And there's a moral to what I've been telling you," Butler said. "When a man in your profession asks for news of an outlaw like Longley, he has a reward on his mind and maybe a killin'. Am I right or am I wrong?"

"Partly right, I guess. I want to kill Bill Longley real bad, but not for the reward on his head."

"You won't be the man to kill him. The only crew lowdown and heartless enough to hang a feller twice is the law."

Sullivan smiled. "Maybe I'll get lucky and the curse won't take."

Butler shrugged. "The Jesuit was in good with God and he said it will. And I believe him."

* * *

Tam Sullivan slept fitfully under his blanket, rising every hour to throw more wood on the fire, check on the horses and the white bundle that was Ebenezer Posey's body. He got up for the last time an hour before dawn, melted snow in the coffeepot, tossed in the last of the Arbuckle, and set the pot on the fire.

Faith Butler, snoring slightly, didn't stir.

Coyotes yipped close, and snow fell in flakes as big as silver dollars and sizzled on the fire. The air was frigid, icy. When first light came, it revealed a sky as black as the inside of a cannon barrel.

Sullivan shook Butler awake. "Coffee's on the bile."

"Damn ye fer a scoundrel, waking a man from the best dream he's had in a twelve-month."

"About women and whiskey, no doubt," Sullivan said.

The old man blinked, remembering. "Not any woman. It was Montana Maine herself come to visit me in a tent on the bank of the Canadian."

Sullivan was surprised. "You've met Montana Maine?"

Butler sat up in his blankets. "Nope, never met her, but I sure hope to remedy that afore I die. They say she's a sight to see." The old man scowled. "Here, have you met her?"

"No. Like you, I never have."

"Well, she's no longer in my head. She just faded away like smoke when you woke me."

Sullivan grinned. "Sorry."

"Maybe it's just as well. They say once a man sets eyes on Montana Maine, he'll never settle for another woman. Now pour me a cup o' that coffee, young feller. It sure smells good."

CHAPTER FIFTY-THREE
A Grieving Widow

After taking leave of Faith Butler, Tam Sullivan headed south as far as Barillas Peak where he swung due west though rugged high country that slowed the wagon in places. It was already growing dark when he reached the Pecos with the temperature hovering somewhere around zero.

Three surviving walls of a burned-out cabin promised meager shelter of a sort, but he spent the last of the light searching for a place to cross the river. He found a narrow point with a stand of shivering willows on the opposite bank, their leaves the color of old gold.

Satisfied that he could get across without too much trouble, Sullivan returned to the ruined cabin. He tried to build a fire with damp wood, failed miserably, and contented himself with a meal of jerky, the last inch of whiskey, and a cigar. For a while at least, the cigar's glowing tip gave him the illusion of warmth.

Ebenezer Posey was beyond feeling cold, but Sullivan

carefully brushed snow from his wrapped body. "Sleep well, old timer. It's going to be a miserable night."

And it was.

Sullivan woke from shallow sleep, stiff and cold, frost in his bones.

The morning offered nothing. Snow fell, the air hurt to breathe, and black clouds hung on the mountain peaks. The Pecos barely moved, flat as a sheet of glass.

His fingers numb in his gloves, Sullivan harnessed up the Morgan, tied his stud to the rear of the wagon, and steeled himself for the last twenty miles of his journey.

Behind him, Ebenezer Posey's body swayed back and forth with every movement.

Sullivan's arrival at the Butterfield stage depot in Santa Fe caused a major stir. Pale clerks, their hands fluttering like moths, worried managers, and even the company's hard-bitten drivers and guards crowded around the wagon, staring in stunned silence at Ebenezer Posey's small, still body.

Finally, a pink-faced man in broadcloth with a silver watch chain across his ample belly took Sullivan aside. "Who is he?"

"One of yours. His name is Ebenezer Posey."

Recognition dawned on the man's face. "Yes, he was one of our junior clerks." His eyes flicked to the wagon. "You'd better come inside . . . Mister . . . ah . . ."

"Sullivan." He grabbed his saddlebags and the valise, and followed the man into the depot.

After waving Sullivan into a chair opposite his desk, he introduced himself as Walt Dexter. "What happened?"

"I could sure use a cup of coffee," Sullivan said.

"Of course." Dexter yelled for someone to bring coffee. After watching Sullivan take his first few sips, he said, "Well?"

Using as few words as possible, Sullivan told Dexter how his employee had died.

The Butterfield man sat in shocked silence for a few moments then said, "And the perpetrators of this vile crime?"

"They're all dead," Sullivan said.

Dexter looked into the younger man's eyes and didn't like what he saw. His quick intake of breath was loud in the room.

"All but one." Sullivan answered the question on Dexter's face. "His name is Bill Longley and I plan to kill him. Real soon."

"The outlaw?" Dexter frowned.

"None other."

"I heard he was in Louisiana."

"Heard that too, but I'll find him." Sullivan tossed the carpetbag onto the desk. "In there you'll find what's left of the money Crow Wallace took from the stage robbery and the reward Ebenezer had with him. We couldn't find the body so he couldn't identify it from the dodger to pay me. Oh, and a passenger's gold watch."

Someone tapped timidly on the door and Dexter bade him enter.

The clerk was tall and thin, and his pale face was flushed across the cheekbones. "Sir, about the body . . . it's attracting a crowd."

"Then get an undertaker, Swenson. Use your initiative," Dexter said. "Later, I'll ask Mrs. Posey what she wants done with her dear departed."

Looking slightly overwhelmed, the clerk left.

Dexter dived into the bag and counted the money. "It would seem, Mr. Sullivan, that a large amount of the ten-thousand dollars from the robbery is gone."

Sullivan nodded. "Crow was a big spender."

"What did we say about the recovered monies?" Dexter asked.

"We said I get ten percent, plus five hundred dollars for the watch."

"It does seem a little excessive, seeing how much of the money was, as you say, spent."

Sullivan smiled and got to his feet. In the dusty, businesslike atmosphere of the Butterfield office the .44 on his hip stood out like a Gatling gun in a convent library. "Eleven hundred dollars, give or take, is coming to me, Dexter. I'm not a friendly man and I'm in a particularly unpleasant mood this morning, so I don't want to hear any argument. On top of that, you make lousy coffee."

He took Crow's wanted poster from the inside pocket of his coat and threw it on the table. "Read it."

Dexter did. "Ah, I seem to have misunderstood."

"Misunderstanding a tired, irritable ranny like me can get you killed, Mr. Dexter."

The man immediately counted out the eleven hundred and Sullivan shoved the bills into his pocket. "Where can I find Mrs. Posey?"

"It's quite all right, I'll break the news to the poor woman," Dexter said.

Sullivan shook his head. "Ebenezer Posey was my friend. I'll be the one to tell his wife."

"And I think you should also know that your husband was a hero," Tam Sullivan said.

"My Ebenezer was a hero?" Mrs. Posey asked, her round, tear-stained face surprised.

"Yeah, he saved a stagecoach from Apaches. They say he killed a half-dozen savages with a borrowed pistol."

"I don't . . . I hardly know what to say. Mr. Posey was the most meek and mild of men."

"Well, I guess a hero lurked inside him, just waiting to break free." Sullivan knew how melodramatic that sounded.

As Mrs. Posey again dissolved into tears, he looked around him.

The Posey parlor had a shabby genteel look, as though the couple had strived to keep up middle class appearances on a clerk's salary and whatever Mrs. Posey made from her bloomers. It seemed that Ebenezer had exaggerated his wife's prowess with the needle and her thriving business. Just one step down and the Posey home would be poor indeed.

"I just don't know what I'll do without Ebenezer." Mrs. Posey shook her head. "I'm lost. He was my life, my everything." She stared into Sullivan's eyes, seeking solace. "And he died such a terrible death."

"The doctor said Ebenezer didn't suffer," Sullivan lied. "It was so fast, you understand."

As many very large women do, Mrs. Posey held a

scrap of a handkerchief no bigger than a postage stamp to her reddened nose.

For a few moments Sullivan thought about what he was going to say. Then, "Can you manage financially, Mrs. Posey? Now that . . . the breadwinner has passed on."

"Ebenezer has no pension, but I do make women's undergarments for the upper classes. But then, the reason they are upper class is because they refuse to pay much, if at all." Mrs. Posey looked around her. "Ebenezer provided me with this home, but now that I am alone in the world, I will have to find cheaper accommodation."

"Do you have relatives?" Sullivan asked.

The woman shook her head. "No. None. On either side." She broke down again. "Mr. Sullivan, I don't know what I'll do. I'm quite alone."

Sullivan felt a pang of sympathy for the woman and it angered him. *Damn it Ebenezer!*

"Well, Mrs. Posey, I know it can't compensate you for the loss of your husband, but the mayor and citizens of Comanche Crossing raised a fund for Ebenezer after he so bravely saved the stage."

"They did?" It was the incredulous question of a woman who'd never before been helped by anyone at anytime.

"Yes, and I was asked to give it to you." Sullivan reached into his pocket and held the money out to Mrs. Posey. "It's eleven hundred dollars. I contributed myself."

That last wasn't any kind of lie.

"But . . . but it's too much," Mrs. Posey said, eyeing

the stack of bills as though they might fly up in her face and smother her.

"It's not too much. It's not enough, Mrs. Posey." Sullivan laid the money on the table beside the woman. "I have to leave now and see to my horses, but I'd like to attend Ebenezer's funeral."

"Of course you shall, Mr. Sullivan. Ebenezer would want that."

"Then I'll take my leave of you," Sullivan said. "If you need anything . . ."

The woman nodded. "I'll be fine."

Sullivan saw that Mrs. Posey wished to be alone in her grief. He stepped to the door and left.

Behind him, a forlorn fat lady sat in a darkened room with her head bowed.

And for the first time in his life Sullivan managed to share the pain of another human being.

CHAPTER FIFTY-FOUR
Colt .45

Ebenezer Posey was laid to rest in a freezing rain under high-banked, gray cloud. Before the preacher finished his words, the rain turned to sleet.

To Tam Sullivan's surprise, Butterfield did right by Posey. The entire depot staff turned out to stand at the graveside. When the burial ended, a knot of mourners murmuring their sympathies surrounded Mrs. Posey and Sullivan stepped away unnoticed.

Later that day, he sold the wagon and the Morgan for a hundred and fifty dollars to a liveryman who must have taken lessons in larceny from Clem Weaver.

Sullivan booked a room in a rundown hotel then headed for the sheriff's office. Despite the weather, the streets were thronged with people and the road-side markets filled the air with the tang of spices, peppers, and the gritty Mexican hot chocolate.

The local lawman was a tall, lanky man who went by the name Card Adams. He wore one of the new-

fangled cartridge Colts in a shoulder holster. Sullivan
envied his mustache, bigger and fuller than his own.

"Sullivan . . . you're the ranny who brung in
Ebenezer Posey," the sheriff said. "Rough trip from
Comanche Crossing, huh?"

"You could say that."

Adams threw himself onto his chair. Behind his
head stood a rack of rifles and scatterguns, each one
gleaming with a sheen of oil.

"Hell, Sullivan, all the halfway decent outlaws have
left the territory on account of the weather. I got
nothing for you. Wait . . ." The sheriff reached into a
drawer and tossed a dodger onto the desk. "There's
him. His name is Dancing Dan Privette, tap dances
and plays the banjo at the same time. He's a pretty
good turn."

"Three hundred dollars reward offered by the Texas
Rangers," Sullivan said, casting his eye over the wanted
poster. "A gentleman of color."

"Yeah, Privette's black as the carl of hell's waistcoat.
He cut up a whore down Nacogdoches way and that
never sets right with the law."

"You got a lead on him?" Sullivan asked.

"A lead? Why, man, he's right across the street. Ol'
Dancing Dan's the main attraction at the Night Owl
saloon."

Sullivan frowned. "So why haven't you nabbed him?"

"And take him all the way to El Paso for three hundred dollars? I think not. Besides, he hasn't broken
any laws in Santa Fe or the New Mexico Territory."

"Did you wire the Rangers?"

"Sure, but they got more to do than ride up from

Texas to arrest a black man for cuttin' on a Mexican whore."

Sullivan thought for a few moments, then he said, "It's better than nothing, I guess. I'm headed for Texas anyway. I'll take Privette with me."

"You're going to make yourself real unpopular, Sullivan. Folks at the Night Owl set store by him."

"Popularity doesn't enter into my line of work."

Tam Sullivan was a man who learned from his mistakes. It was three hundred hard miles to El Paso and for this trip, he laid in plenty of supplies—coffee, tortillas, bacon, cans of peaches, a frying pan, and coffeepot.

He stashed the supplies in his hotel room, then painfully aware that he was down to his last few dollars, he followed the desk clerk's directions to Dirty Sammy's Rod and Gun store on St. Louis Street.

"Nasty out there today, huh?" the grubby man behind the counter said when Sullivan entered in a blast of wind and sleet.

I reckon it is." Sullivan stepped to the counter. "I'd like to see one of them new cartridge Colts they're all talking about."

Sammy smiled. "Got a couple in the case right here." He laid two beautiful revolvers on the glass, symphonies of blue steel and walnut. "The one on the left with the shorter barrel is the Artillery Model, t'other with the seven-and-a-half-inch was the model carried by the gallant Custer and his band of heroes at the Bighorn."

"Didn't do them much good, did it?" Sullivan picked up the shorter barreled revolver and like every ranny who'd ever handled a Colt Single Action Army, he fell in love like a man with a new mistress.

"It's .45 caliber an' she's a shooter." As though Sullivan needed convincing, Sammy added, "Carry her on your hip and fear no man." From long experience around belted men and guns, he read the bounty hunter's eyes and said, "I got a place out back where you can try her. If you don't mind shooting in a blizzard."

Sullivan nodded. "Yeah, I'd like that." Aware of his precarious finances, he asked, "How much?"

"To you, only twelve dollars."

"A bit steep, ain't it?"

"At that price, my wife and kids will go hungry. I'll throw in a box of cartridges and that means they'll starve and I'll go out of business." Sammy looked as though he was about to launch into more of his woes when the bell above the front door opened.

Sheriff Adams stepped inside carrying a Yellow Boy Winchester and a scowl. He nodded to Sullivan then said, "Sammy, you told me you'd fixed this rifle, but it's still throwing my shots a foot to the left of target."

He slammed the rifle on the counter so hard, Sullivan thought the glass had cracked for sure.

The sheriff glared at the shop owner. "Damn you fer a rogue and a swindler, Sammy. What are you going to do about it?"

"Did you go see the doc about your eyes like I told you?"

"No. Not yet."

"Well, you're going to shoot a foot to the left until you get a pair of spectacles. It ain't the rifle, Sheriff. It's you." Sammy picked up the Winchester, levered a .44-40 round into the chamber, and looked around. "See the mouse creeping along the picture shelf above the door?"

"I see it," Adams said. "And it's a rat."

"Watch." Sammy threw the rifle to his shoulder and fired. The wretched rodent blew apart.

He tossed the Winchester to the lawman. "Nothing wrong with that weapon. Get your eyes checked, Sheriff."

Adams cast a measuring glance at Sullivan as one man does to another when his marksmanship is called into question. To save face he said, "You better be right, Sammy. Or the next time I come in here, I'll bend this rifle over your head."

After a follow-up, "Humph!" the lawman jangled out the door and slammed it shut behind him.

Sammy turned to Sullivan. "Want to try the Colt now?"

Twenty minutes later, numbed by cold, Tam Sullivan and Dirty Sammy stepped back into the warmth and gun smells of the store.

"Mr. Sullivan, I've seen a lot of men use the Colt's revolver, but I never seen one who could sling lead like you." Sammy slapped Sullivan on the back. "Man, you're a natural."

"Took me twenty years of practice to become a natural," Sullivan said.

"So, you want the revolver?"

Sullivan nodded. "Seems like."

"I'll give you three dollars for the Navy in your waist-band. You don't need powder and shot no more."

"I reckon I'll hold on to it for now. Newfangled things have a habit of breaking."

"Well, that will be twelve dollars."

Sullivan paid the man and loaded the revolver with the last five rounds from the box of cartridges. He'd left his gun belt and holster in the hotel room so he shoved the Colt into the pocket of his coat.

"A pleasure doing business with you," Sammy said as he dropped Sullivan's crumpled bills into the cash drawer. "And it's been a great honor to meet a real Texas draw fighter.

CHAPTER FIFTY-FIVE
The Dancing Man

More than ever, Tam Sullivan badly needed the three hundred dollar reward on Dancing Dan Privette. He didn't anticipate any trouble taking the man, but bounty hunters are born to caution. He checked with the livery stable to make sure that Privette had a horse. He didn't, but he owned a big government mule with a US brand on its shoulder and the animal looked like it would hold up on the trip to El Paso.

Sullivan returned to his hotel room, buckled on his gun rig, and replaced the cap-and-ball in the holster with the new Colt. He tried his draw a few times and it was as though the revolver leaped into his hand.

Smiling into the mirror, Sullivan said, "You're fast, Tam. Maybe you're as fast as Wild Bill Longley."

Maybe . . .

He left his room and stood on the hotel porch, gauging the weather. Black sky, gloom, sleet, wind, freezing temperatures, snow-capped mountains, and a long, dangerous trail ahead through rough and broken country. He hoped Dancing Dan wouldn't mind the inconvenience.

A sleepless owl silhouetted against a full moon decorated the saloon's glass doors as Sullivan pushed them open and stepped inside. As saloons went, the Night Owl was no better and no worse than others he'd seen. The room was rectangular with an elevated stage at one end and a long mahogany bar that took up most of the far wall, along with the usual scattering of tables, chairs, and polished brass spittoons.

It was not yet noon, but the lamps were lit against the gray day. Only one bartender was on duty, serving the few customers, the sporting crowd sleeping the sleep of the unjust.

Sullivan saw what looked like a doctor appear from behind one of the red velvet curtains that flanked the stage.

His guess was confirmed when the bartender said, "How is he, doc?"

"Broken leg," the physician answered. "He took a bad tumble."

The bartender looked alarmed. "Hell, when can he dance again?"

The doctor shook his head. "When his leg heals. It's a pretty bad break. I'd say ten to thirteen weeks, maybe longer."

Sullivan, felling a spike of panic, stepped to the bar

as the doctor asked for a whiskey. "Doc, who broke his leg?"

"Dancing Dan," the man answered. "He was rehearsing and fell off the stage. It will be months before he dances again, but he can still play the banjo."

"Can he travel?" Sullivan asked.

"Travel! For weeks, he won't be able to walk from his bed to the outhouse."

Suspicious, the bartender said, "Here, mister, are you some kind of law?"

"You could say that," Sullivan said. "Privette is wanted in Texas for a cuttin'. I figure to take him to the Rangers in El Paso."

The doctor snorted. "Not a hope in hell. He'd barely make it out of town without keeling over. You could take him to El Paso, all right, but he'd be a dead man long before you got there."

Sullivan knew a brick wall when he saw one. "Damn it. Can I take a look at him?"

"I don't see why not," the doctor said. "Go up on the stage and turn left. Dan is in a dressing room back there. You'll hear him before you see him."

Frustrated, Sullivan stepped from the bar and crossed the floor, his spurs ringing loud in the sudden silence.

"Be careful you don't fall and break a leg," the doctor called after him.

Somebody laughed.

Sullivan heard the dancer's groans from a ways off before he entered the dressing room.

Dancing Dan Privette lay on his back in a small iron cot, his splinted leg elevated on an empty Arbuckle coffee box. He was a small, compact man with very dark skin and large, expressive black eyes. They expressed pain, suffering, and irritability. "Who the hell are you? Get that damned quack back here."

"Feeling unwell, Dan, are we?" Sullivan said.

"My leg's broke!" Privette yelped. "Get the doc, get my woman, get anybody. Most of all, get me out of here."

"You're such a disappointment to me, Dan," Sullivan said.

"What the hell are you talking about?"

"I'm talking about a cuttin' down Nacogdoches way, Dan. Do you recollect?"

Privette stared wide-eyed at Sullivan for long moments. Then he filled his lungs and shrieked, "Heeelp!"

The doctor and the bartender came running.

"What the hell did you do to him?" the bartender demanded from Sullivan.

"Nothing. I just reminded ol' Danny boy that he's wanted in Texas for cuttin' on a Mexican whore."

"Here, that man has friends in this town," the bartender said. "He will not be abused."

"He's not my friend," Sullivan said.

"As I already told you, mister, he won't make it to El Paso," the doctor said.

"Don't let him take me," Privette wailed. "He'll murder me on the way."

"Shut the hell up." Sullivan looked at the doctor. "He'd be too much of a burden on the trail, I reckon, huh?"

"Well, you'd have to lift him off and on his horse

and carry him wherever you camped, to say nothing of helping him with his body functions."

"Don't plant that picture in my head, doc." Sullivan noticed a wallet and watch laying on a table next to the cot. "His?"

"His," the doctor replied.

Sullivan picked up the wallet. It was stuffed with bills. "Do all right for yourself, Dan, huh?"

"Oh my God, he's robbing me," Privette hollered. "He's taking all my money! Oh . . . ah . . . ah . . . my leg!"

"Lie still, Dan," the doctor ordered.

Sullivan counted out three hundred dollars and tossed the wallet back on the table. "Taking the three hundred dollar reward for your hide, Dan."

"I will not let you remove this man from Santa Fe," the doctor said.

"I won't. But I'll come back for him another day."

"When?" the bartender asked.

"Maybe in the summer," Sullivan said. "His leg ought to be healed by then."

"That's hard, mighty hard and lowdown," the bartender said.

Sullivan nodded. "I'm in a hard, lowdown business." He glanced at Privette. "Feel better now, Dan. Play the banjo to keep your spirits up and I'll see you in July or thereabouts."

"Damn you. I'll see you in hell before I'll let you take me to El Paso," Dan said. "We'll see how big you talk when I'm on my feet, bounty hunter."

"Well, I sure don't want to shoot a dancing man, Dan," Sullivan said. "It just ain't decent. So you just keep calm and let the leg heal."

In between bouts of wailing about his pain, Privette turned the air blue with curses, but Sullivan ignored him.

He touched his hat to the doctor and the bartender. "Good day, gentlemen."

"Hey, do you put out your name, mister?" the bartender called.

"Tam Sullivan."

"Hell, you brung in the dead Butterfield man."

"That I did. His name was Ebenezer Posey."

CHAPTER FIFTY-SIX
Scattergun Justice

Tam Sullivan bought a bottle of brandy and a box of cigars and returned to his room. As was his habit, he carried a chair to the window where he could look out on the street. He was about to sit when a knock came to the door.

Sullivan slid his new Colt from the holster on the bed and stepped to the door. "Who is it?"

"Me. Sheriff Adams.

After unlocking the door and allowing the man inside, Sullivan said, "I guess you heard about Dan Privette?"

"Yeah. You took your reward early. In my day, no bandit, no reward, was the rule."

"Well, I guess I bent the rule a little. Is that what you came here to talk about?"

Sleet melted on the shoulders of Adams' sheepskin and hat, and his mustache was frosted. "No, not that. I got news for you."

"Can it wait until I pour a drink and light a cigar?"

"It'll keep."

"Drink?"

"Of course. And a cigar. I reckon my news is worth it." Adams smiled. "And after all, it is Christmas Day."

"It is? Well fancy that, huh?" Sullivan pulled the chair from the window and bade the lawman sit. He gave him a cigar and whiskey in a chipped, clouded glass.

After he tasted his drink and his cigar glowed, Adams said, "Wild Bill Longley has been took."

Sullivan was stunned speechless for a few moments. "How did it happen . . . I mean, where? Hell man, out with it."

"You going to give me time to tell the story, Sullivan? I can't say it all at once."

"Yeah, sorry. Go right ahead."

"After I saw you at Dirty Sammy's store—the damned scoundrel—a feller up from Texas came into my office abut some claim he had on ten acres of bottomland over on Gallinas Creek. Seems that another feller, a cousin of his, had moved onto the property and built a cabin. Now I don't normally get involved in such—"

"Sheriff, about Longley?" Sullivan interrupted.

"Oh yeah. Well, the feller gave me a *by-the-way* then he asked did I hear that Bill Longley had been took in DeSoto Parish over Louisiana way? 'No,' says I. 'Well,' says he, 'Nacogdoches County Sheriff Milton Mast and a deputy slipped across the border, grabbed Longley, and took him back to Texas.'"

Sullivan smiled. "Sheriff, it sounds like that Texas

feller was pulling a sandy on you. Bill Longley wouldn't let himself get arrested by a pair of hick lawmen."

"How it come up, the feller says, is that Mast and his deputy disguised themselves as a couple harmless old coots, false gray beards an' all, and got close to Longley in a saloon. They threw down on him with Scott ten gauge scatterguns, and he surrendered meek as a lamb."

Sullivan considered that, then said, "That feller of yours doesn't miss a trick, does he? Even knows the make of shotguns the lawmen used."

"Hell, Sullivan, it was in all the Texas newspapers. There's talk that Mast is going to be presented with a gold watch for the capture."

"So where is Longley now? Writing his name on the wall of the Nacogdoches jail.?"

"Yeah, as far as the feller knows, he's still there."

After he refilled Adams' glass, Sullivan thought for a while. Then he said, "The jail hasn't been built yet that will hold Longley. I reckon I'll head for Texas on account I don't want him to escape me again."

"Eight hundred miles from here to there," the sheriff said. "You must want to kill ol' Bill real bad."

Sullivan nodded. "As badly as I ever wanted anything in my life."

"I won't ask you why," Adams said.

"Good, because it's long in the telling."

"You can ride the Southern Pacific cushions at least some of the way. Unless you give Dan Privette his money back and can't pay the fare."

"Did he ask you to get the three hundred from me?" Sullivan wanted to know.

"He sure did. He's feeling mighty low over the busted leg and his stolen money."

"I didn't steal it, Sheriff. I just took my reward early."

"You gonna give it back?"

"Hell, no."

"Well, I asked you and I'll give him your answer."

"Aren't you going to try to arrest me?"

"Hell, no. Just before I got here, Dirty Sammy stopped me in the street and made a point of telling me about how well you shoot."

"You're a wise man, Sheriff Adams."

CHAPTER FIFTY-SEVEN
A Gunman Is Cut Down to Size

It was mid-January when Tam Sullivan rode into Nacogdoches. The town still bore the scars of the War Between the States. The boom times that came with the arrival of the Houston East and West Texas Railroad and an economy shift from agriculture to trade and commerce still lay several years in the future.

The town was a backwater at the northern edge of the Deep South. Heavy winter rains had turned the streets to bogs of red-ocher mud that clung to everything.

He dropped his horse off at the livery and strode to the Sam Houston Hotel & Billiard Hall. After he signed in, he asked the desk clerk if Sheriff Milton Mast was in town.

"I reckon he is. My guess is you'll find him at the Stone House just down the street a ways."

Sullivan nodded his thanks and walked into the muddy street made even gloomier by the overhang of a black and mustard sky.

The Stone House was not hard to find. The impressive, two-story building of sun-dried adobe brick was partitioned into a general store and saloon. The building towered over its neighboring wood stores and offices like a colossus.

Gun-toting men with careful eyes were not rara avis in Nacogdoches, but Sullivan's height and the way he carried himself made heads turn in his direction.

He stepped to the bar, ordered a rye with a beer chaser, then took time to look around him. A dozen men stood at the long bar and maybe twice that number sat at tables and played poker or just stared into their empty glasses, the latter just a few of the many the gallant Lost Cause had plunged into poverty.

The mixologist, resplendent in brocade, diamonds, hair oil, and magnificent mustachio, wafted lavender water in Sullivan's direction. He leaned over the bar and whispered, "Passing through, stranger?"

"I reckon so," Sullivan said.

"Then just mind your Ps and Qs. Don't look now, but the man behind you in the slicker with the ostrich feather in his hat is Courtney Lister. He figures he's the cock o' the walk in this town. He's killed a dozen men, they say."

"Is that so? Well, I'm not here to borrow trouble so I'll step carefully around him. Fact is, I'm here to see Sheriff Mast."

For some reason the bartender looked relieved. Maybe the new French mirror behind the bar had something to do with it. "Milt! Feller here to talk with you."

A voice answered. "Then let him come over here and talk to me. My damned feet hurt."

"In the corner." The bartender pointed in that direction.

"Yeah, I see him." Sullivan crossed the floor, carrying his drinks, keenly aware that Lister watched his every step. "Mind if I set?"

Mast nodded. "Sure. What can I do for you?"

Sullivan pulled up a chair. "Where are you keeping Bill Longley?"

Mast didn't hesitate. "Nowhere. The Rangers took him to Giddings. They're going to hang him fer sure." The lawman's left eyebrow raised. "You a friend of his?"

"No. I plan to kill him when the law lets him go."

"Not this time," Mast said, smiling. "The Rangers have witnesses who swear they saw him kill Wilson Anderson in Bastrop County back in the spring of seventy-five. Anderson was walking behind a plow at the time."

"Yeah. I heard the story," Sullivan said, scowling as he swallowed Mast's bitter pill. The Rangers just might make the murder charge stick this time.

"Not so fast, my buck. Did I hear you right?" Courtney Lister stood near the table, his slicker pulled back from the Colt on his hip.

"What did you hear?" Mast asked.

"I heard this ranny say he aimed to kill Bill Longley." Lister raised his voice so everybody in the saloon would hear him. "Good ol' Bill happens to be a friend of mine."

Sullivan looked hard at the gunman. He felt very tired. "You should choose your friends more carefully, youngster."

Lister didn't like *youngster* one bit.

He needed to prove to everyone on the saloon and to the town of Nacogdoches that he was a man. A man with bark on him, a man to be reckoned with . . . a lean, dangerous draw fighter of the first rank.

Not a kid.

"Look at me. What do you see?" Sullivan said.

Lister's top lip curled in a sneer. "Not much."

"You let things be, Court," Mast said.

"You shut your trap," the young man said. "Your time is coming, Mast."

"What do you see, kid?" Sullivan said again. Quieter this time.

"Hell, I don't know." Lister giggled. "Maybe an hombre so scared he's about to pass out."

"No, that's not it. See, a couple months ago, I killed a kid like you, only a sight meaner, and it got me into a heap of trouble. I don't want to do it again."

Lister seemed uncertain. The big man wasn't scared and that troubled him. "I'm better with a gun than Longley." The boast was as hollow as it sounded.

Somewhere a man laughed.

Lister's uncertainty turned to anger. The situation was slipping away from him and he needed to reassert himself . . . establish that he was a man to be feared. "Get to your damned feet. You threatened my friend and I will not let it stand."

All at once, Sullivan was tired of it—this, and what had gone before. He got to his feet and cleared his gun.

Lister grinned. And drew.

He never cleared leather.

Sullivan's threw a straight right from the shoulder that crashed into the youngster's chin. It was a powerful, on-the-button punch that hit like an axe hitting a sapling pine, and Lister dropped.

Mad clean through, Sullivan kicked away the young gunman's Colt then stripped him of his gun belt. He slid the holster off the belt and threw it away. A big strong man, Sullivan grabbed the kid, threw him over his knee, and paddled his butt with the heavy cartridge belt.

Lister, aware of what was happing to him, kicked and shrieked, trying to swing at Sullivan.

But the big bounty hunter, his teeth bared in anger, was relentless. *Thwack . . . thwack . . . thwack . . .*

The belt rose and fell, each blow that hit Lister's butt a punishing reminder to the youngster not to play with grownups, especially strangers. You never know what you might get.

Courtney Lister finally knew. He'd braced a man he didn't know, a man who'd never done him any harm, and he was paying the price.

As Lister's cries grew into screams for mercy, Sullivan stood up and the young gunman rolled off his knee, thudding to the ground. His blood up, Sullivan lifted Lister, threw him into the street, and tossed his hat after him.

Sullivan picked up the kid's Colt and tossed it onto the table in front of Sheriff Mast.

Ringed by wondering, horrified faces, Sullivan picked up his rye, drained the glass, and set it back on the table. "One thing I cannot stand is an uncivil bully."

Mast shook his head. "Hell, mister. What happens when you get really mad at a feller?"

"You don't want to know."

Ten minutes later, Courtney Lister spurred his horse out of town.

As far as the records show, he was never heard from again.

CHAPTER FIFTY-EIGHT
The Noose Tightens

Tam Sullivan was unimpressed by Giddings, Texas, a small, wooden town in the middle of cotton country that had recently become the county seat.

But the settlement had pretensions to greatness. Its two main thoroughfares, Main and Austin, were a hundred feet wide and the Houston and Texas Railway had a depot in the town.

As far as he could see, the main businesses fronting Main Street, apart from a couple of cotton warehouses, were a saloon, general store, blacksmith's shop, a large store catering to ladies hats and dresses, a saddle and harness shop, and an oil mill.

In addition, the town had a church, school, and Masonic Lodge and behind the storefronts were scores of shacks, set down in no particular order as though they'd wandered into town then lost their way.

The ramshackle livery stable with an adjoining pole corral marked the end of Austin Street, and the owner, a middle-aged man with a strong Yankee accent remarked that Sullivan's big stud was the finest horse he'd ever seen in Giddings.

"Then take good care of him." As he unsaddled the sorrel, Sullivan asked, "Is Bill Longley still here?"

"Wild Bill? He sure is. He's going to get hung later today, though."

"A great loss to the community." Sullivan said.

According to a sign tacked to the door outside, the liveryman's name was Jeff Reilly. He gave a cautious nod. The talk around town was that friends of Longley's might try to spring him from jail. The big man with the fine horse and the iron on his hip could easily be one of them.

"I didn't see the jailhouse when I rode in," Sullivan commented.

That made the livery owner even more circumspect. "That's because we don't have one." Reilly led the sorrel to a stall, scooped him some oats, and then forked some hay.

When he came back, Sullivan said, "Then where is Longley being held?"

Reilly was suspicious. "You a friend of his, mister?"

"No. I'm an enemy of his."

Reilly's clouded face cleared. "Bill's stapled to the concrete floor in a shack behind the blacksmith's shop and he's guarded by four Texas Rangers who ain't real friendly folks."

"I didn't see a gallows, either," Sullivan said. "Is the blacksmith going to hang him?"

Reilly smiled. "No, sir. The Rangers built the gallows on the rise behind town in a pine grove. They're

expecting a big crowd and the trees will stop folks
from getting too close."

"Big crowd, huh?"

"Yeah. A lot of people. There's already a pig on a
spit up there and beer barrels and the Giddings
Ladies Auxiliary is hinting that there may be cake and
ice cream."

"What time's the hanging?" Sullivan asked.

"Four sharp. Rain or shine."

"Wind's coming up," Sullivan said.

Reilly grinned. "Rain, shine, or wind."

The only hotel in town was a one story, false-
fronted log building with a canvas roof. Canvas walls
partitioned the space inside and the Rest And Be
Thankful provided an iron cot with a corncob mattress, a table with a pitcher and basin and, a thoughtful touch, a chamber pot.

"Last room available," the clerk said. "Because of
the hanging, you understand."

After Sullivan stepped outside the clerk hung a sign
on the door. STUFFED TO THE GILLS. It was not yet ten,
but the town was already crowded with people, many
of them blacks who worked for the surrounding
cotton industry.

Giddings was a wide-open town with the usual mix
of hardy frontier types, but Sullivan saw no one who
looked like a gun. The rumor about Longley's pals
trying to free him didn't seem to be true.

Gray clouds scudded across the sky as he crossed
the red mud of the endless street and made the oppo-

site boardwalk after getting cussed out by a freight
wagon driver who figured Sullivan was in his way. He
found the blacksmith's shop with ease.

It was a dark, sooty place with a huge charcoal fire
glowing in a square-shaped forge. "Out back," the
smith said without looking up from an iron he was
shaping.

"That many, huh?" Sullivan asked.

"You're the twelfth this morning. But the Rangers
won't let you see him."

"I'm a friend of his," Sullivan said.

"So were the other eleven," the smith said before
the clang of his hammer on the anvil ended further
conversation.

Sullivan walked through the shop toward the back
and collided with a small man dressed in black, a large
silver cross dangling on his chest.

"Oh, sorry padre. I wasn't watching where I was
going."

"No harm done," the priest said. "Are you trying to
see Bill Longley?"

"That's the general idea," Sullivan said.

"The Rangers won't allow it, you know. They're
very strict."

"Well, all I can do is try."

"Bill is at his holy devotions at the moment."

"At his what?" Sullivan said.

"He's at prayer." The little man smiled as he answered the question he knew was coming. "Bill converted to Catholicism. He has embraced Holy Mother
Church and the Good Lord has forgiven him his sins."

Sullivan shook his head. "Look, ah . . ."

"Father Thomas Muldrow."

"Father Muldrow, he's faking it. Longley's never been near the sound of church bells in his life. He hopes suddenly getting religion will save him from the noose."

"It won't. I know that and so does Bill. He has hope, yes, but of eternal life in the presence of God."

Sullivan couldn't believe what he was hearing. "This I have to see."

"You'll find Bill much changed. Mr.—"

"Sullivan."

"A good Catholic name."

"I came here to kill him, Father. There's my confession."

The priest's serene face didn't change. "Let the law commit the murder, my son. It's so very good at it."

The back entrance of the blacksmith's shop led to an open sandy area, much covered with bunch grass and prickly pear cactus. About ten steps from the shop, four big mustaches, each attached to a hard-faced Ranger, stood in front of a timber shed with a tin roof. The lawmen gathered around a charcoal brazier and one of them poured coffee into the tin cups held by the others.

He turned his head when Sullivan stepped from the shop. "You. Get lost."

"I'm here to see Bill Longley," Sullivan said.

"You and a lot of other people. Now beat it." The man laid the coffeepot on the brazier as Sullivan spoke to his back.

"I came to Giddings to kill him."

That caught the attention of the lawmen and four pairs of cold eyes turned to him as though he'd just crawled from under a rock.

The big Ranger who'd held the coffeepot moved his cup from his right hand to his left. "Shuck that gun belt, mister."

Sullivan, used to the sudden ways of such men, unbuckled and let his gun drop.

"What's your name?" the Ranger asked.

"Tam Sullivan."

"The Denver bounty hunter?"

"Denver. And other places."

"Here, Sergeant Page, ain't he the man who killed Crow Wallace up in the New Mexico Territory?" a young Ranger said.

"Yeah, that would be me." Sullivan nodded.

"You ridded the country of a damned nuisance," Sergeant Page said. "How come you want to kill Longley?"

"He murdered friends of mine," Sullivan said. "I don't want to go into it."

The Ranger's smile was about as warm as a frozen bullet. "Well, Mr. Sullivan, you ain't killing him."

"No. I guess not. I'll let the law do it."

The wind had picked up and the slickers of the lawman slapped around their booted ankles. A scrap of newspaper soared into the air like a flapping dove then swooped to earth again.

"Bill's got religion," Page said.

"Yeah, the priest told me that."

"He's crazy. We'll hang a madman today."

"Maybe he is," Sullivan said. "I'd still like to see him, talk about old times, like."

Page said, "You'll get no sense out Longley. But I don't see any harm in a visit." He turned to the young Ranger. "Luke, take this man inside, but stay with him." Then to Sullivan, "Fifteen minutes. No longer."

CHAPTER FIFTY-NINE
A Crazy Man

Wild Bill Longley was a chained animal. The shackles that bound his ankles and wrists were cruelly looped around a great iron staple driven into the concrete floor so that he could not stand but was forced to crouch like a mad dog. Longley's lips moved.

The Ranger said to Sullivan, "He's praying." To Longley, "Somebody to see you, Bill."

Longley cocked his head and saw Tam Sullivan. "Welcome. Thrice welcome. I'm sorry I can't offer you a drink." Then, as though he just remembered, "They're hanging me today, Sullivan. But I've been hung before and this time, Jesus will take care of me when I descend from the gallows."

"In a pine box, Bill." The Ranger grinned.

"Why are you doing this, Longley?" Sullivan asked.

"Doing what, my dear friend?"

"Faking your religious conversion. No matter what you pretend, you'll hang at four this afternoon."

"I welcome that death," Longley said. "Oh, how I look forward to being gone from this vale of tears."

"You're a lowdown, lying skunk, Longley," Sullivan said, his anger flaring. "Do you remember Lisa York? Do you remember killing her?"

Longley's pale face took on the pious but anguished look of a Christian martyr thrown to the lions. "Yes, I remember her. That terrible sin has been forgiven. I have been led to the light, don't you understand?"

A crafty look transformed Longley's face. "*He* doesn't think so. Can you see him, Sullivan? In the corner over there. He's all on fire?" Before Sullivan could say a word, Longley yelled, "I see you, Booker! I know, I know, . . . You want to drag me down to hell because I won't lift you up to heaven." He yanked on his chains and shrieked, "Don't bring her! No . . . no . . . she's not one of the damned!"

"He's nuts," the Ranger said.

"How long has he been like this?" Sullivan asked.

"Since we picked him up in Nacogdoches, I guess."

"A man just doesn't go insane that quick," Sullivan said.

"He did." The Ranger motioned with his scattergun. "Seems he killed a few people up in the New Mexico Territory and he says they've come back to haunt him." The young Ranger smiled and winked. "The popish priest told Sergeant Page that he drove a demon out of ol' Bill, an evil thing that called itself Clotilde. Page says maybe it was the priest that made him nuts."

"Clotilde *was* an evil thing," Sullivan said.

The Ranger stared at the big man in surprise, trying

to fathom his meaning, but then he was forced to shift his attention to Longley.

"Who the hell are you?" the chained gunman said.

"Me?" Sullivan pointed to himself.

"Yeah, you. I don't know you. Get out of here." Longley began screaming, "Out! Out! Out!"

"We'd better leave. He's getting agitated and seeing ghosts again." The Ranger grinned. "Still want to kill him, Sullivan?"

"No. But I'll watch the law kill him."

"Damn it all," said a man in the saloon. "There's never been a wind like this in Giddings."

"Or anywhere else, for that matter," another said.

The wind was raging, howling, threatening to tear the roof off the saloon. Looking around him, Sullivan saw that a few faces showed fear. He smiled at a saloon girl in a pinafore dress who clutched a serving tray to her breast.

The girl smiled back, but her eyes were wide and frightened.

Sullivan picked up his beer from the bar and stepped to the window, looking out at the street and a day gone raving mad. Wind-driven sand rampaged wherever it pleased and rat-tat-tatted on windows that were already taking a beating, rattling in their frames. Across the wide street, the canvas roof of the hotel billowed like a ship's mainsail in a storm, threatening to split open and let the sand cover everything inside. The sky was a strange, dull crimson color, flat as a plate with no sun or cloud to be seen.

"Hell of a day for a hanging, huh?"

Sullivan turned to the man who'd stepped beside him. "Seems like."

The man took a watch from his vest pocket, thumbed it open, and snapped it shut again. "Three-fifteen."

"Reckon the sandstorm will keep the crowd away?" Sullivan asked.

The man looked at him as though he was crazy. "Not a chance. Wild Bill Longley's is a big, big hanging. You going?"

"I guess," Sullivan answered.

"I hear there'll be cake and ice cream."

"Cake, ice cream, and sand."

The man looked quite distressed. "Hell, I never thought about that." He walked away.

Sullivan finished his beer, then left in plenty of time to see Bill Longley die.

CHAPTER SIXTY
The Demon

The tall pines around the gallows tossed their heads in the wind as the thirteen-coil hangman's noose danced a merry little jig.

Hundreds of onlookers had gathered for the big event, some living in makeshift tents. The air smelled of the roasting pig that turned on a spit over a guttering fire. The crowd was noisy, good-humored, eager to the see the Baddest Man in the West, as the local newspaper described him, meet his deserved fate.

As he walked among the throng Sullivan heard all kinds of rumors.

"Wild Bill converted to Catholicism and was having visions of the Virgin Mary."

"The hangman is an expert brought all the way from the notorious Four Corners district of New York."

"John Wesley Hardin, killer of forty men, busted out of jail and is on the way with a gang of desperadoes to save his old friend."

"Bill blamed his downfall on strong drink and fancy women." "Cake and ice cream is expected . . ."

Sullivan ignored the talk and walked through the trees to the gallows.

The wind had torn away the decorative red, white, and blue bunting that had covered the front of the rickety structure and the drop was visible. He frowned, thinking the distance Longley had to fall before the noose broke his neck didn't seem high enough. He was a tall man, several inches over six feet.

One of the local lawmen, wearing a deputy's badge pinned to the front of his vest, stood on the gallows platform and jumped up and down on booted feet, testing the structure's stability.

Sullivan looked up at the man and yelled above the roar of the wind. "Hey!"

The deputy, a stocky man of medium height who seemed to have lost his hat, looked down at Sullivan and hollered, "What do you want?"

"The drop's too short!"

"What?"

"The damned drop's too short."

The deputy shrugged. "Look's long enough to me."

"It won't let the rope tighten and break Longley's neck," Sullivan said.

"Then go tell that to the Rangers," the deputy said, waving his hand. "I'm too busy."

Sullivan wanted to see Bill Longley die, not another bungled hanging. He turned away and made his way through the crowd in search of Sergeant Page.

A huckster selling some kind of patent medicine had attracted a large audience and Sullivan paused long enough to hear him yell his pitch.

"I have this very day, with this very hand"—he slapped his left hand with his right—"paid *one hundred dollars* to the Texas Rangers for yonder rope. Yes, the very rope that will choke the life out of Wild Bill Longley, the most notorious, the deadliest, the lowest down killer who ever walked the west."

This drew wild cheers, as Sullivan knew it would.

The huckster, whose slicked-down hair didn't move in the gale, held up his hands for silence. "Now, here's bounty for you," he yelled. "For this day only, every man, woman, or child who buys a bottle of Dr. Drub's Miracle Liver Tonic will receive for free, not one inch! Not two inches! But *three full inches* of the rope that hung Wild Bill Longley!"

There were more cheers and folks seemed eager to buy. Sullivan reckoned the medicine man had already cut up a few hemp ropes into three inches as a reserve.

He found Sergeant Page at the blacksmith's shop.

"You back, Sullivan?" the Ranger said with no particular friendliness.

Sullivan got right to the point. "The drop is too short. It won't kill him."

It took Page a moment to figure out what the big bounty hunter was telling him. "It looks fine to me."

"Page, when the trap's sprung, Longley will hit the ground feet first. Like the last time, he'll only be half hung."

"Then we'll have to hang him twice." Page noted the horrified look on Sullivan's face and his own features hardened. "I've got a crowd of maybe a thousand people to manage. I have to be on guard against a rescue attempt and I'm hanging a man who's a raving lunatic. Sullivan, I've got more to worry about than the length of the gallows drop. You see how it is with me?"

"I see how it is with you."

"Good, now get the hell away from here and let me get on with my job."

"One last thing," Sullivan said. "Did the priest really chase a demon out of Bill Longley?"

The Ranger's eyes were guarded, uncertain. "The priest called it an exorcism, or a word like that. But I don't know anything about spooks and ha'nts and such."

"Did you see the . . . whatever it was?"

Page was silent for a long while, so long that Sullivan thought he'd say nothing more. But then, "There was something inside him. I saw it leave."

"A demon? Did it call itself Clotilde?"

"Whatever it was, it drove Longley crazy." Page held up a hand. "All right, Sullivan, enough. We go on talking like this, my boys will drag us both to the booby hatch." He turned his back, then said over his shoulder, "I'll look into the drop."

CHAPTER SIXTY-ONE
A Dreadful Hanging

Gone was the raving lunatic. The Bill Longley the Rangers led through the jeering crowd, at least half of them black, was a man of quiet dignity and he displayed considerable courage. He carried a small, pink rosary in his shackled hands and his lips moved constantly around a slight smile.

The town marshal and his three deputies kept the onlookers away from the gallows but allowed Sullivan closer since he seemed to be a friend of the Ranger sergeant.

The wind howled, scattering spots of rain, and the surrounding pines performed a frenzied dervish dance. The pig on the spit turned and fat sizzled.

Despite the chains on his legs, Longley took the eight steps to the gallows platform unaided then stood on the trapdoor as Page directed.

Sullivan searched the gunman's face, looking for fear, remorse, anything. He saw only a beatific expression.

In his mind, Bill Longley was determined to die a martyr.

The drop under the gallows was still the same. No effort had been made to dig out the ground and make it lower.

Page, the marshal, and the other Rangers crowded around the condemned man. Father Muldrow stood to one side, reading aloud from his Bible. Longley took no notice, his eyes on the torn sky where a flock of crows wheeled in the wind like pieces of charred paper.

"William Preston Longley, do you have anything to say before sentence is carried out?" Page asked.

At first, it seemed that the man would keep his mouth shut. Then, shouting against the wind, Longley spoke. "Good people!" he yelled. "Answer me this. How come John Wesley Hardin got jail time after killing forty men and I killed but a score and I'm getting hung?"

The crowd jeered and there were cries of, "String the rascal up!"

"I'll tell you why," Longley yelled. "It's because I'm a Roman Catholic and I'm dying for my faith."

That brought a cascade of boos, but a couple of roosters who'd already gotten into the beer held each other up and yelled, "Huzzah!"

A moment occurred that Tam Sullivan remembered for the rest of his life—the instant when Longley's eyes locked on his . . . piercing blue eyes . . . too bright, too glittering, too filled with hate to be human.

"Sullivan!" the condemned man screamed. "You killed her. She told me. She came unto me, entered into me, and told me. She spoke in tongues with the voice of a snake."

Not only was Sullivan struck dumb, but the whole crowd was silenced. For a few moments, the only sound along the thronged rise was the lament of the wind.

The medicine man broke the spell.

Apparently worried that he'd lose the crowd and his profit, he yelled at the top of his lungs, "Get on with it, for God's sake!"

As the crowd cheered him on, Sergeant Page stirred like a man wakening from sleep. He settled the noose around Longley's neck, stood with the black hood dangling from his hand and stared at the man as though seeing him for the first time.

"Dave, get it done," a Ranger said.

The crowd was restless. Impatient voices raised, and a few thrown rocks thudded against the gallows.

"Dave!" the Ranger said again, more urgently.

Longley turned and snapped, "Damn your eyes, hang me!" He smiled. "If you dare."

Page stood immobile, his face working as sweat beaded on his forehead.

Sullivan stepped closer to the platform and yelled, "Page! Fight back!"

The big Ranger said nothing, frozen in a moment of time he could not comprehend.

"Don't let it get inside you!" Sullivan roared.

"Clotilde!' Page cried. He staggered a step and crashed on his back.

As the town marshal and an alarmed Father Muldrow knelt beside the unconscious man, the young Ranger named Luke grabbed the hood from Page's hand.

"Damn you, Longley!" He yanked the hood over

the gunman's head and buckled a leather strap around his neck. The Ranger stepped off the trap-door and yelled to the deputy at the lever, "Do it!"

The crowd yelled their approval as the man sprang the trap and Bill Longley plummeted through, plunging straight down like a coin dropping into a slot.

It happened as Sullivan knew it would.

The drop wasn't high enough and Longley hit the ground feet first. With a terrible, strangled cry, he fell forward onto his knees. The rope vibrated like a fiddle string, but the noose did not break his neck.

He struggled against the noose, slowly choking to death as the crowd reeled in horror. Longley's swollen face turned purple and saliva dripped from his mouth as he fought for air.

The Ranger, a tough young man in a hard line of work, recovered quickly from his shock and yelled, "Pull him up!"

Willing hands untied the rope from the gallows crossbeam and Longley was hauled back onto the platform by the neck.

The hanging had been bungled and the crowd was incensed. The cries were to let Longley go.

"He's been punished enough!" yelled a red-faced woman near Sullivan.

The very mob who'd been baying for Bill Longley's blood demanded that Longley walk free.

Sullivan watched history repeat itself. Longley was half hung yet again, and again he'd beat the noose.

But Sullivan hadn't counted on the determination and sense of duty of the young Ranger.

"Yank him higher and tie him off!" he yelled. "Close the trap!"

As the trapdoor thudded shut again, Longley was hoisted high until he was up on his toes, his neck stretched, head lolling to one side.

The angry crowd cursed and yelled, but a deputy stepped to the front of the platform, a scattergun in his hands. His voice breaking from strain, he vowed to blow the guts out of anyone who attempted to thwart the course of justice.

From under the hood, Longley let out a low moaning sound. Women in the hushed crowd had tears in their eyes.

The young Ranger stepped over, put his arms around the groaning man's neck, and clenched them behind Longley's head. He looked at the deputy at the drop handle and yelled, "Let 'er rip!'

The lawman didn't hesitate. He yanked the handle and Longley and the Ranger hurtled through the trap.

Sullivan, standing close, heard the snap of Longley's breaking neck, like the sound a dry twig makes when it's snapped in half.

The Ranger, seemingly unhurt, crawled out from under the gallows . . . to a dreadful, wailing shriek that rang through the crowd with the awful clarity of a tolling bell.

Heads turned in every direction as people tried to pin down the source of the woman's scream. But it had come from the very air, high up where the pine trees danced, and it's origin could not be found.

Sullivan looked at Bill Longley's body ticking back and forth on the hangman's rope like a clock pendulum and knew full well who had emitted the fearful cry.

* * *

"You all right, Page?" Sullivan asked. "Let me buy you a drink."

The Ranger bellied up to the bar, his face ashen. "Brandy."

"Make that a large one, bartender," Sullivan said.

Page sampled his drink "I had a bad turn up there on the gallows. Like I felt sick all over."

Sullivan nodded. "Something you ate, I'm sure."

"Yeah, that's it. Or too much coffee."

"That will do it."

Page built a cigarette with hands that were not still.

Sullivan lit it for him, and then the Ranger said, "Hell of a death for any man, wasn't it?"

"I'd say," Sullivan agreed. "The young Ranger did well."

"He ended it."

"It needed ending." Sullivan s moved away from the bar. "Well, so long and good luck, Ranger."

"You too, Sullivan. See you around."

"Yeah. See you around."

EPILOGUE

Bright morning sunlight streamed through the tall dining room windows of Denver's Excelsior Hotel as Tam Sullivan refilled his coffee cup and lit his first cigar of the day. Gone, at least temporarily, were his rough trail clothes, replaced by the finery of the broadcloth and frilled linen of the prosperous sporting gent.

"I say, sir," the man at the next table said, nodding to the newspaper in his hands. "Did you read the good news?"

"No, sir. I haven't yet read the paper this morning," Sullivan said. "Something interesting?"

"I'll say it's interesting. Here, it's short. I'll read it to you. 'We are delighted to inform the male citizens of Denver, to the chagrin of the female order we're sure, that Miss Montana Maine will once again grace the luxurious Rochester Hotel with her presence, beginning this Friday evening.

"'Miss Maine returns from a winter sojourn in the New Mexico Territory where she spent her time studying the works of the philosopher René Descartes and dabbling in local folklore about the raising of the dead.

"'We believe we must add our own two cents' worth to this wonderful occasion by raising our glasses to the glorious Miss Maine as we observe that there's a hell of an excitement in this town.'" The man stared at Sullivan, bright eyes reflecting his question. "Well, sir, what do you think of that?"

Sullivan smiled and pinkied ash from his cigar into the silver ashtray in front of him. "I was planning to leave for Texas on business tomorrow, but I think I've changed my mind."

TURN THE PAGE FOR AN EXCITING PREVIEW

THE GREATEST WESTERN WRITERS OF
THE 21ST CENTURY

*William Johnstone and J. A. Johnstone are the acclaimed
masters of the American frontier and national bestsellers.
Now, they take on the deadliest and most feared outlaw to
ever walk the Old West—John Wesley Hardin.*

**First he became a killer . . .
Then he became a legend.**

He was fifteen when he killed his first man.
Before his murderous ways ended, Hardin had
killed forty-four men in cold blood—one, the
legend goes, because he snored too loudly.
From then on John Wesley Hardin stayed true
to his calling, killing man after man after man,
spending most of his life being pursued
by local lawmen and federal troops.

Hardin lived a fever dream of lightning fast draws
and flying lead. By the age of seventeen, he had
earned a deadly reputation for cold-blooded killing
that drew traitors, backstabbers, and wannabe
gunslingers—all for a chance to gun down
the man who had turned killing into
an all-American legend . . .

FORTY TIMES A KILLER!
A Novel of John Wesley Hardin

by WILLIAM W. JOHNSTONE
with J. A. Johnstone

On sale now, wherever Pinnacle Books are sold!

CHAPTER ONE
Death in the Street

"John Wesley Hardin! I'm calling you out, John Wesley!"

My friend turned to me and his left eyebrow arched the way it always did when his face asked a question.

"All right. I'll take a look," I said, laying aside my copy of Mr. Dickens' *The Life and Adventures of Martin Chuzzlewit*, partially set, as you know, on our very own western frontier.

I rose from the table and limped to the saloon's batwing doors, more a tangle of broken and missing slats than door. I guess so many heads were rammed through those batwings that nobody took the trouble to repair them any longer.

Three men wearing slickers and big Texas mustaches stood in the dusty street. All were armed with heavy Colt revolvers carried high on the waist, horseman-style. They glanced at me, dismissed me as something beneath their notice, and continued their wait.

I told John Wesley what I saw and he said, "Ask them what the hell they want."

"They're calling you out, Wes. That's what they want."

"I know it, Little Bit. But ask them anyhow." Wes stood at the bar, playing with a little calico kitten, the warm schooner of beer at his elbow growing warmer in the east Texas heat.

The railroad clock on the wall ticked slow seconds into the quiet and the bartender cleared his throat and whispered to the saloon's only other customer, "James, this won't do."

The gray-haired man nodded. "A bad business." He stared through the window. "Those men are pistol fighters."

He was not ragged, as most of us Texans were that late summer of 1870. His clothes were well worn, but clean, and spoke of a good wife at home. He might have been a one-loop rancher or a farmer, but he could have been anything.

I stepped outside into the street, if you could call it that.

The settlement of Honest Deal was a collection of a few raw timber buildings sprawled hit or miss along the bank of the west fork of the San Jacinto River, a sun-scorched, wind-blown scrub town waiting desperately for a railroad spur or even a stage line to give it purpose and a future.

I blinked in the sudden bright light, then took the measure of the three men. They were big, hard-eyed fellows. The oldest of them had an arrogant look to him, as though he hailed from a place where he was the cock o' the walk.

That one would take a heap of killing, I figured. They all would.

I swallowed hard. "Mr. Hardin's compliments, and he wishes to know what business you have with him."

"Unfinished business," the oldest man said.

Another, tall and blond and close enough in looks and arrogance to be his son, said, "Gimp, get back in there and tell Hardin to come out. If he ain't in the street in one minute, we'll come in after him."

The man's use of the word *gimp* surprised me. I thought the steel brace on my left leg covered by my wool pants was unnoticeable. Unless I walked, of course. I'd only taken a step into the street, so I could only assume that the tall man was very observant.

Wes was like that, observant. All revolver fighters were back in those days. They had to be.

Measuring him, it seemed to me that the younger man was also one to step around, unless you were mighty gun slick.

"I'll tell Mr. Hardin what you said." I smiled at the three men. I had good teeth when I was younger, the only part of my crooked, stunted body that was good, so I smiled a lot. Showing them off, you understand.

I figured I knew why those three men didn't want to come into the saloon after Wes unless they had to. The place was small, little bigger than a railroad boxcar, and gloomy, lit by smoking, smelly, kerosene lamps. Only Yankee carpetbaggers could afford the whale oil that burned brighter without smoke or stink. If shooting started inside, the concussion of the guns would extinguish the lamps and four men would have to get to their work in semidarkness and at point-blank range.

356 William W. Johnstone

Against a deadly pistol fighter like Wes, those three fellows were well aware that no one would walk out of the saloon alive. They wanted badly to kill Wes, but outside where they would have room to maneuver and take cover if necessary.

I can't say as I blamed them. A demon with ol' Sammy's revolver was Wes, fast and accurate on the draw and shoot.

That's one of the reasons I idolized him. I'd never met his like before . . . or since.

Well, I turned to go back into the saloon and tell him what the three gentlemen outside wanted, but I'd taken only one clumping step when Wes stepped around the corner of the saloon, a smile on his face and a .44 1860 Army model Colt in each hand.

All his life, Wes favored those old cap-and-ball pistols, and he would often say that they were both wife and child to him.

He wore black pants held up by suspenders and a vest of the same color over a collarless white shirt. Shoulder holsters bookended his manly chest and he sported a silver signet ring on the little finger of his left hand, the hallmark of the frontier gambler.

"You fellows wish to speak with me?" he said, making the slight bow that he considered the stamp of a well-bred Southern gentleman.

Well, the three men had been caught flatfooted and they knew it.

The oldest of them was the first to recover. He pushed his slicker away from his gun and said, "You know why we're here, Hardin."

"Damn right you do," the blond man said.

They were on the prod, those two, and right then I

knew there would be no stepping back from this, not for Wes, not for anybody.

"I'm afraid you have the advantage over me," Wes said. "I've never seen you gentlemen before in my life."

"You know us, damn you," the older man said.

"We're here for my brother Sonny," the blond man said.

Wes smiled again, showing his teeth.

Lord-a-mercy, but that was a bad sign. John Wesley was never a smiling man . . . unless he planned to kill somebody.

"I've never heard the name Sonny, nor can I attach it to a remembered face," he said. "How do you spell it, with an *O* or a *U*?"

"You're pleased to make a joke." This from the man who hadn't spoken before, a lean, hawk-faced man whose careful eyes had never left Wes, reading him and coming to a decision about him.

He was a gun, that one, He'd be mighty sudden and would know some fancy moves.

"I made a good joke?" Wes asked. "Then how come I don't hear you gentlemen laughing?" His Colts were hanging loose at his sides as though he had all the time in the world.

"You go to hell." The hawk-faced man went for his gun.

Years later, I was told that the lean man was probably a ranny by the name of Hugh Byrd who had a vague reputation in Texas as a draw-fighter.

Word was that he'd killed Mason Lark up El Paso way. You recall Lark, the Denver bounty hunter with the Ute wife? Back then nobody considered Lark a bargain and even John Wesley once remarked that the man was fast on the draw and a proven man killer.

Well, for reasons best known only to himself, Byrd—if that really was his name—decided to commit suicide the day he drew down on Wes.

His gun hadn't cleared leather when two .44 bullets clipped half-moons from the tobacco tag that hung over the pocket of his shirt and tore great wounds in his chest.

I didn't watch him fall. My eyes were on the other two.

The blond man got off a shot at Wes, but he'd hurried the draw and the slug kicked up a startled exclamation point of dirt an inch in front of the toe of Wes's right boot.

The towhead knew he'd made a bad mistake. His face horrified, he took a step back and raised his revolver to correct his aim.

But the young man's hurried shot had been the kind of blunder you can't make in a gunfight . . . and Wes made him pay for it. His bucking Colts hammering with tremendous speed and accuracy, he slammed three or four bullets into the man's upper chest and belly.

Gagging on his own blood, the yellow-haired fellow dropped to his knees.

Wes ignored him. He swung on the older man who hadn't made a move for his gun. His reactions slower than the others, the fight had gone too fast for him and there was no way he was going to play catch-up.

He tossed his Colt away and raised his hands to waist level. "I'm out of it, John Wesley. Now you've killed both my sons and I want to live long enough to grieve for them."

The man was not scared or afraid to die, but I knew living would be hard for him, each passing day another little death. Blood had drained from his features and I looked into the gray, blue-shadowed face of a corpse.

"No, mister, you're in it," Wes said, smiling. "There ain't a way out. You brought it, and now you pay the piper." He raised his Colt, took careful aim and shot the old man between the eyes.

The blond man was clinging to life, coughing up black blood. He turned his head as the older man fell into the dirt beside him. "Pa!" He reached out and put his hand on his father's chest. His mouth was a shocked, scarlet O. "Are you kilt dead, Pa?"

"Yeah, he's kilt dead," Wes said. "Now go join him in hell."

The Colt roared again . . . and then only the desert wind made a sound.

I reckon the whole population of the town, maybe a dozen men and a couple women, young'uns clutching at their skirts, stood in the street and stared at the three sprawled bodies. The faces of the men and women were expressionless. They looked like so many painted dolls as they tried to come to grips with the violence and sudden death that had come into their midst.

"This won't do," the bartender said. "This is a job for the law." He glanced hopefully around the crowd, but nobody had listened to him.

Fat blowflies had already formed a black, crawling crust on the gory faces of the dead and I fancied I already got a whiff of the stench of decay.

The bartender, who seemed to have appointed himself spokesman for the whole town, looked at Wes. "Who were they, mister?"

"Damned if I know."

The bartender made it official. He reached into his vest pocket and took out a lawman's star that he pinned to his chest. The star looked as though it had been cut from the bottom of a bean can. "I heard one of them say they were here for Sonny," the bartender-sheriff said. "You ever hear of him?"

Wes shook his head. "No, I don't reckon I have. Unless his name was spelled with a *U*."

"You ever hear of a man named Sunny, with a *U*?"

"No. I don't reckon I have." With every eye on him, Wes made one of those grandstand plays that helped make him famous. He spun those big Colts and they were still spinning when he dropped them into their holsters. "Sheriff, a man in my line of business makes a lot of enemies. Hell, I can't keep track of all the men who want to kill me."

"And what is your business?" the sheriff said.

"I'm a shootist," Wes said.

Me, I looked into John Wesley's eyes then. There was no meanness, no blue, luminous light I've seen in a man's eyes when he takes pleasure in a killing . . . but there was something else.

Wes looked around the crowd, his gaze moving from face to stunned face, and his eyes were bright, questioning. *Look at me! Look at me everybody. Have you ever seen my like before?*

Right then, John Wesley was Narcissus at the pool, the man who fell madly in love with his own reflection.

And the people around him, as soon as the gunshots stopped ringing in their ears, fed his vanity.

All of a sudden, men were slapping him on the back, shaking his hand, telling him he'd done good. The women looked at him from under lowered eyelashes and wondered what it would be like to take a gladiator to bed.

Even the sheriff stepped off the distance between Wes and the dead men and grinned at the crowd. "Ten paces, by God. And three men hurled into eternity in the space of a moment!"

This drew a cheer, and Wes bowed and grinned and basked in the adulation.

He was but seventeen years old and he'd killed eleven white men.

The newspapers had made him a named gunfighter, up there with the likes of Longley and Hickok, and he'd have to live with it.

And me, I thought, *But in the end they'll kill you, Wes. One day the folks will forget all about you and that will be your death.*

CHAPTER TWO
The Dark Star

"I got an idea, Little Bit," John Wesley said. "Hell, it's a notion that can make us both rich."

"Wes," I said, laying Mr. Dickens on my lap, my thumb marking the page I'd been reading by firelight, "does your brain ever stop?"

Wes grinned, glanced at the full moon riding high above the pines, and pointed. "No, I'm like him up there, always shining. And when I get an idea, I shine even brighter."

We'd left Honest Deal at first light that morning, heading west for the town of Longview over to Harrison County where Wes had kin. I was all used up. The dog days of summer were on us and the day had been blistering hot and as humid as one of those steam baths that some city folks seem to enjoy.

The night was no better, just darker.

My leg in its iron cage hurt like hell and all I wanted

was to read a couple chapters of *Martin Chuzzlewit* and then find my blankets.

But Wes, who had a bee in his bonnet, wouldn't let it go. His shirt was dark with arcs of sweat under his arms, and his teeth glinted white in the moonlight. "Well, don't you want to hear it?"

"Hear what?" I asked.

"Don't mess with me, Little Bit. I told you I have a great idea."

I sighed, found a pine needle that I used to mark my page, and closed the book. "I'm all ears," I said, looking at Wes through the gloom.

"All right, but first answer me this. Do you agree that I'm a man destined for great things?"

I nodded. "I'd say that. You're a fine shootist, Wes. The best that ever was."

"I know, but I'm much more than that."

"So, tell me your idea."

"Listen up. My idea is to star in a show. My own show."

"You mean like a medicine show?" I smiled at him. "Dr. Hardin's Healing Balm."

"Hell no. Bigger than that and better." Wes raised his hands and made a long banner shape in the air. "John Wesley Hardin's Wild West Show."

His face aglow, he said, "Well, what do you think? Isn't it great, huh?"

"I don't know what to think. I've never heard of such a thing."

"A . . . what's the word? . . . *spectacular* show, Little Bit. With me as the hero and you as . . . as . . . well, I'll think of something."

"On stage in a theater, Wes? Is that what you think?"

"Maybe. But probably outside in an arena. We'll have drovers and cavalry and Indians and outlaws and cattle herds and stagecoaches and . . . hell, the possibilities are endless." Wes leaned closer to me and the shifting firelight stained the right side of his eager, handsome face. "I'll be the fearless frontiersman who saves the fair maiden from the savages or captures the rustlers singlehanded, stuff like that."

"Sounds expensive, Wes. I mean, paying all those hands and—"

"Damn it, Little Bit, that kind of thinking is the reason you're not destined for greatness. I'll get rich backers, see? They'll bankroll the show for a cut of the profits."

Wes smiled at me. "Hell, we got three hundred dollars for the horses and traps of them dead men back at Honest Deal, so we already got seed money." He read the doubt in my face and said, "It can't fail. Nobody's ever had an idea like mine and nobody else is going to think of it. Man, I'll make a killing and a fortune."

He again made a banner of his hands and grinned. "John Wesley Hardin's Wild West Show! Damn, I like the sound o' that." He let out a rebel yell that echoed like the howl of a wolf in the silence. "Little Bit, it's gonna be great!"

Around me, the pines were black, and they leaned into one another as though they were exchanging ominous secrets. I felt uneasy, like a flock of geese had just flown over my grave. "What do I do, Wes?"

"Do? Do where?"

"In the show, Wes. What do I do in your Wild West Show?"

Wes's eyes roamed over me and I was well aware of what he saw . . . a tiny, stunted runt with a thin, white face, boot-button brown eyes, and a steel brace on his twisted twig of a left leg.

I wasn't formed by nature to play any kind of western hero.

John Wesley was never one to get stumped by a question, but he scowled, his thick black brows drawn together in thought. Then his face cleared and he smiled. "You read books, Little Bit, don't you?"

I nodded and held up my copy of Mr. Dickens.

"Then there's your answer." Wes clapped his hands. "You'll be my bookkeeper! And"—he beamed as he delivered what he obviously believed was the snapper—"a full partner in the business!"

I said nothing.

"What's wrong? I thought you'd be happy with that proposition."

"I am, I really am."

"Then why do you look so down in the mouth you could eat oats out of a churn?"

"Because the thought just came to me that before you can do anything, Wes, you'll have to square yourself with the law."

John Wesley sighed, a dramatic intake of breath coupled with a frustrated yelp that he did often. "Little Bit, are you talking about Mage again?"

"Well, Mage for starters, but there are others."

"Mage was your friend, wasn't he?"

"Not really. We were together a lot because he wanted to learn how to read and do his ciphers."

"Negroes are too stupid to learn to read," Wes said. "Hell, everybody knows that."

"He was doing all right. He liked Sir Walter Scott."

"He wasn't doing all right in my book," Wes said, his face tight. "Mage was an uppity black man who needed killing."

I smiled to take the sting out of a conversation that was veering into dangerous territory. When Wes got angry bad things happened.

"Ah, you were just sore because he beat you at rasslin'," I said.

"Yeah, but I bloodied his nose, didn't I?"

I nodded. "You done good, Wes. Mage was twice as big as you."

"And ugly with it."

Wes was silent for a while. A breeze spoke in the pines and a lace of mist frosted by moonlight drifted between their slender trunks. I fancied that the ghosts of dead Comanches were wandering the woods.

"You know what he said, don't you?" Wes asked.

"Let's drop it. It isn't that important."

"You know what he said?"

I shook my head. I didn't feel good that night. My leg hurt and the salt pork and cornpone we'd eaten for dinner wasn't sitting right with me.

"He said that no white boy could draw his blood and live. Then he said that no bird ever flew so high that could not be brought to the ground. He was talking about a shooting, Little Bit. He planned to put a ball in my back."

"Mage shouldn't have said that."

"Damn right he shouldn't. And he shouldn't have tried to pull me off my horse, either."

I made no comment on that last and Wes said, "All I did was shoot him the hell off'n me."

I felt his angry blue eyes burn into my face.

"You would've done the same."

"I guess so. If I could shoot a revolver, I might have done the same."

"Everybody in Texas knew it was a justified killing. Everybody except the damned Yankees."

"That's why you should make it right with them, Wes," I said.

"Damned if I will. Since when did the killing of an uppity black man become a crime?"

"Since the Yankees won the war."

Wes spat into the fire. "Damn Yankees. I hate their guts."

"A lot of Texas folks think like you, Wes."

"And how do you feel, Little Bit? Until real recent, I never pegged you as a Yankee-lover."

"Wes, my pa died at Gettysburg, remember. How do you think I feel?"

"Yeah, you're right. I forgot about that. You got no reason to cotton to Yankees, either." Wes grinned at me, his good humor restored. "I'll pour us some coffee, and before we turn in, we'll get back to talking about my Wild West Show for a spell." He frowned. "Damn it. We'll have no Yankees in it, unless we need folks to shovel hoss shit. Agreed?"

"Anything you say, Wes. Anything you say."

CHAPTER THREE
"I Don't Enjoy Killing"

I saw John Wesley Hardin being born, I was with him
when he died, and in between I was proud to call him my
friend. He was everything I wanted to be and couldn't.

Wes was tall and slim and straight and moved with
the elegance of a panther. He'd a fine singing voice
and the very sight of him when he stepped into a
room set the ladies' hearts aflutter. Many men admired him, others hated him, but all feared him and
the wondrous things he could do with revolvers.

Like England's hunchbacked king, I was delivered
misshapen from my mother's womb. My frail body did
not grow as a man's should, and even in the full
bloom of my youth, if you'd be pleased to call it that,
I never weighed more than eighty pounds or reached
a height of five feet.

Do you wonder then that I admired Wes so, and
badly wanted to be like him? He was my noble knight

errant who sallied forth to right wrongs, and I his lowly squire.

I think I know the answer to that question.

And why I pledged to stay at his side to the death.

As I told you earlier, we were headed for Longview to visit with Wes's kin for a spell, but he wanted to linger where we were for a day longer.

"This is a pleasant spot and we can talk about my idea some more. Sometimes it's good to just set back and relax."

I had no objections. I felt ill and my leg continued to give me trouble.

The day passed pleasantly enough. I sat under a tree and read my book and Wes caught a bright yellow butterfly at the base of a live oak. He said it meant good luck.

But when he opened his hands to let the butterfly go, it could no longer fly and fluttered to earth, a broken thing.

Wes said not to worry, that it was still good luck. But he seemed upset about the crippled butterfly and didn't try to catch another one.

The long day finally lifted its ragged skirts and tip-toed away, leaving us to darkness and the Texas stars.

Wes built up the fire and put the coffee on to boil. Using his Barlow knife, he shaved slices of salt pork into the pan and said there would be enough cornpone for supper with some leftover for tomorrow's breakfast.

I was pleased about that. It was good cornpone, made with buttermilk and eggs, and I was right partial to it back in those days.

After supper we talked about the Wild West Show, then, as young men do, about women. After a while, I said I was tired and it was about time I sought my blankets.

I stretched out and tried to ignore the pain gnawing at my leg.

Night birds fluttered in and out of the pines making a rustling noise and a puzzled owl asked its question of the night. A pair of hunting coyotes yipped back and forth in the distance and then fell silent.

I closed my eyes and entered that gray, misty realm between wakefulness and sleep . . . then jolted back to consciousness when a shout rang through the hallowed quiet.

"Hello the camp!"

I sat upright and saw that Wes was already on his feet. He wasn't wearing his guns, but stood tense and alert, his eyes reaching into the darkness.

Even as a teenager, John Wesley's voice was a soft baritone, but to my surprise he pitched it near an octave higher and broke it a little as he called out, "Come on in. There's coffee on the bile."

I wondered at that, but didn't dwell on it because the darkness parted and two men rode into the clearing.

Men made a living any way they could in Texas when Wes and I were young, and those two strangers looked as though they were no exception. They were hard-faced men, lean as wolves. I'd seen enough of their kind to figure that they were on the scout.

Astride mouse-colored mustangs that couldn't have
gone more than eight hundred pounds, they wore
belted revolvers and carried Springfield rifles across
their saddle horns. As for clothing, their duds were
any kind of rags they could patch together. The effect,
coupled with their dirty, bare feet, was neither pleasant nor reassuring.

But the Springfields were clean and gleamed with
a sheen of oil.

Whoever those men were, they were not pilgrims.

One of the riders, bearded and grim, was a man
who'd long since lost the habit of smiling. "You got
grub?"

"No, sir," Wes said, using that strange, boy's voice.
"Sorry, but we're all out."

The man's eyes moved to our horses. "Where did
you get them mounts?"

Wes didn't hesitate. "We stole them, sir. But we're
taking them back to Longview to square ourselves
with the law."

The man turned to his companion, "Lem, how
much you figure the paint is worth?"

"Two hundred in any man's money," the man
called Lem said. He looked at Wes. "You stole a lot of
horse there, boy."

Wes nodded. "I know, sir. And that's why we're
taking him back to his rightful owner."

"Who is his rightful owner?" Lem asked.

"We don't rightly know," I said. "But we aim to find
out, like."

"Well, you don't have to worry about that, sonny,"
Lem said. "We'll take the paint off your hands, and
the buckskin as well. Ain't that so, Dave?"

The bearded man nodded. "Sure thing. Pleased to do it. And, being decent folks, we'll set things right with the law for you."

"We'll do it ourselves," Wes said . . . in his normal voice.

And those two white trash idiots didn't notice the change! They sat their ponies and heard what they wanted to hear, saw what they wanted to see.

What they heard was the scared voice of a half-grown boy, and what they saw was a pair of raw kids, one of them a crippled, sickly-looking runt.

Beyond that they saw nothing . . . an oversight that would prove their downfall.

It was a lethal mistake, and they made it.

They'd underestimated John Wesley Hardin, and as I said earlier, you couldn't make mistakes around Wes. Not if you wanted to go on living, you couldn't.

"Lem, go git them horses and saddles," Dave said. "Now, you boys just set and take it easy while Uncle Lem does what I told him."

"Leave the horses the hell alone," Wes said.

Lem was halfway out of the saddle, but something in Wes's tone froze him in place. He looked at Dave.

"Go do what I told you, Lem," the bearded man said. Then to Wes, "Boy, I had it in my head to let you live, since you're a good-looking kid and could come with us, make yourself useful, like. But my mind's pretty close to a-changing, so don't push me."

Lem dismounted and then, rifle in hand, he grinned at Wes and walked toward the horses.

"I told you, leave the horses be." Wes stood very still, his face like stone.

I swallowed hard, my brain racing. *Wes, where the hell are your guns?*

"Boy, step aside," Dave said. "Or I'll drop you right where you stand."

"And you go to hell," Wes said.

Dave nodded as though he'd expected that kind of reaction. "You lose, boy." He smiled. "Sorry and all that."

He brought up his rifle and John Wesley shot him.

Drawing from the waistband behind his back, Wes's ball hit the Springfield's trigger guard, clipped off Dave's shooting finger, then ranged upward and crashed into the bearded man's chin.

His eyes wide and frantic, Dave reeled in the saddle, spitting blood, bone, and teeth.

Wes ignored him. The man was done.

Wes and Lem fired at the same instant.

Unnerved by the unexpected turn of events, Lem, shooting from the hip, was too slow, too wide, and too low. Wes's bullet hit him between the eyes and he fell all in a heap like a puppet that just had its strings cut.

Never one to waste powder and ball, Wes didn't fire again.

But something happened that shocked me to the core.

Despite his horrific wound, his face a nightmare of blood and bone, the man called Dave swung his horse around and kicked it into the darkness.

Wes let out a triumphant yell and ran after him, holding his Colt high.

They vanished into the murk and I was left alone in silence.

In the moonlight, gun smoke laced around the clearing like a woman's wispy dress wafting in a breeze.

The man on the ground lay still in death and made no sound.

A slow minute passed . . . then another. . . .

A shot! Somewhere out there in the dark.

Uneasy, I picked up a heavy stick that lay by the fire and hefted it in my hand. Small and weak as I was, there was little enough I could do to defend myself, but the gesture made me feel better.

"Hello the camp!" It was John Wesley's voice, followed by a shout of triumphant glee.

The black shades of the night parted and he walked into the clearing, leading the dead man's mustang.

I say dead man, because even without asking I knew that must have been Dave's fate.

"You should've seen it, Little Bit," Wes said, his face alight. "Twenty yards in darkness through trees! One shot! I blew the man's brains out." He laughed and clapped his hands. "If he had any."

Without waiting for my response, he said, "Now we got a couple more ponies to sell and two Springfield rifles. Their Colts are shot out and one has a loose cylinder, so I'll hold on to those." His face split in a wide grin. "What do you reckon, Little Bit, am I destined for great things or ain't I?"

I didn't answer that, at least not directly. "John Wesley, the killing has to stop."

He was genuinely puzzled and toed the dead man with his boot. "You talking about these two?"

"No, I guess not. I mean, the killing in general. You have to think about the Wild West show."

"These men needed killing, right?"

I nodded. "Yeah, I guess it was them or us." I was still holding onto the stick and tossed it away. "Maybe you could've let the other one die in his own time and at a place of his choosing. I say *maybe* you could. I'm not pointing fingers, Wes."

"Name one man I killed who didn't need killing, Little Bit. Damn it, name just one. And don't say Mage. He was a black man and don't count."

He waited maybe a full second then said, "See, you can't name a one."

"Wes, there are some who say you pushed the fight with Ben Bradley."

"He cheated me at cards and then called me a coward. A man who deals from the bottom of the deck and calls another man yellow needs killing. At least in Texas he does."

"I was there, Wes. You kept right on pumping balls into him after he said, 'Oh Lordy, don't shoot me anymore.' I remember that. Why did you do it?"

"Because in a gunfight you keep shooting till the other man falls. And because only a man who's lowdown asks for mercy in the middle of a shooting scrape, especially after he's gotten his work in."

I was silent.

Wes said, "Well, did Ben Bradley need killing?"

I sighed. "Yeah, Wes. I guess he did at that."

"Then what's your problem?" Wes's face was dark with anger. "Come on, cripple boy, spit it out."

"Don't enjoy it, Wes. That's all. Just . . . just don't enjoy it."

Wes was taken aback and it was a while before he spoke again. "You really think I like killing men?" he finally asked.

"I don't know, Wes."

"Come on, answer me. Do you?"

"Maybe you do."

"And maybe I was born under a dark star. You ever think of that?"

Above the tree canopy the stars looked like diamonds strewn across black velvet. I pointed to the sky. "Which star?"

"It doesn't matter, Little Bit. Whichever one you choose will be dark. There ain't no shining star up there for John Wesley Hardin."

Depression was a black dog that stalked Wes all his life and I recognized the signs. The flat, toneless voice and the way his head hung as though it had suddenly become too heavy for his neck.

In later years, depression, coming on sudden, would drive him to alcohol and sometimes to kill.

It was late and I was exhausted, but I tried to lift his mood. "Your Wild West show is a bright star, Wes."

I thought his silence meant that he was considering that, but this was not the case.

"I don't kill men because I enjoy it. I kill other men because they want to kill me." He stared at me with lusterless eyes. "I just happen to be real good at it."

"Get some sleep, Wes," I said.

He nodded to the body. "I'll drag that away first."

"Somewhere far. You ever hear wild hogs eating a man? It isn't pleasant."

Wes was startled. "How would you know that?"

Tired as I was, I didn't feel like telling a story, but I figured it might haul the black dog off Wes, so I bit the bullet, as they say. "Remember back to Trinity County when we were younkers?"

"Yeah?" Wes said it slow, making the word a question.

"Remember Miles Simpson, lived out by McCurry's sawmill?"

"Half-scalped Simpson? Had a wife that would have dressed out at around four hundred pounds and the three simple sons?"

"Yes, that's him. He always claimed that the Kiowa half-scalped him, but it was a band saw that done it."

"And he got et by a hog?"

"Let me tell the story. Well one summer, I was about eight years old, going on nine, and you had just learned to toddle around—"

"I was a baby," Wes said.

"Right. That's what you were, just a baby." I hoped he wouldn't interrupt again otherwise the story would take all night to tell.

"Well, anyhoo, Ma sent me over to the Simpson place for the summer. She figured roughhousing with the boys might strengthen me and help my leg. Mrs. Simpson was a good cook and Ma said her grub would put weight on me."

"What did she cook?" With the resilience of youth, Wes was climbing out from under the black dog, and that pleased me.

"Oh, pies and beef stew, stuff like that. And sausage. She made that herself and fried it in hog fat."

"I like peach pie," Wes said. "And apple, if it's got raisins in it."

"Yeah, me too."

"And plenty of cinnamon."

"She made pies like that." Then quickly, before he could interrupt again, I went on. "I was there the whole month of June, then on the second of July, the day after my ninth birthday, the cabin got hit by a band of Lipan Apaches that had crossed the Rio Grande and come up from Mexico."

"Damned murdering savages," Wes said.

"The youngest of the Simpson boys fell dead in the first volley. His name was Reuben or maybe Rufus, I can't recollect which. The others, myself included, made it back into the cabin, though Mrs. Simpson's butt got burned by a musket ball as she was coming through the door."

"Big target."

"Yeah, I guess it was."

"Hold on just a minute." Wes grabbed the dead man by the ankles and dragged him into the brush. When he came back he said, "Then what happened?"

"Well, Mr. Simpson and his surviving sons held off the Apaches until dark when all went quiet. But they were afraid to go out for the dead boy's body on account of how the savages might be lying in ambush."

"Damned Apaches. I hate them."

"Well, just as the moon came up, we heard this snorting and snuffling sound, then a strange ripping noise, like calico cloth being torn into little pieces."

"What was it?" Wes asked.

"It was Reuben or maybe Rufus being torn into little pieces."

"The big boars have sharp tusks on them. They can rip into a man."

"They ripped into the dead boy all right. Come first light all that was left was a bloody skeleton. But the head was still intact. The hogs hadn't touched it." I stared at Wes. "Why would they do that?"

"I don't know, Little Bit. There ain't no accounting for what a hog will do."

Wes stepped to the brush, then turned and said, "I'm taking this feller well away from camp. Your damned story about them hogs has me boogered."